Buried in Clay

Buried in Clay

PRISCILLA MASTERS

First published in Great Britain in 2009 by
Allison & Busby Limited
13 Charlotte Mews
London W1T 4EJ
www.allisonandbusby.com

A CIP catalogue record for this book is available from
the British Library.

10 9 8 7 6 5 4 3 2 1

13-ISBN 978-0-7490-7913-0

Typeset in 12/17 pt Sabon by
Terry Shannon

The paper used for this Allison & Busby publication
has been produced from trees that have been legally sourced
from well-managed and credibly certified forests.

PEFC
PEFC/06-31-02
CATG-PEFC-052
www.pefc.org

Printed and bound in Great Britain by
MPG Books Ltd, Bodmin, Cornwall

Born in Yorkshire and brought up in South Wales, PRISCILLA MASTERS is the author of the popular series set in the Staffordshire moorlands featuring Detective Inspector Joanna Piercy. She has also written several medical standalone mysteries. Priscilla has two sons and lives in Staffordshire. She works part time as a nurse.

'No *art with potters can compare*
We make our pots of what we potters are'

AN ANONYMOUS STAFFORDSHIRE POTTER

'*...everyone that works in this place suffers more or*
less with coughs, and we are all stuffed up; we have
known a great many deaths from it'

SCOURER FANNY WOOD, AGE 33

'Clay lies still, but blood's a rover;
Breath's a ware that will not keep.
Up, lad: when the journey's over
There'll be time enough to sleep.'

AE HOUSMAN, 'A SHROPSHIRE LAD'

AUTHOR'S NOTE

I started writing this manuscript in the mid 1980s in response to an aunt's challenge about what I was going to do with the rest of my life. At the time I was running a small antiques business in Leek, Staffordshire, specialising in Staffordshire pottery and period furniture, particularly old oak. Travelling to salerooms in Nantwich and Chester I would take the road past Balterley and my eye was caught by a black-and-white house set prettily on a hill. I found out it was called Hall o'th'Wood and dated from the sixteenth century. Each time I passed it my imagination would be activated and I began to weave stories about the people who might have lived there linked with my appreciation for the erstwhile potters of Staffordshire. These stories grew into a manuscript which I entitled 'Hall o'th'Wood'. I wrote it on a manual typewriter, using Tipp-Ex each time I rewrote. I kept no copy!

The manuscript found its way to London and was

rejected by all the well-known publishers then adopted by a literary agent who also failed to place it. The sole copy was accidentally destroyed and I came to believe that the story of Hall o'th'Wood would exist only in my imagination. Years later, after I had made my name as a crime writer, my publisher questioned me about my early work. On learning that my first novel had been destroyed she challenged me to rewrite it. I did wonder whether I could remember the story more than twenty years later but as I typed I recalled words, phrases, events and the story unfolded.

This, then, is that story and who else could I dedicate it to but Susie Dunlop who has resurrected my first novel, Juliet Burton, my current literary agent and David Shelley who has been with me for almost all the way. With thanks to all of them for their enthusiasm, patience and loyalty.

With apologies to Sotheby's Chester saleroom. I know you did not open until the 1980s but this is fiction and it suited my purpose to have you open for business in 1967...

PROLOGUE

Hanley, Stoke-on-Trent, 1787

Time. He barely had enough. Two days at the most before they would come for him and his opportunity would be lost for ever. He must work fast. There was much to do if he was to create this dumb witness. And so he worked furiously, trying to do the work of minutes in seconds – of hours in minutes – listening all the time for the knock on the door which he knew would come – finally. He only prayed for two days' grace. He needed no more.

But there were parts of the production that would not be hurried.

And the first of these was the forming of the pot.

With a potter's eye he selected a lump of pale clay of the right size and texture for his purpose, kneading it until he had removed all the bubbles of air which would otherwise destroy it when it was fired. He took his customary care, ignoring the hourglass pouring sand through his brain, concentrating only on the slippery smoothness of the clay. Its familiar texture calmed him so he worked now rhythmically, almost in a trance.

First he centred the clay on the potter's wheel, then he stroked it, feeling as though by instinct the form that would rise up from it. From time to time he dipped his hands in the bowl of water by his side. It would not do to let the clay dry out. It would stiffen the fluidity which was necessary to mould it. He worked his feet on the pedals, slow and steady, up and down, up and down, keeping the timing regular enough to turn the wheel at precisely the right speed so it would cooperate with his hands and find the shape hidden in the lump of clay. He had noticed before that if he could not keep up a steady rhythm the clay would slide off centre and the pot be spoilt. He could not afford that. He would have only this one opportunity to turn this pot. If he lost it its story would be lost for ever.

Now his concentration was all absorbed in the shape that rose, as though by magic, a phoenix from ashes, within his hands and he the creator. His feet, hands, eyes, heart, all worked together as one organ; his breathing slowed, his heart stopped racing. If he could only finish this jug, fire it, enamel it and paint it with his accusation it would exist into time's future, as an accuser, a silent witness, a testimony to justice and the man whose guilt he did not doubt.

That was all he asked, that this piece of pottery would survive him. He might have a few days' grace but he knew that he would die soon. All he asked was that he could leave this one object behind him so it might survive the years and one day...

It was not in his nature to dream. He was a humble, simple potter, not imaginative or fanciful but a man whose nature was bound up with the clay which he worked so competently with his fingers. It did not do to dream. And yet... His eyes peered darkly into the future. Perhaps his vision included hands picking his pot up.

But the lack of concentration brought its price. His own hand slipped and the jug wobbled and was almost spoilt but he kept his fingers firm, his forearms rigid, his shoulders relaxed and brought it back gently into shape. One could only coax clay, forcing nothing. And now it was time to take it from the wheel. He slid the wire underneath the soft, malleable clay and placed the finished object on the shelf.

He allowed himself to study it for a moment. Yes, it was fully formed but it was not yet complete. He took a long piece of clay, rolled and flattened it, then delicately bonded the handle to the body with slip – liquid pottery.

The kiln was hot enough now for the first gentle firing – biscuit firing, they called it. He slept beside the kiln while it baked the clay pot, wrapping himself up in a couple of the hessian sacks which lay nearby. While he dozed he listened but no footsteps came. The glaze had to be fired at a higher temperature to melt the lead and seal the pot. As he worked he sensed that time was running out, almost felt the noose tightening around his neck, pulled at the collar of his shirt. The collar would be replaced by rope – he knew.

Finally it was time to paint the jug with the words that would testify to the world the truth about the accursed name, the accursed place and the accursed man. The story in its bald entirety. Matthew Grindall stopped for a moment, his dark eyes seeing her face which was hot with shame, the determination and horror of her death, and the fingers which held the paintbrush shook with rage so the lines were not true. Suddenly he gave in to tears. All had promised so well. But now he would never look on her face again, hear her merry laughter, listen to her voice again. He was so overcome with sudden hatred he almost dropped the precious pot. He would be with her soon, but not lying by her side in the churchyard. A convicted murderer could not lie in consecrated ground but he had arranged that he would be interred by loyal friends at dead of night beyond the wall which lay nearest to the wooden cross which marked her plot.

He took malicious delight in the execution of the picture, detailing the grotesque, the man hanging from the gibbet, his neck awry. But his face changed as he painted the crooked walls of the great house. No one could fail to appreciate the beauty of it. Ah, he thought, if only.

At last he had finished his work and laid down his paintbrush.

It was only minutes after he had placed the jug in the kiln, as he was still washing the paint from his fingers, that he heard the commotion outside the door.

They were coming for him.

Two Days Later

They were removing the jug from the cooled kiln. Whatever the surrounding drama Staffordshire potters are not used to waste. David Cridman picked it up. 'It seems a shame to spoil it, such a fine piece.'

Stuart Moncliff was more dubious. 'Oh, I'm not so sure. It's tainted. Bad luck. A cursed piece of clay.'

But Cridman was his senior and, it was rumoured, a partner in the potbank. 'Perhaps I'll take it home.'

And so the saga began…

Susanna's Story

We cannot help but walk over the past. In our towns and pavements, along streets and rivers, through the air which hangs with the cries of those who have gone before us. Why say walk when I mean trample? For our lack of awareness makes us careless and cavalier with all that has gone before. No person more so than an antiques dealer as I was. I might handle a piece of pottery or an item of furniture. But do I consider the lives and sufferings of the men or women who made it? Do I think of their stories and emotions as I touch wood, fabric or pottery or stare at a painting? Sometimes I do – as with a sampler of a child made to sit out her Sundays sewing when probably she would have preferred to romp in the garden. On very rare occasions I have no choice but to confront the anguish that lies beneath a piece commemorating a battle, a life or a death. The jug was such an object. It was impossible to ignore its history.

There is a Chinese philosophy that life is a tangle of many threads. We select a thread and follow it through until the skein of life is laid before us. I do not agree. We have no real choices in our lives. Threads present themselves and we tug at them blindly, without any understanding of where fate is leading us. The threads themselves are malicious, waiting to entangle us, bind us and make us fast.

The jug was such a thread and I was destined to follow it through, from its angry conception on a potter's wheel, thrown, originally, as a lump of clay but formed through skilled fury into a fine piece of pottery. Fired, enamelled, painted and glazed, somehow it survived, though its story was lost along the way. It seems strange to think that my entire life relied on so slender a thread. But such is fate. We can only wonder at it.

It is the joy of an antiques dealer to unearth the provenance of just such an object and it became my life's task to untangle its story.

From the moment when I first cradled it in my hands, feeling the clay warmed by the sunshine that spring day, I was somehow aware that the thread of my life had tangled and when I unravelled it I was starting along a new course. My fate was now in the hands of others – the potter Matthew Grindall, Luke Chater, Rebekah, Richard Oliver both past and present, Richard's family and, above all, that beautiful house, Hall o'th'Wood.

CHAPTER ONE

'There is no armour against fate'
James Shirley 1596-1666

April 1967

Looking back I find it hard to believe that at that time, on that day, I was so unaware of the fact that the past was about to creep up on me and engulf me with its stories and legends, tricks and tales. Yet as an antiques dealer I should have been aware of the effect the past can have on the present, of the legends attached to an inanimate object which can increase its price tenfold – particularly if the story is a dramatic one – one of tragedy, murder, love or hatred. If you doubt me look at the prices fetched by the ephemera connected with the Titanic or commemorative ware of the untimely death of Princess Charlotte, daughter of the Prince Regent, who died in childbirth in 1817 to the grief of the entire nation.

I remember that morning as a sparkling spring day, with lawns fresh and full of promise, gardens colourful with daffodils and tulips, prettily showy, celebrating the end of winter. Everywhere there was this same optimism in people's step as the April sun beamed down on what my aunt used to call a Persil world, one washed clean, hanging out to dry. My aunt, Eleanor Paris, had this habit of coining phrases which exactly describe a thought, a day, a picture, a sentiment. It is the mark of an artist. I am told frequently that I am very like her. This I find flattering.

So – back to the day itself.

At nine o'clock that morning I was driving from Stoke-on-Trent to Chester, filled with the anticipation of attending a Sotheby's Fine Art sale. I was humming a Supremes tune, 'You Can't Hurry Love', the window of my car wound down three inches or so, letting my hair blow free. Perhaps the title of the song was itself a portent of my future.

Because of my mission, the bright weather, and a rather smart, new, navy blue miniskirt which I was wearing with a white, crêpe blouse, I felt infused with happiness and optimism. I never could rid myself of the conviction that in this sale or the next I would find a 'sleeper' – a piece which I and only I would recognise for its age, authenticity and value. I would buy it for a bargain price and sell it for more – much more. In knowledge could be hidden a fortune and, more importantly to me, kudos. Such finds were important to establish a reputation in the competitive antiques world. It was a world which thrilled me with its secretiveness and stealth.

A little before ten I reached Chester.

I parked my car in the street, near to the saleroom, and walked briskly through the spring sunshine, passing the tiers of black-and-white shops to Sotheby's auction room in Watergate Street.

My shop in Stoke-on-Trent had been visited by an American dealer from Texas the previous week and he had virtually cleaned me out of stock. My windows currently sported empty shelves. Empty shelves earn no money so it was imperative that I filled them quickly. But there is always the caveat: fill your shop only with the right pieces, bought for the right price. A few wrong purchases and an antiques business can quickly come crashing round your ears. So I needed to be vigilant.

Outside the saleroom I paused, just for a moment, to savour the name. Sotheby's, the proud epitome of the quality antiques world; the familiarity with which I treated it, as though an old friend, always touched me. As I entered the door I breathed in the indefinable scent which is patina – age, dust, history and legend mingled with woodsmoke and sealed in with beeswax and lavender polish. The very scent of a saleroom sends my senses reeling – even today.

The next second I ran up the stairs, two at a time, straight up to the second floor which led to the viewing room, scanning the scene from the doorway.

It was a familiar sight, dusty sunshine slanting down through high windows onto glass-topped cabinets, tables of Staffordshire pottery, jugs, plates, figures, pieces of blue-and-white china and dealers moving slowly and quietly between them, up and down the aisles, picking over the pieces carefully – always carefully, sometimes with an eyeglass jammed into their eyes. There was very little consultation. Antiques dealers are happiest when they work alone. Naturally suspicious and considering everyone else to be a potential rival – someone who will outbid them and deprive them of stock, rob them of business, bid higher than them on the prize lots of the day and ultimately deprive them of income.

From my perusal of the saleroom advert in the trade press I already knew that all the great names of the Potteries were represented: Wedgewood and Spode, Whieldon, Minton and Obadiah Sherratt. And so many more anonymous potters whose names would never be known. For their pieces were unmarked, entire families who had all worked in the industry, their wares often containing spelling mistakes in their titles or letters turned around the wrong way because to the unschooled people of the Potteries they were as unfamiliar as Arabic. And yet these illiterates' imaginations could run wild so they produced blue horses, impossible lovers, pirate kings and mandarins, dwarfs and giants, exotic animals – cheetahs and jumbo elephants and an animal even they could not quite picture so they named it a camelopard. To them it was half-camel, half-leopard; to you or I, a giraffe.

A hand reached out from behind me to pick up a blue-and-white turkey plate and I recognised Eric Goodwood, a dealer I knew well, who would prove strong competition later on in the morning. He greeted me with a nod and we moved aside for one another. I would study the plate later after he had moved around the room.

As for me I had my own methods, working my way through the lots, beginning at Lot number one, considering it – rejecting it if it was a commonplace piece, too badly damaged or even, horror of horrors, a sneaky reproduction. As I worked I marked my catalogue with a coded guide price. The paranoia of the antiques world affected me too. I did not want anyone to know what my top bid could be.

My own guide prices were usually somewhere between the reserve price and my instinct for what I could sell it for minus the profit I expected to make and the cost of any restoration. To me it was a simple, almost instinctive formula which had worked well in the years since I had begun my business.

The atmosphere was soft, quiet and secretive, whispered comments wafting through the air unclear, tangled up like Chinese whispers. A time or two a phrase would unravel itself quite clearly – 'eighteenth – not nineteenth century... Alpha piece...commonplace... damaged.'

It would all affect the price.

* * *

I worked steadily for two whole hours, absorbed in the task, until I reached the far side of the room and a tall glass-fronted cabinet with a brown-coated porter standing guard, holding the door open, observing the activities. And there it was, on the top shelf – a tall creamware jug with the most exquisite design on the front. I felt my pulse quicken in recognition of its quality as I moved forward to pick it up. It was eighteen inches tall, perfect and undoubtedly late eighteenth century.

Dealers have an almost fey superstition for a piece of singular beauty. It happens rarely but sometimes an object will wind its way towards your heart. It is a dangerous thing because it robs you of every ounce of business sense you might have built up over the years but it is unavoidable in a business which relies on your aesthetic sense.

I knew before I picked it up what it would feel like in my hands, lighter than expected, the body soapy smooth, almost warm. But what was remarkable for a jug of this age was that the transfer design on its front was unrubbed so the design was still perfectly clear. It must hardly have been handled, lived its life inaccessible, on a high shelf, rarely dusted – or else preserved in a glass-fronted cabinet with its doors locked. Either that or some miser had concealed it, wrapped it in tissue paper and hidden it in a box, away from avaricious eyes. I also knew that for me this beautiful jug was the prize lot in the entire sale.

I would have it.

And so my fate was sealed. The thread of fate had bound me to this object and all that it represented. I was now powerless.

I bent my head and studied the design.

The picture on the front was of a house which looked sixteenth century. It was black-and-white, wattle and daub crooked walls, half-timbered in the intricate Cheshire design known as magpie work which was peculiar to Cheshire three centuries ago. Casement windows stared out blindly from beneath heavily carved eaves and a roof which dipped down low then rose steeply. Beneath the transfer was the name of the house, *Hall o'th'Wood*.

I remember wondering then whether such a place really existed, whether it ever had or whether it was yet another figment of the potter's mind.

Like the camelopard.

I turned the jug around. On the back was confirmation of my dating. *Rychard Oliver*, I read. *Hys jug*. Below was the date, *1787*.

But what struck me was the macabre scene depicted. It was of a public hanging, the man's head lolling at such an angle there was no doubt that the man was dead and of a broken neck. A ring of faces mocked. Yet I shouldn't have been so intrigued by the depiction of a gruesome subject. The Staffordshire potters had loved a whiff of crime and mystery. Lucrezia Borgia, Mazeppa (stealer of women's hearts, strapped to the back of a wild horse which was then whipped into a gallop), William Palmer (the poisoner) and the Red Barn and Stanfield Hall, both houses connected with murder, always fetched a good price. Even the Tichborne Claimant was a popular piece.

I held the jug for a moment, intrigued by this glimpse into an unknown story and reluctant to put it back on the shelf, still wondering why the potter had decided to paint such a macabre scene on the back when the exquisite Hall o'th'Wood was on the front. I turned the jug round again to look at the house, wondering what 'hys story' was, then noticing that on the bottom, in hand-painted, tiny lettering, was something which made the jug even more of a treasure. The potter had signed it.

Matthew Grindall, hys work.
Rebekah Grindall, hys sister.

And with these added crumbs, the Ring of the Tolkien stories could not have held more power over me than this simple piece of domestic pottery. I felt then that I had to have it, to possess it, to own it and to keep it.

But for what price? I was a dealer, existing on profit, occasionally forced to swallow a loss on an ill-advised buy.

But I could afford, on odd occasions, to indulge myself as another woman might do with an expensive gown or exotic holiday. But these baubles did not interest me so much as holding a piece of beautiful history in my hand.

I struggled to screw my business head back on.

Normally such a jug, in 1967, in such fine condition, might have fetched ninety pounds. With provenance providing a back story, possibly double that. The price I wrote in my catalogue was more than three times the estimate.

'Nice little piece.' The voice came from behind me.

John Carpenter was an antiques dealer who had a shop in Chester, less than a mile from here. We were friendly rivals. He dealt in much the same sort of stock as I. But because more people come to Chester as tourists than visitors to Stoke-on-Trent he had a healthier list of customers than I. I clutched the jug and he looked hard into my face and must have read some of my determination because he looked thoughtfully at me.

Dealers can work together at salerooms. They can ring pieces – that is buy an item for a knock-down price and then bid between themselves later. Or they can simply stand aside on the understanding that you will accord them the same courtesy. 'Ringing' is illegal and it goes on in salerooms up and down the land. But I had already made a bad move if this jug was to be 'ringed'. To display too obvious an enthusiasm is always a mistake. Your colleagues can bid you up – and up – and up. So I smiled at him and put the jug back in its place on the top shelf of the cabinet, near the back. There is even the slimmest of chances that a fine piece such as this might slip by unnoticed. On such luck fortunes are made.

'Time for a coffee?' John asked and I nodded. This was a coded message for a swapping of intention.

* * *

Next door to Sotheby's salerooms an enterprising woman called Sandra Pool had opened a coffee bar. Full of smoke and hot as the Black Hole of Calcutta. We found an empty table and a pert, blue nylon-overalled waitress brought us two mugs of steaming coffee. Moments later Eric Goodwood joined the party.

'So, Susie,' John said slyly. 'What are you after today?'

I laughed. Because I was young they often tried me like this. But I had learnt not to be too open.

'The usual,' I said vaguely. 'A few of the Staffordshire flatbacks, one or two of the figures, some of the plates. You know.'

Eric spoke next. 'Anything special?'

This put me in a dilemma. I wanted to tell them that I would buy that jug. As there is honour amongst thieves so too there is honour amongst antiques dealers.

Of a sort.

If I really desired the Hall o'th'Wood jug they would let me buy it. If it was so important I could have it – at a price. The trick was to affect indifference, buy it for the lowest possible price, without them knowing quite how much I had wanted it and was prepared to pay.

'A few things,' I said casually. 'Bits and pieces.' I diverted the subject, spooned some sugar into my tea. 'Anything you're particularly interested in?'

'I'd like to have a go at the Meissen,' John said. 'I've done well out of that in the last couple of months.'

I nodded. I had no interest in German porcelain.

'What about you, Eric?'

'I'm buying a lot of the transfer blue-and-white printed ware at the moment. Particularly Spode.'

I nodded again.

John Carpenter was eyeing me. 'Funny,' he said, smiling, 'I could have sworn you had your eyes on that nice creamware jug.'

'I might have a go at it,' I said, struggling to keep my voice casual.

'It's a lovely piece,' he commented. 'In nice condition too.' Interestingly his next comment reflected my own observation. 'Must have been put away,' he said. 'It's never stood on a dresser for nearly two hundred years. The enamelling's not rubbed at all. Did you notice?'

Of course I'd noticed. I'd noticed everything about it.

Eric Goodwood was watching me slyly. 'Know the place, do you, Susie?'

That was when I first learnt that Hall o'th'Wood was real, and still stood today. I would not have believed such a place could exist outside a particularly pleasant dream – had it not been for the hanged man depicted on the same object which turned the dream into what? A nightmare?

Surely not. Surely the house had too much perfect beauty to be that. I pictured it again, as a real place, and did not know whether I wanted it to exist outside my own imagination and on the jug.

'No,' I said baldly. 'I don't know it.'

Eric Goodwood spoke. 'It's in Balterley. I'd have thought you'd have seen it, Susie. Don't you drive from

Stoke to Chester that way? It stands back on a hill. Quite visible from the road. Beautiful house. Been in the same family for generations, I believe.'

'Really?' I had never taken that particular road.

My affected casual tone must have sounded fake. Eric and John exchanged amused glances. 'OK by us,' they said. 'You may have competition, Susie, but it won't be from us.'

So it was settled. I would be quiet when the Meissen and blue-and-white was being held up and they would not bid against me for the jug.

The business was over.

We discussed a few further lots and the tacit deal was set. There would be no saleroom battles between us today.

I wasn't naive enough to think that there would not be other competition. John was only one dealer, Eric one more. There would be others – and that was discounting any private customer who braved the jungle of an antiques auction.

But John and Eric would have been serious competition and at least they were out of the running.

Ten minutes before the sale was due to start I took up my place – half-hidden behind a pillar but in full view of the auctioneer, a young, ginger-haired public schoolboy named Saul Winters about the same age as myself. He was confident and loud and could move swiftly through the lots which suited us all. We dealers wanted to be back at our shops by lunchtime.

I did not want to attract attention but to blend in with the background. I was well known in the salerooms as a dealer in pottery. My reputation was fast growing and anything I gave too much scrutiny to would inevitably invite interest. This, in turn, could force the price up. Dealers could, on occasions, be petty, or influenced by rivalry, or even just plain greedy. If they knew that I was interested in a piece they may well try to bid me up or even affect interest simply to squeeze some more money out of me. It was simply a way of making money in a tricky, volatile world. Added to that the vendor could be at the sale, note my interest and push the bidding up. And it is a well-known fact that an auctioneer might take bids 'off the wall'.

There are as many pitfalls in a saleroom as there are sharks in the sea around Australia. One does not have to be bitten by one to know that they are there.

There is an air of tension as the pieces are held up by the porter and the bidding opens. The trick is to catch the auctioneer's eye early on. Only your initial bid needs to be showy, to attract his attention. After that the slightest movement will be interpreted. You will have more trouble giving that final shake of the head than getting your bids accepted. Auctioneers know the serious bidder. They won't miss their bid. It's their business and their profit. Saul Winters moved swiftly through the lots, pointing here and there, giving the sale an air of excitement, banging his gavel down noisily for each sale.

I was soon in the rhythm of things, bidding on a few lots and marking my catalogue, watching who was buying what, noting that John was successful buying his Meissen while Eric had trouble acquiring the blue-and-white against stiff opposition, but really my mind was fixed on the beautiful jug and I had great difficulty not turning my head every few minutes to look at it, sitting proudly on the top shelf of its cabinet to the left of the auctioneer.

I had been dealing in antiques for almost six years – ever since I had left university, the proud possessor of a BA in Fine Art. I had opened a shop and from then on I had learnt and the shop had flourished. I was now worth four or five times my initial investment and had even taken on a girl, Joanne, to manage the shop while I was away buying. But even though I was a hardened dealer, gaining experience, I still felt the familiar jolt in the pit of my stomach when the porter finally held the jug up and Saul Winters started extolling its beauty.

'What a lovely item this is. Eighteenth century jug in perfect condition...'

He stopped. The porter was whispering something to him. It was causing some concern. And the confusion was doing nothing for my nerves. I nibbled at my index fingernail – a habit my aunt had told me off for since I was a child, painting it with cloves and aloes and mustard and finally nail varnish which had virtually cured me of it – except in cases of extreme anxiety.

Like now.

Finally the auctioneer straightened and smoothly continued praising the jug. 'Lovely piece here. We have one or two bids on the books… Start me at fifty pounds.'

No one moved. Certainly not me. It was better to lurk in the deep, dark water before splashing around in the shallows, attracting attention and making that first bid. Because once I had made my first bid I would hang on tenaciously, until the jug was mine.

'Twenty pounds then,' the auctioneer said.

John put his hand up. He would take the bidding up until I entered the battle. For make no mistake about it, it is a battle, to own the piece you have decided is your star lot of the day and fight off the opposition. To go home without it would have been a battle lost.

The auctioneer looked straight at me, waiting for my bid. Winters had an instinct and he must have known, even before I waved my hand, that I would be interested in this piece. Perhaps he had seen the way I had handled it with that reverence we dealers reserve for only the most special of pieces.

I still didn't move.

The bidding reached eighty pounds and Saul Winters caught my eye. I nodded and he smiled. He knew he had me by the fish hook of desire. I felt myself flush with the exhilaration of it all.

'One hundred pounds. Saying once, saying twice. Oh – one hundred and ten pounds is that, sir?'

I did not look around but fixed on Saul Winters and gave the most imperceptible of nods.

'One hundred and twenty pounds. Saying once. Twice. Sold.' The gavel slammed down. 'Sold for one hundred and twenty pounds to Susanna Paris of Bottle Kiln Antiques.' I let out a sigh of relief.

The jug was mine.

But the sale was not over. I bid, almost casually, on a few more lots, bought a nice collection of Victorian chimney pieces for a knock-down price, and a set of three graduated earthenware plates with a rare blue-and-white pattern which Eric obviously didn't want. They weren't Spode and I suspected this was why.

Stock replenished. My shop would look good tomorrow.

But already I doubted that the creamware jug would ever sit in the window of Bottle Kiln Antiques. I didn't think I would be able to part with it.

'That ends this sale of pottery. Our next sale is...'

I moved across to pay for my lots. It was lunchtime. I was hungry and anxious to return to Bottle Kiln Antiques and gloat over my purchases. I queued behind a man I did not know. My eyes ran over him casually as I waited. He was not tall – only an inch or two taller than myself. I had an impression of square shoulders, a grey suit, very well cut, short, greying hair – and intense anger.

I corrected myself. No – not anger. Fury. He was furious with the cashier.

'I left an order to buy.' His voice was clipped. Public school. Autocratic.

The girl was very young and red in the face. Close to tears. 'I'm sorry, sir. I did try and explain over the phone. We're not allowed to take instruction merely to buy. We must have a ceiling bid.' She appealed to him. 'I mean – the lot could have fetched anything. Anything.'

The man wasn't mollified. 'I'll speak to the director.'

'Yes, sir.' The girl picked up the telephone. Then she caught my eye. I gave her a smile of shared sympathy. She spoke quickly and put the phone down. 'If you'll excuse me,' she said, 'perhaps I could sort out someone else while you're waiting.'

The man stood aside.

I put my catalogue on the counter and the girl and I ran through the lots, ticking them off, checking prices. 'Lot 4...Lot 185...246.'

'246?' The man spoke from behind me.

I turned around. And met a pair of very clear, grey eyes, a firm, full mouth, smooth skin with the faintest of tans. 'Yes.'

'The jug?' he said eagerly. 'The jug with Hall o'th'Wood on it?'

'Yes,' I said again.

'I'd like to buy the jug from you. I left an order to bid but...'

Behind me the girl was watching curiously, wondering how this encounter would end.

'I'm sorry,' I returned, angry at his peremptory tone, 'but the jug isn't for sale.'

He had a flash of temper. 'Are you a dealer?'

'Yes.'

'Well – surely dealers buy items to sell for profit.'

I was astonished at his tone. Who did he think he was?

'I'm offering you a profit on the jug,' he continued. 'A good one. So?'

'I don't sell everything I buy,' I said angrily. The man was riling me. 'I haven't quite decided what to do with it yet.'

He put his hand on my arm. 'Please,' he said, 'I really want to buy that jug.'

Something in me smiled.

Didn't he know the classic rule of purchase – never to let the possessor know your desire?

'I'm sorry,' I said a little more gently. After all – he simply wanted the piece as I did – and his leak of enthusiasm marked him down as an amateur buyer – someone unused to saleroom manners.

'It isn't for sale.' I fumbled in my bag, found a card and handed it to him. 'If I do decide to sell I promise you can have first refusal.'

But he wasn't going to give up. 'That isn't good enough.'

'I won't sell it to anybody else,' I promised.

For the first time since I had met him he smiled and I caught the full force of his charm. White, even teeth, the frown lines melting away. He was, I decided, about fifty and had a very attractive face. 'I want to... Look,' he said, changing his mind quite abruptly. 'Why don't I take you for lunch and I can explain?'

I was taken aback. 'I don't know.'

'Please,' he said. 'I know you'd find it interesting. You see...' He was about to add something else but instead he simply smiled again and I was drawn inside that magic circle of charm.

I made my decision then. After all – I was intrigued to know the history of the jug. 'All right.'

He held out his hand. 'Oliver,' he said. 'Richard Oliver.'

It was one of the three names on the jug. Perhaps I had already sensed some connection. It partly explained why he was so anxious to buy it. 'Susanna Paris,' I said.

He shook my hand and stood back while I finished settling my bill.

So together we walked out of Sotheby's, back out into the spring sunshine, and strolled through the streets of Chester.

That was how I first met Richard Oliver.

CHAPTER TWO

As we walked along the street Richard Oliver made small, chivalrous gestures: he took my arm as we crossed the road, walked along the outside of the pavement. He was a man of both charm and manners, I decided.

I was never more aware of this as on that first day in his company. We climbed the steps of The Rows and walked between the stone arches until we found a trattoria on the upper gallery, gaily decked with red-and-white gingham café curtains and wafting a scent of garlic as we opened the door. A waiter gestured us towards an empty corner and we weaved towards it, threading around tables laid with gingham cloths, lit by candles set in Mateus Rosé bottles grotesque with dripped wax. A soprano warbled an aria in the background. It was a glimpse of little Italy.

Richard held my chair for me and I sat down, intrigued by this polite, chivalrous man and his connection with my jug. The waiter hovered while we scanned the menu and we gave him our order – lasagne, salad and a bottle of Chianti. I wasn't really concentrating that hard on the food. I wanted to know the story.

'Do your friends call you Susanna?' His eyes were warm and held mine with a very direct gaze. I wasn't sure what lay behind them. It is never easy to tell when people hide behind the shield of politeness. Was this simply a ploy to persuade me to sell him the jug?

Probably.

'No,' I said, laughing. 'It's a bit of a mouthful. My friends call me Susie.'

I noted the rather distant politeness and again this old-fashioned formality.

'Would you mind if I called you Susie?'

I shrugged. 'Not at all.'

I knew, without even asking, that no one ever shortened his name. He would always be called Richard.

As the waiter poured the wine I opened the subject.

'Tell me about Hall o'th'Wood,' I said softly. 'What's the story behind the pictures on the jug?'

Richard put his knife and fork down then took a sip of wine and swallowed it. 'I don't know the story,' he said. 'At least not all of it. I live at the Hall o'th'Wood. It's my family home. It's been in my family for generations. Ever since the early eighteenth century.'

I smiled. 'It looks wonderful,' I said. 'Does it still look like that today?'

He nodded. 'Exactly. Practically nothing in Hall

o'th'Wood has changed in four hundred years.' There was an obvious pride in his voice.

I took a forkful of lasagne. 'Then it's no coincidence that your name is on the jug?'

'Not exactly my name,' he said gently, a touch of humour lighting his eyes. 'My great-great-great-grandfather's.'

'I couldn't work out from the design,' I said, probing, 'whether he was the hanged man.'

Richard Oliver shook his head. 'No,' he said. 'He wasn't hanged. He was, so family legend has it, murdered – or so I've always believed.'

I was surprised at his lack of curiosity. Perhaps it was an affectation. Surely he couldn't be ashamed of something which had happened almost two hundred years ago? I took a look at the proud face and thought, yes. It was possible.

'Who was he murdered by?'

'I don't know,' he said, his mouth straightening. 'It wasn't something I was interested in. It was not really talked about,' he added stiffly.

I didn't believe him. 'Was he murdered in the house?'

His lips tightened. He didn't like my interest in his family skeleton. 'I don't know.'

I tried another tack. 'It's a long time ago, Richard,' I said. 'It hardly reflects on your life today, surely. Aren't you just a bit curious?'

He took a long draught of wine, his eyes not leaving my face. When he set his glass down it was with a firm hand. 'There are some secrets best left secrets,' he said. 'None of it can benefit people living today.'

'But it's your history,' I persevered. 'Most people would find it interesting.'

'Not I.'

I knew it was bordering on intrusion but I could hardly contain my curiosity. 'And the potter, Matthew Grindall? His sister, Rebekah? Do you know nothing about them either?'

'No.' His curtness was bordering on rudeness.

What was the significance of the gallows, I wondered, and did not dare ask? But if he was so disinterested in the story behind the jug why did he want it so much?

It was obvious Richard Oliver would only be drawn on one subject – the house – so I returned to that.

'Describe it,' I said. I could settle for that – for the time being.

His face changed completely. It lost the shuttered look. It was as though he was two people. A Jekyll and a Hyde. His eyes returned to my face. 'As you could probably tell from the picture on your jug Hall o'th'Wood is a very old house. Sixteenth century. Built in the style of the time, in the shape of a letter 'E', in tribute to the queen. Susie,' he said, warming now to his subject. 'It is in fabulous condition. Practically all of it is authentic. The panelling, the doors, the fireplaces and the most wonderful carved oak staircase which splits in front of a huge stained-glass window, almost like a church.' He was smiling – not at me but, I felt, at the window.

'Is it a religious window?'

'No – more pastoral. The trees and animals, sheep, cows, grazing in the fields. In the centre a crusader stands.' He paused, as though about to say something but changed his mind and continued. 'When the evening comes and the light streams in through it I could almost believe in Heaven.'

And Hell? I thought. Surely the man hanging in the gallows was nearer to Hell? So was it his ancestor or the potter? Or the killer? Was Matthew Grindall the killer? Or was there another man – or woman – involved? Rebekah, perhaps?

He was watching me very carefully and I knew he was gauging my reaction. It was all a sort of test. He continued talking about the house. 'So many old properties have been vandalised,' he said, warming to his subject, 'in this decade in particular.' 'The Sixties are completely lacking in respect for tradition but Hall o'th'Wood has never been touched. It is as it always was. I feel more a caretaker than an owner. A custodian, almost.'

Of its reputation too?

But something in me connected with this sentiment. I met his eyes and my cynicism melted away. 'I feel like that too when I handle a particularly good piece,' I said.

He looked at me, a little startled but made no comment. I pushed all my questions to the back of my mind. They must wait, I thought.

It was I who broke the silence with a joke designed to

probe beneath the surface. 'And your wife?' I queried lightly. 'Does she have to cook in a sixteenth century kitchen, roasting a sucking pig with an orange jammed in its mouth?'

He laughed out loud at this quip, opening his mouth wide without self-consciousness. 'I'm not quite such a Luddite, Susie,' he said. 'I have bowed to the twentieth century, fitted it out and put an Aga in. Maria has pine cupboards for her equipment.' His face was full of fun now. He looked boyish – almost mischievous. 'And no spit for the Sunday roast either.'

'Maria?'

'Housekeeper.' He shook his head. 'My wife. Ex-wife, Julia.' He drew breath. 'Well – let's just say she didn't really care for the place. It wasn't her cup of tea. She was a modernist and hated living in what she called 'the mausoleum.' It was a mistake to have married her in the first place. We've been divorced for years now.' He gave a harsh, cynical laugh. 'Hall o'th'Wood is very choosy whom she allows to live within her walls and from the first Julia didn't fit. The minute I took her there I knew it.' His eyes looked beyond me. 'She was miserable there. If she could have had her way she would have jazzed the place up.' He practically shuddered.

'Oh dear,' I sympathised.

We ate in silence. 'How good a portrayal of the house is the picture on the front of the jug?' I was learning to skirt round inconvenient subjects.

'Perfect,' he said, instantly regaining his enthusiasm.

'Right down to the very last timber. The potter must have spent a long time studying the structure. In fact it's so accurate you can see my bedroom window on it.' His flirtation was a challenge. It made me realise how much I was enjoying his company.

My turn to dig again.

'Do you know anything about the provenance of the jug, Richard? Has it been in your family since the eighteenth century?'

The chilly look he had given to the cashier at Sotheby's was returning and it was obvious Richard Oliver only wanted to talk about the house and probably persuade me to sell him the jug. That was his agenda. If he knew the story he was not going to share it with me, an antiques dealer, who would copy the entire tale onto a large label, tie it round the handle of the jug and inflate the price accordingly. Therefore I must steer a neutral course. 'I wonder,' I said fatuously, 'where it came from, why it was made, where it's been in the last hundred and eighty years, how it ended up in Sotheby's and what the story which lies behind it is – if anyone knows it at all?' I watched him, plastering a bland expression on my face.

He shook his head. 'I didn't even know of its existence. You can imagine how I felt when a friend saw it photographed in Cheshire Life in Sotheby's advertisement. I was intrigued.'

I looked away.

'All Sotheby's would tell me was that it had been the property of a local farmer. That is it.' He was looking at me again. 'Sum total of what I know about the jug.'

And now it was mine.

He poured me another glass of wine and filled his own glass up. 'Now you,' he said. 'Tell me about yourself, Susie. Where do you come from? How did you put yourself into the antiques business? Is it a family tradition?' He was teasing me. 'Are you part of Paris & Daughter?'

I laughed with him, liking him in this light mood. I put my chin in my cupped palm and looked into the grey eyes, marking how dark the pupils were. 'Absolutely not,' I said. 'My father was a diplomat.'

He dipped his head towards me. 'Was?'

'My parents were killed when I was a child,' I said. 'I was brought up by an aunt. She's an artist. She lives near Soller – on the island of Majorca.'

'I see,' he said. 'A bohemian childhood.'

I nodded.

'So where is your shop?'

'In Hanley. Right in the middle – just down from Lewis's department store. It's in a disused bottle kiln, on the site of an old potbank.' It was my turn for enthusiasm now.

I was studying his face and thinking how pleasing his features were – neat, regular and now his temper had melted away I was aware of very great charm and warmth. I judged him then a man who could be a good friend. A deep and committed lover – or a bad enemy. His eyes were fixed on mine with a flattering absorption.

His face, which could look hard, was now softened with amusement and interest. His lips were full and a well-shaped Cupid's bow and I found myself wondering what they would be like to kiss. Hard? Soft? Warm? His eyes were still on me and I felt myself flush with embarrassment. I was not a natural coquette. I poured myself a glass of water and offered him one. He accepted and sipped it as slowly as the wine.

I continued to wonder about him, agreeing with my earlier estimate. Early fifties. His face was dominated by the clear gaze of his eyes and I found my glance returning to them. Even when I was looking away from him I could feel the heat from them as hot as a laser beam. His skin was smooth and faintly tanned, not the dark playboy tan of foreign holidays in Europe but the healthy glow of someone who enjoys striding through English countryside. I searched again at his mouth and found no trace of the anger he had shown to the cashier at Sotheby's. In repose it looked sensuous. He was watching me, still smiling. I wondered which was the real Richard – the angry, almost spoilt man, furious at being thwarted by the Sotheby's system or the charmer in a Saville Row suit, plain maroon tie and very white shirt, neatly pressed and starched. By Maria presumably.

I breathed in and caught his scent, the faintest waft of cigars, mixed with expensive soap, spice and something else indefinable, perhaps the same scent that I associated with antiques – honey, lavender, beeswax.

He continued firing questions at me about the antiques

business but I suspect he was aware of my scrutiny. 'Do you have a partner?'

I can remember thinking that if this was simply a preamble to persuading me to sell him the jug it was a very good attempt but wasted. However I determined to enjoy his company.

'I don't have a partner,' I said.

'So who is watching the shop now?' His eyes were on mine and he was gently teasing again.

'Did you simply close the door and put a sign up – Gone to the saleroom. Back tomorrow?'

I laughed then. 'No, I do have a girl called Joanne who looks after the place. She manages the customers very well. Better than me actually. She's much more patient.'

He murmured something.

'I shall call in later on this afternoon and see what she's been up to but I had to come to Sotheby's today. An American buyer cleaned me out last week. The cupboard was bare. Empty shop windows are not a good idea, Richard Oliver. People soon go elsewhere unless I fill them up which is a full-time job.'

'Quite,' he said dryly and I knew he was picturing what he considered as his jug centrepiece in my shop window. 'Hence the long list of lot numbers you gave the girl at Sotheby's.' He was scrutinising me as intently as I had been watching him.

I had a strange sensation of being out of my depth. The background noises had stilled; the soprano was quiet. The restaurant had ceased to exist outside this table and this one man. I didn't know then which was the stronger emotion – curiosity to know the story of the jug, bold attraction for Richard Oliver or something else, some recalled elegance and sophistication. I realised that this was dangerous. In minutes he would ask me to sell the jug to him and I would not resist. Then he would vanish from my life for ever.

It was he who broke the silence. 'How long have you had the shop for?'

I pulled myself back to the present. 'Six years. I did a Fine Art degree in London and couldn't wait to leave the smoke. I came up here initially to learn about pottery manufacture and never quite moved on.'

His eyebrows rose. 'I suppose you'd find it patronising of me to comment that you don't look old enough to run your own business at all – let alone for a number of years.'

Yes, I thought. I would.

'I inherited a legacy which gave me the opportunity to buy the shop and open up. It was a good start.'

'And do you buy anything?'

'Some furniture, a few clocks, bits of silver. I specialise in Staffordshire pottery, particularly Victorian portrait figures. It's my passion.' As yours is your house, I could have added.

He raised his eyebrows. 'Why portrait figures?'

Was he interested? Really interested – or was this polite affectation? I was finding it difficult to gauge. But it might be an idea to share confidences. I wanted the story behind the jug and so I tried to put my passion into words.

'Because the whole world is there seen through the honest eyes of the potter. It's a naive microcosm. Politicians, criminals, royalty and circus performers. Animals they would never see, famous people they would never meet. All fashioned in simple clay to stand on their customers' chimney breasts.'

'I see. And are some of them valuable?'

'Some of them – yes. Very. Others you might buy for as little as three pounds.'

'I see,' he said again and fell quiet.

The silence between us grew as I waited for him to broach the subject of the jug but he didn't. He poured me another glass of wine, met my eyes, smiled, and continued to eat his food.

I knew I would have to ask him. In fact, as I looked up from my food, I caught him looking at me, his lips twitching into an almost-smile.

He was waiting for me to open the subject.

Well, I thought, two can play at this game.

It was a good salad, in an olive oil and balsamic vinegar dressing and the pasta al dente, full of garlic. I wondered if he had been here before. With a wife? Mistress? Girlfriend? I was full of questions about him as I watched him eat but we were largely silent for the rest of the meal, both sipping the wine very slowly as though to delay departure.

I looked across at him and caught him watching me. I knew then that I should sell him the jug, that however

much I wanted it it should return to Hall o'th'Wood –
whatever the story. I could have named a price and he
would have paid it without argument. But some
possessiveness, some mischief, some Midas complex held
me back from offering to let it go and take a small profit.
I know now that in my heart I wanted to retain
something of Hall o'th'Wood and of its owner. But now
I can be honest with myself. Then I was making excuses.
Once I'd found out the provenance and the story which
lay behind this lovely piece of pottery I could either
treasure it myself or take a good profit. It is often not a
good idea to sell your best pieces without considering
them for a while.

We lingered over coffee, finished the bottle of wine.
And temporarily we moved on to other subjects, to travel
and paintings, the horrors of thalidomide, the tragedy of
Campbell's death, at growing ease with each other.
Reluctant for the meal to end we ordered a second coffee
and sensed that the waiters were hovering, ready to close
the empty restaurant for the afternoon. We were the only
people still sitting.

We skirted round the subject of the jug but I knew he
would return to it before we parted.

He asked for the bill and paid it and I felt suddenly
awkward. I stood up, knocking a knife from the table as
I did so. I bent to pick it up but he was there before me.
He picked it up, setting it back on the table.

My conscience pricked me. 'Richard,' I said.

He met my eyes and I had the fleeting suspicion that he

believed his charm would have worked and I was about to offer him the jug. But the demon within me whispered objections. It is a valuable piece.

You should take it to David, in the museum, and at least find out a little about it.

In your cottage it would look wonderful on the shelf above the fireplace.

Soon it will be all you have left to remind you of this lunchtime interlude and the man who has shared it with you.

'Richard,' I said again.

The grey eyes warmed as he inclined his head towards me. 'Susie?' I caught a look of amusement flash across his face.

I had been wrong, I thought. He was not so much manipulating me as mocking me.

'I don't want to sell the jug. Not just yet,' I said quickly. 'But I promise I won't sell it to anyone else. I shan't put it in the shop. It won't be for sale. I'll keep it at home, with me.'

Being thwarted didn't dent his good humour. 'I shall enjoy thinking about that,' he said, 'my jug on your mantelpiece.' He put his hand on my arm. 'So that's your decision, is it?'

I nodded.

'Well – it will have to be good enough for me, won't it, Susanna Paris?'

By being so very formal and good humoured at my refusal to sell him the piece he had taken the wind out of my sails. I had expected a battle. Not such an easy victory. I was taken aback. It had the effect of making me feel I was playing his game rather than my own. I still had the strange, drowning sensation. And I didn't want to surface.

We walked slowly back through the streets, finally separating at Sotheby's front door. He shook my hand. 'Well, Susie,' he said. 'I can tell that you are a very determined woman. I've failed to persuade you to sell me the jug. It's possible then that having set eyes on it only via a catalogue photograph I never will see it again. But...' Again the grey eyes flickered over me. 'I hold you to your promise,' he said. 'You have given me your word that you will not sell it to anyone else.'

I met his eyes as I repeated my vow – that I would sell it to none other than he and that until I did feel I could part with it, it would remain in my possession and not grace the windows of my shop. He turned on his heel then while I walked slowly back up Sotheby's stairs.

I packed my pieces carefully into boxes, including the precious jug. Then I fetched my car round to the back door, loaded up and drove back towards Stoke.

But the return journey felt nothing like my outward trip. Something had changed irrevocably. I sensed it even then. Everything had changed. The sky was a different colour. Flowers were colourful, even the tarmac of the road had a pretty sheen on it, like jet. It wasn't just the acquisition of the jug. Something in me was singing along with the music on my car radio.

All the way home I tried to analyse what had happened. I ran through the light conversation, recalled his deep, clipped tones and decided. There was an aura around Richard Oliver, I realised, a few people have it, this ability to charm people, like the man playing his slow flute to the swaying cobra. He holds the animal in its thrall. Richard Oliver had that effect on me – the magnetic gaze which attracted mine. The aura around him was like that which clings to the air around a piece of fine and expensive furniture or an Old Master painting. The best way I could ever put it into words was that he reminded me most of the lovely jug which was mine – for now: beautiful, unforgettable and potentially dangerous. He could be, I decided, a treacherous mystery.

I reached the shop just before five – much later than I had planned but once there I soon regained something of my normal, exuberant spirit. Turning into the car park always gave me a frisson of pure liquid joy. My shop, Bottle Kiln Antiques, was long and low with a stumpy bottle kiln at one end. It had once been a small potbank. But during the early part of the twentieth century it had finally closed. The kiln was now a round showroom with glazed shelves and spotlighting all the way round. This held most of the pottery while the long, low building which had once been glazing sheds and painting tables now held the furniture. From the day I had opened my doors it had been a successful business and I loved the place. It was mother, father, lover and child to me. One cannot plan to become an antiques dealer. You either have it in your blood or you do not. No amount of money can select the right stock and no amount of charm can sell so-called naughty pieces – items which have had substantial alterations done to them, cutting down large pieces to make them small, dainty, desirable and much more expensive – or downright cheats – wardrobes made into chests of drawers, square pianos turned into bookcases. There is no end to the antiques dealer's wicked inventiveness. While the buyer needs to be wary the dealer needs the rare combination of knowledge, taste, money and luck. Luck? How so? You need to be in the right place at the right time – a field at dawn in Stratford -on-Avon, a little known saleroom in the industrial north, a bleak country-house sale on a chilly November evening. It is not always so glamorous as that sunny, April day, in Sotheby's Chester saleroom.

I was one of the chosen few.

Susanna Paris's Bottle Kiln Antiques had become famous in the antiques world and the more my fame grew the faster my turnover increased. I worked hard and travelled many miles to keep the shop filled with good quality pieces. It could seem a losing battle. I was constantly chivvying my ceramic and furniture restorers to speed up their 'turnaround' time to keep my windows filled. The Sixties were heady days for 'the trade'.

Carrying one of the boxes of china I shouldered open the door. Joanne had been about to switch the lights off and go home but she stayed and watched as I unpacked my trophies. She picked each one up and made her comments.

'Shame about the broken ear.'

'You could easily have the horse's head repainted.'

I smiled at her. Plump and pretty with olive skin and thick, curly dark hair, she was a farmer's daughter from the Moorlands who had left school with no GCEs and no idea of what she wanted to do with her life. She had answered my advertisement and as much to her own surprise as mine had taken to 'the trade' like the proverbial duck to water. I had become really fond of the girl with her honest ways, her broad Potteries accent and her ability to deal with the most difficult of customers. A useful talent. Most buyers of antiques were discerning.

I think what had impressed me too was the way she had learnt quickly and seemed to feel, as I did, respect for the work of her ancestors, the Staffordshire Potters. It sometimes struck me as ironic that while pottery firms were being soaked up by the few big names, Wedgewood, Portmeirion, Doulton, she was busily selling – often for export – the wares of her Stoke-on-Trent forefathers.

I sorted the pieces out. Some would have to be taken straight to my pottery restorers, Steve and Jules; others could be priced up and put straight in the showroom. I could see Joanne's fingers itching to place them around the kiln. Finally I fetched in the last box, the one containing the creamware jug and flourished it proudly. 'What do you think of this?'

Her mouth dropped open and she reached out to take it from me.

It is a strange thing. I trusted Joanne implicitly. I knew she would not drop the jug. In the years she had been with me she had never broken a single piece. And yet I was reluctant to hand it even to her.

But I did and she gazed at it with its due admiration.

'Oh, Susie,' she said, holding it at eye level and turning it around. 'It's so – perfect.' She stopped as she studied the hanged man. 'And so horrible,' she said.

I nodded, mesmerised by the words, *Rychard Oliver, hys jug* and the magic date, *1787*.

And to myself I whispered the name, *'Hall o'th'Wood.'*

'It's a real place,' I said dreamily. 'And what's more – its owner, also, coincidentally', I smiled, 'called Richard Oliver, took me out for lunch today.'

She looked again. 'Was one of his ancestors the hanged man?'

'He says not.'

She shuddered. 'Well however lovely the house is,' she said, 'I wouldn't want this piece standing on my mantelpiece. Too spooky by half.'

She looked at the bottom of the jug. 'Well, well, well,' she said. 'A signed piece. That gives you a great excuse to spend some time with your friend David, at the museum.'

'I wonder what...' She traced the words, *Matthew Grindall, hys work.*

Rebekah Grindall hys sister...'a humble potter has to do with a house as grand as Hall o'th'Wood and what connection Rebekah Grindall has with...' She turned the jug round again, '...Rychard Oliver.'

'Nothing pleasant, I suspect.'

'I'm surprised the current Mr Oliver didn't buy the jug himself,' she said.

I took the jug from her and held it myself. 'He tried to. Luckily for me he didn't really understand the way salerooms work so his bid wasn't accepted.'

She was watching me now. 'Didn't he try and buy if off you?'

'Why do you think he bought me lunch?'

'But you didn't sell?'

'I promised him first refusal but no I didn't sell.'

'Good for you,' she said then added, 'What's he like?'

'Very suave,' I said smiling. 'And very nice too.'

She smiled. 'Well if I were you I'd give him a wide berth. There's a murky connection somewhere.' She gave me a playful punch. 'And bad blood will out.'

'Yes.' I stood up. 'Maybe. But he wasn't telling me any of it. Anyway. I can look after myself. Now then I've kept you late. I'll give you a lift home.'

We set the alarm and locked up the shop. I left behind the pieces which would be for sale. Joanne and I would price them up tomorrow. I loaded the pottery that needed restoration back into my car, together with the box containing the precious jug.

CHAPTER THREE

After dropping Joanne off at the house she shared with two other girls in Milton I drove towards my home.

My home was a grey-stone cottage in a tiny hamlet called Horton, north-east of the Potteries, just off the A53 road to Leek. Horton was a small village with little more than a pub, a thirteenth century church and a group of farm workers' cottages clustered round a large, elegant, stone farmhouse. Mine had been one of the farm workers' cottages set a mile along a narrow road. This road skirted a shallow, marshy valley populated by cows – and little else. It was a haven of peace and tranquillity and I loved it.

Horton Cottage too was my idea of perfection. Built in 1847 it had a small sitting room with views right across the valley, a dining room just big enough for four chairs round a Victorian, walnut loo table and a narrow kitchen at the back which overlooked my patch of garden – now bright with daffodils. Upstairs it had two bedrooms with low, sloping ceilings and gabled windows and a good-sized bathroom. I had bought Horton Cottage not long after I had bought the antiques shop and soon after I had moved in I had resolved that I would never sell it. It was such a comfortable home. A haven. My stability. Perhaps even then I sensed that it would, one day, become both a retreat and a refuge.

I reversed my car into the drive and carried the boxes inside. There was no hall. The front door opened straight into the sitting room, small and square with a brick fireplace, a comfortable sofa, a table, two chairs and beneath the leaded lights of the window an oak coffer. I set the boxes down on the table and, as I inevitably did when I had been out for the day, crossed the room to stand in front of the fireplace and stare up at a painting I had bought last year. I had known at the time that it was valuable but at dawn in an open-air antiques fair, people are not quite concentrating and the vendor had failed to recognise the antiquity and quality of the picture. This, of course, is the very fish hook which drags dealers out of their beds even at dawn on a cold, winter's morning. I had felt the quickening almost before I had spotted it on the floor, on a grubby sheet, propped up against a cartwheel. I had picked it up, affecting nonchalance. This affectation of nonchalance is as important an attribute to a dealer as that great well of knowledge. The dealer had demanded fifteen pounds for it, eyeing me slyly and though I had known it was worth more than a hundred times that amount I had demurred and grumbled. It was all part of the game; he had let me have it for fourteen.

Haggling becomes a habit and to agree too readily to a price implies that the object is worth more. Far more.

The subject should have told the vendor of its value but I'd realised he had assumed that it was a recent copy. True it was dark and unattractive. It needed cleaning. It was a portrait of a Tudor woman, painted in muted colours on an oak panel and the dealer had wrapped it up for me in newspaper tied with twine. I had no sympathy for him. If he had no eye for art he should, at least, have recognised the antiquity of the oak panel the portrait was painted on. There was no signature on the bottom. Possibly there never had been one and that was another reason why he had undervalued it and missed its worth. I was wary of signatures anyway. They are easy to fake. But the lack of one did not detract from my instinct for the portrait. Besides – behind the lady was a dark linen fold panel draped with a curtain and from my experience it was possible that the artist had concealed his mark amongst the drapes of the material.

She was wearing a fine dress bordered with Brussels lace. Around her neck was a ruff. Her hands were white and slim and sported one large ruby ring set in gold. Her hair was a lighter shade of brown than mine and her eyes seemed to me to hold a certain compassion. She was not, in my opinion, a beautiful woman but she had a fine face, pale porcelain skin (probably aided by lead), an obstinate, strong chin and intelligent eyes. I did not know her name but between myself and this nameless woman in her fine clothes and hard stare had sprung up an odd acquaintance. She had become both friend and confidante. At times I almost felt a physical bond between myself and this unknown woman from four hundred years ago. The picture felt part of my heritage now, as I believed the jug might soon become. Other women may have a cat or a dog or a budgerigar to welcome them home from a day's work but my welcome was this proud friend who never even looked at me other than coldly, with her own brand of supercilious hostility, as though my very presence offended her.

And yet we were friends. I stared up at her. Oh, she was a haughty one, this Tudor woman, studying me proudly from the wall, in her feathered cap, richly embroidered gown and pearls in her ears. Eyebrows and hairline plucked, lips full and reddened yet without seduction.

All I had done to the painting was to have it professionally cleaned. And that was what had thrown up the details of the work, the richness of the colour and the intricacies of her costume. It was even better than I had anticipated when I had handed over my fourteen pounds.

It is these lucky buys which keep antiques dealers chasing so hard. I had gambled and won.

I unwrapped the jug from its layers of newspaper and cradled it in my hands, feeling again the warm, waxy feel of the creamware body and the thrill which its sinister decoration gave me. With my finger I traced over the name, Rychard Oliver, and wondered whether I would ever meet the current owner of Hall o'th'Wood again or ever go there. The crooked walls of the house held a great magnetism for me, its casement windows staring blindly out with an obscure invitation. I wondered which one was his bedroom window. Using a magnifying glass I made out the detail of the panels of the great, oak front door and the face on the knocker. I turned the jug around and ran my fingertips again over the picture of the man hanging. As often happens I could see so much more now. The agonised expression, the rough shirt open-necked, the hands flailing against his fate, the bulging staring eyes. It was, in fact, horrible. Mesmerising, fascinating and ultimately horrible.

Why did he want it so much? Was it his obvious love for the house or was this jug the only witness to some family secret? Was it important? Did Richard Oliver want to keep it hidden? Was it so shameful?

Perhaps I should have paid better attention to the simple statement. Rychard Oliver, hys jug.

Tomorrow, I decided, I would take it into the museum and let David take a look at it. Together we would unearth the story.

And then I would decide whether to sell it or not.

I believed that it would be my decision.

I turned the jug upside down to study again the two names, Matthew and Rebekah Grindall. They sounded like fine Potteries names.

I set the jug down on the coffer and went to make myself a cup of coffee, then sat down on my sofa, picked up my eyeglass and studied my acquisition again.

It was skilfully painted in overglaze enamels in colours rather lurid for the late eighteenth century. I moved the glass over the man's face. The painter had taken great trouble to show the results of a slow hanging – the face was bluish, the tongue protruding, the eyeballs bulging. Peered at this close it was even more horrible. In all my years of dealing in Staffordshire pottery I had never seen anything quite so graphic as this. And that added value.

So what was the story behind it? A poacher caught on the land of Hall o'th'Wood? A murder? Who was Rebekah – apart from being 'hys sister'?

I couldn't wait to show it to David. I held the jug up to my Tudor woman. 'So what do you think of this then, madam?'

Needless to say she didn't answer.

I spent the next hour sorting out my other purchases of the day, deciding what restorations I would organise. Sometimes I had to refer to a book to decide whether a hand had held a bird, a staff, a book but Gordon Pugh's Guide to Staffordshire Portrait Figures provided all the answers.

It was too late by the time I had finished to bother with supper. Besides – I had eaten well enough at lunchtime. I read a book until I was tired then lay in the bath until I was sleepy enough to go to bed. I see now it was a solitary life – talking to a painting, reading books and spending evenings alone – but I was content.

I did not dream that night and for that I was glad. The dreams would inevitably have been a wander through the dark corridors of Hall o'th'Wood, and around every corner I would happen on a man hanging.

Next morning I drove early into Hanley and parked outside Bottle Kiln Antiques. Early though I was I still arrived a little after Joanne and found her busily dusting and polishing and setting the new pieces out, some in the windows, others already in the showroom. I laughed at her.

'Leave a bit of dust on them, Joanne, it makes people think they've found a hidden treasure. People like their antiques a bit dusty – a bit mysterious.' I made a face at her.

She dressed me down with a severe look. Joanne was a prosaic Potteries lass who had a great conscience about cleaning. Her very character would be judged by her prowess with a duster – or so she felt.

'You're looking very pleased with yourself,' she said.

'I am,' I said. 'I see you've put the new pieces around already.'

'It was getting embarrassing, Susie,' she protested. 'The shop was so empty. There was nothing here and someone came all the way from London yesterday on a buying trip for Staffordshire pottery and was most put out that we had nothing for him.'

She winked at me. 'I still managed to flog him a few pieces though. The nice big figure of Victoria and Albert and two blue-and-white Spode serving plates.'

'Good,' I said and Joanne looked smug. 'Fancy a coffee?'

'Thanks.'

She vanished into the back leaving me to think. I could feel some curious stirrings. I knew that at some point I would drive out to Hall o'th'Wood. Not simply out of curiosity to compare the house on my jug with the real thing but I have a true appreciation of all things old. And I have to confess I wanted to see the place where Richard Oliver lived. On the other hand I didn't want him to catch me spying on him.

Joanne was back, a steaming mug in each hand. She handed me one.

'I'm off to the museum in a bit,' I said. 'I want David to take a look at my new acquisition, see if he can tell me anything about it then I'll go to Steve and Jules. The sooner I get these pieces restored and up for sale the sooner I can buy some more.'

We sat and drank coffee for an hour or so, gossiping and serving the few customers who wandered in. Antiques shops are rarely busy and never crowded. In fact they should not be crowded for two reasons. The first is that you cannot appreciate fine pieces when they are hemmed in by people and the second is that their value attracts the light-fingered. The shop owner needs to be vigilant and it's hard to keep an eye on more than a few people at a time. At twelve I stood up. 'I'm off,' I said.

David Bradshaw had been a friend of mine ever since I had first come to the Potteries to live. He had run a course on Teach Yourself Staffordshire Portrait Figures and I had attended, knowing the museum possessed hundreds of figures which were never put on show but kept in locked vaults. During the course we had been allowed access to these vaults and encouraged to handle these rarities. There is no substitute for touching the real thing. Every week after the talk David and I had gone out for a drink and the friendship had blossomed. In fact, he was not only one of my closest friends; he had become almost my best customer, acquiring pieces both for the museum and his own personal collection.

I found him in his office, a tall, bony man in his early thirties, with mouse-brown hair that flopped over his brow. He wore a shapeless tweed jacket and faded brown corduroy jeans with saggy knees. I could not help contrasting his appearance with the neatly suited Richard Oliver. And David came a very poor second.

Which made me feel guilty as I plonked the box on his desk.

'Look what I bought yesterday.'

His long, bony fingers probed the newspaper. 'A jug?' he ventured.

'Right.'

He pulled it out of the box.

'Wow!' he said, holding it up. 'Wow! What a fantastic piece!'

I was so pleased. David was the one person who would

really appreciate the quality of the jug, know that its subject matter, attribution and condition made it a unique piece. David and I shared a passion for such objects and I drew in a deep breath.

He whipped out a magnifying glass from his desk drawer and spent minutes peering at the jug, scrutinising the two pictures – the beautiful house contrasting with the ugly scene.

After a few minutes he gave me a sneaky smile. 'Where did you buy it?'

'Sotheby's. Chester. Yesterday.'

He set it down. 'I hardly dare think what you had to pay for it.'

I told him and he whistled. 'Doesn't surprise me. I bet you had stiff competition.'

Stiffer than you think, I thought.

He peered again at the name of the potter. 'I don't recognise the name Matthew Grindall,' he said, 'which surprises me. He's obviously a painter of great skill. How come his name is unknown? I should know of him.'

He was silent for a further minute. 'And another thing,' he said. 'Who would commission this odd choice of subjects? I mean if someone wanted a jug with Hall o'th'Wood on why would they put such a grim scene on the back?'

He paused. 'And if it was to commemorate a hanging why not put the man's name, and the date and place of the execution? That would have been more usual.' He turned to look at me. 'I have no doubts that the piece is genuine – eighteenth century Staffordshire – but I need to do some research – dig around and find out exactly what went on.'

He picked the jug up again. 'It must have been in a private collection,' he mused. 'It's in near perfect condition. Did you ask Sotheby's what its provenance was? That might give us a clue.'

'No. I understand it came from a local farm,' I ventured.

'But there's no damage,' he enthused. 'The enamel's not rubbed. It's so perfect. Not a crack – not a chip. It must have been kept wrapped up – or in a cabinet. It's flawless.' He frowned. 'How odd. That means it hasn't even been touched.' He put his face near it, scowling. 'It's strange,' he said.

His offer came suddenly. 'I'll give you a profit on it.'

I felt immediately awkward. 'I can't sell it to you.'

He grinned. A wide, boyish, toothy grin. Both ugly and beautiful at the same time. Its ugliness was in its asymmetry; its beauty in its genuineness.

'Come on, Suse,' he coaxed. 'You shouldn't hang on to such a nice piece. It belongs here, in the museum. It should be on public show. Balterley's near here. The house is one of the great listed buildings in this area. In fact I think the Oliver family still live there.'

I met his eyes. I knew that they did.

Again I shook my head.

But David was undeterred and like Richard Oliver he thought he could persuade me to change my mind by offering me lunch. 'Then come for something to eat,' he said cheerily, 'and a quick drink? It is lunchtime.'

I had a pang of conscience. 'You won't persuade me, David.'

He grinned again. 'I can try. You'll sell it in the end.'

So for the second time in two days I was having lunch with someone who was trying to persuade me to sell them the jug. But this was in a different place than the Italian trattoria in Chester. It was at a small bar in Hanley round the corner from Museum Place. As we downed our pints and tucked into a Staffordshire oatcake with bacon and cheese oozing out, I felt I must come clean with my friend. 'Actually, David,' I said awkwardly, 'I might sell it one day, but it'll almost certainly not be to you.'

He raised his eyebrows and his green-grey eyes narrowed.

'The current owner of Hall o'th'Wood was at the sale. He missed the bidding and so I managed to buy it but I promised him first refusal so you see, David, I couldn't possibly sell it to you. It wouldn't be fair.'

He looked sulky. 'He doesn't have any right over it just because his house is on the front.'

'I know,' I said just as awkwardly, 'but he seems to love the place so much and you must admit the picture's brilliant. It's natural he's really desperate for it.'

I could feel his eyes on me.

'You could make a heap of money out of him.'

'It isn't that.'

'So what is it?'

Like many people David's real questions were often uttered in a silky tone.

But I couldn't answer something I didn't really know myself.

'I think he feels he has a sort of moral right,' I said. 'Obviously owning the house makes him want the jug.' I looked up. 'And I sort of feel it belongs to it.'

'And the hanged man?'

I was silent because I did not know. I opened my palms. 'We just don't know. We don't even know who he is.'

David misguidedly launched into a peevish attack on Richard Oliver. 'He shouldn't have been so careless, missing the bidding.'

It put me in the position of defending him. 'I don't think he buys much at auction. He doesn't understand how it works. He instructed Sotheby's simply to buy it.'

'Then he's careless with money too. They could have run him up to hundreds. Thousands even.'

Privately I agreed but this time said nothing. Richard didn't need any more defence from me.

We finished our meal and went our separate ways. I had to call in to the ceramic restorers. I returned to Bottle Kiln to pick up my car, loaded the two boxes of china into the back then drove to Tunstall, to the restoration studios.

This is one of the joys of dealing in pottery in the Potteries. There is an absolute wealth of talent here – in danger of going to waste since the pottery industry is slowly returning to its place of origin – the Far East. Pottery restoration is a highly specialised skill. You need to understand about kilns and glazes, modelling and firing, feckling and draining slip from moulds. But you need to be much more than that. You need to be an obedient copier because hands and heads, birds' wings and any other small projection can so easily be knocked off. So reference books are always spread. We discussed, drew diagrams and studied moulds until I was satisfied. I spent more than an hour with Steve and Jules poring over these books to see how best they could restore the pieces to near perfection. And almost as long again haggling and arguing over the prices, Jules with her Mia Farrow hair cut, shaking her head, wringing her hands and telling me my meanness would put them out of business. It was all an act. I returned to the shop well pleased with my day's work. But one of the frustrations and limitations of antiques dealing is that you cannot force the pace. Pieces need to be considered, studied and evaluated. You can attend ten sales and buy only one choice piece. You can put that choice piece in your shop window and wait months for it to sell. At times the antiques trade is like a snail – at others it is more like the wildebeest migration, frenetic, excited, noisy and crowded.

Joanne must have been watching for my car. The minute I reached the door she pulled it open to me, her eyes sparkling. 'Guess who's been on the phone?'

I shook my head. 'Mick Jagger? Paul McCartney?'

'Don't be silly,' she scolded. 'No. Richard Oliver,' she said. 'He asked where you were. I said out with a friend. He said would you be back by four-thirty. I said yes I thought so and he said he'd ring again. He doesn't give up, Susie, does he? He wants that bloody jug.'

I was thoughtful. So the jug was enough of a lure to keep him dangling. The thought rather pleased me.

But how had he got my telephone number?

Then I remembered. I'd given him my business card.

At four-thirty the telephone rang and I picked it up myself. 'Bottle Kiln.'

'Susie.' I recognised his voice straight away. It was deep, a pleasant, mellow tone – with a hint of uncertainty?

'Yes.'

'It's Richard Oliver here,' he said unnecessarily. 'I wonder...' He stopped. And began again. 'Would it be presumptuous?' He gave a short, dry laugh. 'If I promise not to mention the jug – not even once – would you have dinner with me one night?'

I didn't even hesitate. 'Yes.'

'Tomorrow?'

'Yes.'

'I'll come and pick you up. Eight?'

'Yes.' I couldn't think of anything more to say and he must have marked this because he gave a rich chuckle. 'You'll have to give me instructions how to get to your house or I shan't find you.'

I told him, put the phone down and ran the gauntlet of Joanne's open-mouthed gaze.

CHAPTER FOUR

The following night I left the shop early and drove home. I couldn't deny it, I was looking forward to an evening in Richard Oliver's company – whatever the hidden agenda. But I was also very conscious of the difference in our ages which in turn made me apprehensive too.

I bathed and shampooed my hair then wrapped myself up in my biggest towel and sat in front of the mirror to dry my hair and apply my make-up.

My hair always took ages to dry. It was thick, curly and unruly. My aunt would often comment, laughing as she tugged at the comb, that the unruly bit was me and I should be pleased that I was not 'thick' too but the quip never brought a smile to my lips. I was more likely to scowl into the mirror until Aunt Eleanor teased me about looking like a frog. Tonight it seemed determined to be awkward, taking twice as long as normal to dry, however hot I switched the hairdryer setting to. I had another quarrel with it. The fashion then was for dead straight locks, shining, glossy as satin. Mine was – quite simply – a disaster.

I sighed and turned my attention to my face.

I creamed some Max Factor Sheer Genius foundation over my cheeks and patted my face with some pale powder. I decided against false eyelashes. Sometimes they really irritated my eyes, which made my eyes water which in turn led to them becoming unstuck. And the last thing I wanted when dining with the suave Richard Oliver was for one of my eyelashes to land in his soup! The vision it threw up made even me smile. I suddenly wished I had time to ring my aunt and share this little image with her. She and I would have laughed together. But it was already a quarter to eight and I hadn't even decided what I was to wear. I returned to the face in the mirror, ringed my eyes with black kohl pencil, brushed on some eyeshadow, smeared on Biba lipstick and looked again at my face. I looked anxious and apprehensive. But then I was apprehensive about how the evening would turn out.

I stuck my tongue out at myself, winked and felt marginally better.

I knew the reason I felt as I did. The face that looked back at me was too young for him. Too eager, like a boarding school child being treated for dinner out by a relative, preparing herself for the adult world. It reminded me too much of my own boarding school days, of the occasions when my parents had arranged to take me out for the afternoon and the sudden end of these treats when I was returned to school. I was not elegant or sophisticated like the women I felt sure Richard would associate with. I felt suddenly unsure of myself. About to enter a strange world. And now I felt even more nervous.

I hadn't felt like this since I was fifteen and the son of one of the holidaymakers staying near my aunt's house had asked me to go to a beach party with him.

I'd gone and felt awkward for most of the evening until we'd gone for a swim and I had managed twice as far as he.

It seemed a long time ago now. I'd thought I'd outgrown such adolescent behaviour and was disappointed in myself. I tried to remind myself that I was a grown woman of twenty-six years old. I had run my own successful business for six years. I fought at the local salerooms with other dealers and I believed they respected me as an equal. I didn't need to put myself through this doubt.

But it didn't work.

I stared anxiously at my reflection and tried to calm myself but it didn't matter how many times I told myself that this was silly, I still had butterflies in my stomach.

I glanced at my watch. It was ten to eight.

I tugged at the bath towel and gave an unhappy look at myself in the full-length mirror. The fashion then was to look emaciated with a flat chest and bony hips and on this I didn't score too high either. The idol of the time was Twiggy who must have weighed a stone and a half less than I did. Her skin was fashionably pale with huge, panda eyes and I looked nothing like this. Good food and plenty of swimming and sailing off the coast of Majorca throughout the summer had given me a healthy body, full breasts, and a year-round tan. All girls and young women want to look like the icons of the day and I didn't. More than ever before I wished passionately that I was one of the thin, enigmatic women who stared at me from the covers of Vogue or Elle or Honey.

And now I had completely lost my confidence and criticised every aspect of myself I couldn't decide what to wear. The fashion that year was for short skirts – really short skirts – of which I had plenty. But I didn't think that miniskirts were Richard's style. In the end I settled on a black crêpe dress, its length just a little above the knee, empire line, with a slash in its puffed sleeves. Over the top I wore a maroon velvet jacket and on my feet high-heeled, black shoes with a T-bar. Over my shoulder I slung a black leather shoulder bag with a buckled front which I had acquired mail order from my favourite, Honey magazine.

I glanced at my watch. It was five minutes to eight. I sprayed on some Chanel No 5 and heard a car struggling to turn into my drive.

I took a final glance at myself in the mirror and met anxious eyes.

It was puerile to wait for the man to knock on my door so I simply opened it to him.

A maroon Rolls Royce had somehow backed into the narrow track behind my car. A chauffeur sat in the front and Richard had climbed out and was approaching my front door, his hand already raised to knock.

He smiled and behind that smile I saw that he too was nervous. Did the jug mean so much to him? Or did he feel apprehensive about me?

'Hello again, Susie,' he said. 'You should have warned me about the drive. Jenkins has had the hell of a time squeezing in.' Sudden warmth in the grey eyes robbed the words of any criticism and I knew that he had simply struggled for something to say. His discomfort put me at my ease.

'Shall we set off straight away? I have a table booked for eight-thirty. I don't like to be late.'

His punctuality pleased me. 'I'm ready.'

I locked the door behind me and climbed into the back seat of the Rolls, Richard next to me, while Jenkins drove gingerly along country lanes not designed for Rolls Royces but haywains and pony traps, tractors and the odd Land Rover.

Richard made some conversation, asked me what I'd been doing all day, whether I'd attended another sale and I told him I'd been busy at the pottery restorer's and the shop. I didn't mention my trip to the museum.

'Where are we going?'

'The Old Beams – Waterhouses.'

I loved the place. Again I was pleased. 'I couldn't have picked better myself.'

He turned his head to look at me. 'So you approve?'

I nodded. Not only was the restaurant good but it would be a lovely drive, through the Staffordshire

Moorlands, Leek and out onto the Ashbourne road for just a few miles.

The sunlight was slowly fading as we turned out onto the A53 road to Leek. It danced low through the trees, gleaming orange, transforming the rural scene into a fading Constable painting. I sat back and simply enjoyed the drive.

Richard too seemed content not to force the conversation but to enjoy the evening sunshine as it dropped behind the hills. Once or twice he looked across at me and smiled. A time or two more I felt his eyes on me but when I turned around he was looking out of the window. He spoke only once, to comment on the scene.

And yet I did not feel awkward in his company.

We reached The Old Beams in good time and Jenkins dropped us off at the door. Richard smiled indulgently when I thanked the chauffeur but he said nothing.

The Old Beams catches the eye as you drive through Waterhouses. On the left-hand side, at a sharp bend, long and low and fancy built it is one of the gourmet's places to eat in this part of the world. There are other, less obvious choices, pubs which cook local dishes and serve mainly to the natives but The Old Beams is where foodies find themselves.

The maître d'hôtel rushed over towards us as we entered. 'Mr Oliver,' he gushed. 'This is indeed a pleasure. It's a while since we've seen you. How are you, sir?' He pumped his hand.

I sensed that Richard did not like the attention. He merely nodded and frowned, answering curtly – bordering on rudely. 'Well, thank you.'

The maître d'hôtel gave me a curious glance and ushered us towards a table for two, in the farthest, darkest corner of the small restaurant as though we needed to be hidden away.

We ordered aperitifs and took our time choosing our food.

When we had ordered and the wine had been opened Richard poured us both a glass and settled back in his chair. 'Now then, Susie,' he ordered, as we sipped ice-cold Chablis, 'tell me about yourself. Start at the beginning.'

I smiled back. 'What do you want to know?'

'Tell me about your childhood, your hobbies, your friends, your family.' He shifted in his seat. 'Your life, Susie.' He leant forward, suddenly intense. 'What makes you tick?'

And quite suddenly this was not polite conversation but someone wanting to understand my very essence. And unusually for me, for I was a private person, I did not mind telling him.

'My parents died when I was eight.'

He lifted his eyebrows.

'They were in an air crash.'

He was still enquiring. 'My father was the pilot,' I said quickly. 'We don't know what the cause of the crash was. There was an investigation but it happened while they were abroad in the Gulf and it was apparently difficult to obtain any facts. I'll probably never know whether it was pilot error or a problem with the plane. I was at boarding school at the time and they don't exactly encourage you to spill out your emotions.'

I fell silent, recalling the summons to the headmistress, the clipped words and the terrible, empty feeling which had washed over me as I had returned to class – changed for ever. I looked up to see his eyes on me.

'I was simply told that my parents were dead, with little detail. My aunt tried to find out exactly what had happened but it was all so difficult. My father had been working out there and communications were poor. They simply vanished from my life.'

Again his eyes were on me, appraising, and I felt he had seen something of the lonely girl stifling her sobs in a dormitory.

I drank some of the cold wine which checked my emotion. 'I spent the summers with my aunt. She was wonderful. She simply stepped in and took our upbringing over. My father's sister,' I explained. 'Eleanor Paris. She's an artist. You may have heard of her.'

He shook his head.

'She's getting quite well known. She lives on the north-east coast of Majorca, between Deja and Soller. There are a lot of artists there.' I smiled. 'It's a sort of colony. I spent all my holidays with her, at Casa Rosada. Her paintings are...' I struggled to describe her frenetic, moving paintings.

He was listening very intently.

'...well – I think they'd be classed as surrealist.' I laughed and tried to explain. 'They're very distinctive. I could recognise one of hers from the other side of a gallery. She uses the colours and textures of the island but *her* style.' I laughed and watched him smile. 'That's all her own. Think somewhere between Rousseau and Chagall. Lots of flying houses and distorted people who, when you look, are actually someone you know.'

His eyes gleamed. 'She sounds interesting. I'd like to meet her.'

I was as sure that she would like to meet him. And as for painting Hall o'th'Wood I could imagine the way her brush would twitch from the moment she saw it, even perhaps see the house and the painting through her eyes. She would have made the house full of movement, peopled with the three persons from the jug – Rychard Oliver, ancestor of the man who sat opposite me, giving me all of his attention, and the potter too, Matthew Grindall and his sister, Rebekah. The gallows would hover, threatening, over the house, its significance unknown. 'She is interesting,' I said. 'In fact I think she's probably the most interesting person I have ever met.'

I pondered. 'It was probably her influence on me that gave me the confidence to open the antiques shop.'

'And have you found it hard?'

'At times. I made some pretty awful buys right at the beginning.' I laughed. 'I lost money for the first six months.'

'And then?'

'Something clicked. I found my taste and my market.'

'Is it difficult to be accepted in the business?'

'The trade,' I corrected, still smiling. 'No – not really. As long as you don't act like a complete prat at the saleroom other dealers don't care whether you're young or old, male or female, rich or poor. In some ways it's a very egalitarian existence. Nothing is important but your knowledge and the way you use it.'

He poured me another glass of wine and led the conversation in another direction. 'Do you have other family besides your aunt?'

'I have a sister.' I made a face. 'Sara. Five years older than me. She sort of looks after me. Takes charge. She's quite bossy really. She's always interfering in my life and thinking she knows what's best for me.'

'And does she?' He was smiling.

'Absolutely not,' I said firmly.

'Where does she live, this bossy sister?' I think it was at this point, when he shared my humour and kept his gaze firmly on my face as though he would drink it, that I began to feel that this was no ordinary man.

I answered his question. 'Newcastle-under-Lyme. Not far from here. Sometimes I think not far enough,' I added darkly.

We ate our food. I know it was good but I cannot remember what it was. We chatted some more but I can't remember now what turn the conversation took. I wanted to ask him about his life but didn't feel comfortable intruding. I had the impression that Richard Oliver was an intensely private man who would not welcome prying. In that way we were alike.

The dessert menu arrived and we chose. Then followed the cheese and biscuits. There were some good local cheeses, one from Hartington, and they came with seedless grapes which we ate sporadically. I wanted the evening to extend into the night.

When coffee came I bit the bullet.

'What about you? I know nothing about you apart from the fact that you live in Hall o'th'Wood, that you are divorced and have a housekeeper called Maria.'

He made a wry face and chose to talk about the easiest subject. 'I don't know what I'd do without Maria – and Jenkins, the chauffeur and Elijah Hobson, the man who lives in the Lodge and does the garden. They run the house – and my life – for me.' He smiled and something in that smile made me catch my breath. He did not strike me as a man prone to sentiment yet the affection in that smile was warm.

We talked of other matters then, and finished our food while all the time I was thinking that I did not want the evening to end.

Ever.

And we did not mention the jug. It lay between us, cold and threatening, a dark side to this wonderful evening. We did not need to speak of it but it was still there.

Jenkins drove us home at the same sedate pace as our

outward journey. Richard was quiet for most of the drive. A few times I felt his eyes on me and wondered what he was thinking. As we turned off the Leek road onto the narrow lane that led towards Horton he suddenly looked straight at me. 'How old are you, Susie?'

I said something fatuous about never asking a lady her age then answered him. 'Twenty-six.'

'I have a son of the same age.'

I tried to make a joke of it. 'Let me guess his name. Is he called Richard too?'

'No.' He caught my mood and tossed it back. 'He's called Michael. As I said – Julia – my ex-wife – did not care for tradition. She insisted he was not called Richard and I capitulated.' He bit his lip. 'I was still at that stage in our marriage when I was prepared to try compromise. It was a waste of time.' He stared out of the window again even though now it was dark.

It broke the moment and we were both quiet again.

When we reached the cottage Jenkins again reversed the car into the track at the side and then switched the engine off.

I asked Richard if he would like a coffee and he accepted. He muttered something to Jenkins while I opened my front door and put the kettle on. I felt the draught as the door swung open again and then heard it close behind him. When I brought the coffee into the sitting room he was standing in front of the portrait of the Tudor woman, staring up at her.

I put the tray down on the coffee table, next to the jug, turned and met her black eyes suspiciously. Was I imagining it or did they warm when they rested on him?

'That's quite a painting,' he remarked before moving on.

I told him the history of my Tudor friend but I could tell he wasn't really listening. His mind was not on my story. Possibly it was on his.

He was prowling around the room, picking things up, asking me about them, hardly listening when I spoke, and putting them back down again. He was like this until he reached the oak coffer. Then he bent and picked the jug up.

'It's even more perfect than I had thought,' he remarked, turning it around. 'I knew the picture of the house was detailed and faithful from the photo in the magazine. But this...' he indicated the hanged man. 'This is horrible. Quite horrible.'

'I imagine,' I said carefully, 'that the story behind it must be gruesome?'

'Hmm,' he said and set it down.

He was giving nothing away and again I was full of doubts.

Perhaps this night had been a set-up. Whatever he had said it was the jug which connected us. Nothing else.

But surely all that conversation, I argued, his attitude...? Had I been so deceived? Kidding myself? Whatever he had promised would he now offer me a profit on the jug, write out a cheque and vanish from my life?

He smiled at me politely.

I have a natural suspicion of polite men. Their politeness can hide so many things – boredom, manipulation, connivance. Determination.

He looked back at the jug and I caught a tightening of his mouth and remembered the fury he had vented on the cashier at Sotheby's. I was uncomfortable. I knew how very much he wanted it.

'When did it leave your family?' I asked. 'Surely it was at one time at Hall o'th'Wood?'

'I don't know that it ever was in my family,' he said curtly.

I realised that even if he knew the history of the jug he would not share it with me but bury it.

I also knew that it shed some ugly light on his forbears. I could have argued that what our grandparents do does not necessarily reflect on our own character but perhaps even then I knew that this charming and polished man concealed a flaw which had been present in his great-great-great-grandfather.

His eyes flickered away from me. 'I've never heard it mentioned,' he said. 'I didn't even know it existed until that friend of mine saw it pictured in the magazine and rang me up. The minute I saw the picture I knew without doubt that it was authentic. There is no mistaking Hall o'th'Wood.'

There was no mistaking the pride in his voice either.

'I strongly suspect if it ever was in the family that it would have been my grandfather who would have sold it.' He smiled but it was not at me. 'He was a very sticky Victorian gentleman who had a penchant for gambling. Stories go that he all but gambled Hall o'th'Wood away.' His eyes moved across to the jug. 'I wouldn't be at all surprised if he would have gambled this away if it ever came to the Oliver family.' He said no more, except, tersely, 'I should be going, Susie.'

Maybe I should have repeated then that I would not sell the jug to anyone else, that I had already decided that it would return, one day, to its rightful place and rightful owner, that I simply wanted to possess it for a little while longer. Perhaps the next few weeks would have been different. But I said nothing and he walked towards the door, I with him, when quite suddenly he turned around, put one arm around my head, pulled me towards him and kissed me on the mouth. It wasn't a hard kiss, more exploratory, almost a brush, a hint, velvety and soft but even so I caught the first indication of the full passion that I had already guessed at. When I did not pull away he put his hands either side of my face and this time the kiss was different. It was hard and lingering, his body bent in towards mine.

My aunt told me once, when I was about fourteen and curious about such things as love, that you know when you are falling in love because when they kiss you it is a little like drowning. You do not lose consciousness or hear bells and yet all sensation is altered. I did not know whether she had ever felt like this. I never asked her but I felt like that now. I knew that I was being sucked into this man's life and love and was unsteadied by it. My perception of the world was altered for ever.

'Susie,' he murmured, his lips brushing my cheek, my hair and finding my mouth again.

Then he broke away and stared at me. 'Will you come and spend a day with me at Hall o'th'Wood?'

'Yes.' There was nothing in this world I wanted more.

'Saturday?'

I nodded.

'I'll ring you first thing in the morning,' he said, 'and tell you how to find it. My darling,' he said, pushing my hair away from my face and kissing me again, 'come early and stay late.'

Then he was gone. I heard the door close behind him, the car pull away and stood for a while in the same spot, not moving from the air which he had breathed. In it I caught again the faint tang of a cigar and an even fainter tang of aftershave, scents which now would always mean him.

I took the coffee cups back into the kitchen, switched the lights off and went to bed knowing my dreams would be all of him. I wouldn't sleep but would touch my lips and recall the feel of him against me.

I couldn't wait for Saturday.

CHAPTER FIVE

I was wakened early the next morning by the telephone and Richard's voice. 'Morning, Susie,' he said and I sensed he was smiling. 'I hope I haven't woken you up.'

I said no and he laughed and I knew that he knew I was lying. I felt warm, comfortable, intimate and snuggled down under the blankets.

'Have you got a pen handy? And some paper?'

I fumbled around and found some.

'Fire away,' I said.

'Right. Take the A525,' he said, 'from Newcastle towards Balterley. As you reach the village look up to your right and you'll see the house on a small hill.' He gave a short laugh. 'You should recognise it. Come as early as you like,' he said again, 'and stay late.' I promised I would.

'I'll see you tomorrow then.'

The last day of the week dragged and more than once I caught Joanne watching me, curiosity sharpening her features but I said nothing. And later I was glad of that.

Sara rang me on Friday evening and asked me to spend Saturday with her and the children. 'John's away,' she said, 'playing golf. We could do with the company. Maybe go to the pictures, Susie.'

'I can't,' I said. 'I'm busy.'

I should have remembered that no corner of my life was ever safe from my sister's prying.

'What are you doing?' she asked suspiciously. 'Surely Joanne can manage the shop and there aren't any auctions on a Saturday, are there?'

'I'm spending the day with a client.' The words were out before I could think and they invited her curiosity.

'What for? Who is he?'

'How do you know it is a he?'

'Because you're being evasive, little sister.'

'Well – it is a he. I bought a jug he's anxious to buy and we'll discuss it tomorrow.' It was probably the truth anyway. Any feelings I thought he had for me were probably imagined. Taking me to Hall o'th'Wood was likely to be simply a clever ploy.

'All day?' she asked incredulously.

'He's asked me to spend the day at his house.'

'The evening too?'

'Well, I don't know how the day will pan out,' I said desperately. 'But I can't make arrangements.'

'Hmm,' she said suspiciously. 'You're up to something, Susie. I shall ring you first thing Sunday morning.'

I made a half-promise to see her on the Sunday then put the phone down.

Others, it seemed, were also sensing something different about me. David rang later that evening and asked me to have dinner with him, also on the Saturday night. 'I've done a bit of digging,' he said. 'I haven't got the full story behind the jug. It seems some details are missing from church records and such but I can shed a bit of light.'

'I'm sorry, David,' I said. 'I've made arrangements.'

'Oh.' I knew from the hurt in his tone that he was offended.

'Sunday lunch,' he said brightly. 'We could go to the pub.'

Again I refused. 'I've promised to see Sara,' I said.

'But I had something special planned, Susie,' he said.

This was unusual. We more often shared lunchtime drinks than dinners. I made another half-promise – to have dinner with him one night during the following week.

'Suit yourself, Suse,' he said. 'I just had something to celebrate, that's all.' Which immediately made me feel guilty. For having a prior engagement?

'Next week,' I said. 'I will be in touch. I promise.'

I was destined to break all my promises.

To myself, even then, I had to confess that none of these arrangements seemed real. The fact was I could not see beyond tomorrow and my day at Hall o'th'Wood. I was excited that I would be finally seeing the place and for the umpteenth time that evening I picked the jug up from the table and stared at it, turning it around in my hand and read the words, again and again, and wondered when I would understand the significance of the names and the pictures so carefully painted on it.

I awoke at seven on the Saturday morning and wondered how early was Richard's early. Not this early. Not before ten, surely?

I bathed and washed my hair, ate the smallest of breakfasts, a bowl of Shreddies and milk, two cups of coffee, and found I could not even contemplate the piece of toast which popped out of the toaster. I drank a glass of orange juice and asked myself the question again.

How early is early? How late is late?

I dressed with care in white, bell-bottomed, linen trousers, a striped skinny-rib jumper and a navy jacket, wedge-heeled shoes and sat for a while, trying to touch my face up invisibly with make-up. At nine o'clock I drove slowly through Newcastle then turned along the A525 towards Balterly, in Cheshire.

As long as I live I shall never forget my first sighting of Hall o'th'Wood. It has burnt itself into my memory now but on that day I could only think that the house was even more beautiful than its picture on my jug. No mere picture even executed by the most skilled artist could ever do it justice. It stood, timeless and proud, on the top of a small hill, nestling in a few trees, walls crooked, black and white, just as I had seen on the jug. It had been truly portrayed by that unknown potter. No artist's licence but an accurate picture – but I had been unprepared for its sheer grace. I turned into the daffodil-lined drive, pulled up and stopped the car to stare at it for a moment, absorbing its beauty, thinking I had never in my life seen a house which seemed to hold history so completely in its grasp.

I would have stopped for longer but a man who had been trimming the verges crossed over to me and leant in through the window. 'Morning,' he said politely. 'Is it Mr Michael you're wanting to see?'

I shook my head. 'No, Mr Richard.'

'Right then. Up you go.' He tipped his cap and stepped back smartly while I drove towards the house leaving Elijah Hobson standing, staring after me. There – I knew his name already.

The main entrance was reached at the side, under a wide archway which led into a square, cobbled courtyard. To my right two huge doorways marked the old coach houses, beyond those various gardener's sheds and stables. But straight ahead were the crooked, intricate walls of the old house, casement windows reflecting the gold sunshine of the morning and black beams which stood out starkly against the old, white walls. I climbed out of the car, looked up and saw the window Richard had spoken about, the crusader. Bewitched, I stood still and stared at the house until the studded, black, oak door opened and Richard was walking towards me. 'Susie,' he said, gladness making his voice rich and welcoming. 'Welcome to Hall

o'th'Wood.' He bent and kissed my cheek. 'Welcome,' he
said again. 'It's so good to see you here.' He dropped an
arm casually around my shoulder. 'So,' he said, standing
alongside me and staring up, with me, at the house.
'What do you think?'

I chuckled. 'Need you ask?'

We entered the hallway, still laughing, and I gazed
around, speechless, absorbing it all, from the wide,
polished oak floorboards scattered with Turkish rugs, to
the huge, stone fireplace, the gleaming panelled walls
hung with portraits, and Carolean stump work. The
staircase swept majestically upwards, splitting in front of
the huge window, the crusader staring down
benevolently, as though protecting the people who lived
here. I scanned the minstrels' gallery and finally tipped
my head right back to stare at the high ceilings with their
plaster mouldings.

I turned towards Richard and said nothing. I had no
words to describe the emotion this place aroused in me.
But by his silence I had the feeling that he knew just how
much I appreciated the antiquity of the place.

Elizabeth herself might just have stepped out into the
garden. I caught a waft of a rose petal nosegay and
beeswax polish mingled with lavender and a tinge of
rosemary.

He watched me for a moment then led me into the
kitchen with a 'Come and meet Maria. Let's see if she
approves of you too.'

The kitchen was long with a low-beamed ceiling and

scrubbed pine cupboards all around. The floor was red quarry tiles, polished to a dull sheen. On the rack, over a cream-coloured Aga cooker, clothes were drying filling the room with a warm, steamy scent.

I could smell onions and garlic being fried gently in olive oil.

A stout woman in a black dress was silhouetted against the window. She turned around as I walked in and stared at me with dark, hostile eyes. Richard did the introductions. 'So,' she said. 'You are the Susie he has been talking about.' She had a strong Spanish accent.

'Buenos días, Maria,' I said. 'Hola. ¿Cómo está?'

She faced me with astonishment. '¿Habla español?'

'Sí,' I answered. 'Crecí en Mallorca.'

She hugged me then, and chattered in a mixture of Spanish and Mallorquí while Richard watched with an indulgent expression on his face.

After a few minutes Maria shooed us out of the kitchen, scolding Richard. 'How you think I make you deener when you make me to talk talk talk? How I get things done?'

He took me then through the rest of the house. From the long dining hall, with its oak refectory table and the coat of arms over a fireplace big enough to roast a pig in, and the library, to the pretty sitting room with its casement windows which overlooked a knot garden, then the lawns and the trees beyond – the very wood from where the timbers of the house must surely have come? When we walked up the wide, carved staircase I

stopped in front of the stained-glass window and turned
to Richard. 'You were going to say something about the
window when we were at the restaurant the other night,
weren't you?'

He was staring at it as he spoke, dropped his arm
around my shoulders. 'Yes.' He laughed and pulled me
closer to him. 'Silly really, only a silly confidence about
pretending the crusader was asking me to join him in the
Holy War.' He was smiling, looking relaxed and happy
and I reflected how different he seemed from the angry
man at the saleroom who had been thwarted by the
system. Here, surrounded by the portraits of his
ancestors, he was not an enigma at all but someone who
knew exactly where he belonged in the order of things.
And that was here, in this house. I could not imagine him
anywhere else. As he led me up the stairs I understood
then that this man could not exist outside these ancient
walls. Here, all at the same time, he was the small boy,
the child, the grave-eyed lad, the young man, the son and
the father.

It was a powerful thought.

We walked along the galleried landing hung with
portraits of his ancestors. I studied each one and found
what I had searched for, a strong family resemblance.
Here the grave, grey eyes with their steady, unflinching
gaze, there the full mouth – the tightening of the lips
leaking an impatience with the sitting, as though they
urged the artist to work quicker. As I looked at each one
I found elements of Richard's face mirrored here and

there throughout the generations. It pleased me.

He stopped in front of one, on the upper landing – a rakish-looking fellow, with the same eyes, but an even harder line to his mouth. He was wearing tight trousers and bent forward, leaning on a walking stick. In the background was a coach and horses. Peering out of the coach was the frightened face of a young woman. It was a curious subject for a family portrait. I peered closer. His eyes stared out at me with a lascivious look and I stepped back.

'Before you ask, Susie,' he said, 'this is the Rychard Oliver who was murdered. I don't know the story – not anything about it. I understand he was in his late thirties when he was killed. What do you think?'

'What did he do,' I mused, 'that Matthew Grindall painted gallows on the back of the jug? He wasn't hanged, was he?'

'Perhaps it was Matthew Grindall who was hanged and threw this pot anticipating his fate.'

'Perhaps.'

Richard's mouth tightened. 'Not all families,' he began, 'are perfect. Some families are fatally flawed, Susie,' he said softly.

I looked at him and he gazed beyond me.

'I suppose I'm trying to explain that there are skeletons in cupboards. This man had the very worst of the Oliver tendency.'

'To what?' I looked at the face again and felt troubled.

No man is really perfect. What did Richard hide behind his urbane and charming exterior?

'It might have been a duel,' I said lightly, 'over the woman in the coach.'

He touched my hair. 'I really don't know,' he said softly.

I remember wondering then what story David had turned up.

The bedrooms were all huge with four-poster beds draped with thick, brocade hangings. Maria had opened the windows to each one to air it and there was here and there a strong scent of lavender and rose petal potpourri combined with the beeswax polish which made every piece gleam. I wondered which one was his bedroom, the one whose window had been faithfully copied onto my jug. Then I caught the lingering scent of aftershave and cigars and knew the room with the wine-coloured bedspread was his. The room with a huge key in the door.

I loved the place. Everything seemed to have sat in the same position for years. The silver-backed brushes on the dressing table, the paintings, even the books on the side table by the bed. It all belonged so perfectly.

Studying the objects made me share an understanding with him that the jug too belonged back here. It had no business being in my cottage. I would have to sell it to him. Now that I had come here I shared that moral obligation, to return what was rightfully his. Whatever the story it was his story – not mine. I made a vow not to be greedy with my profit. At the time I felt his friendship was of more value than a few pounds.

'Show me your grandfather,' I said suddenly, 'the gambler.'

He stopped in front of a portrait of a heavily whiskered man in Victorian dress, a pack of cards scattered across the table in front of him. I stared at the background of the portrait, wondering if I might see some evidence of the jug – its spout, a portion of handle, something – anything – but it was not there. Perhaps the old scoundrel had already sold it. Or perhaps the jug had been secreted by the potter and never had found a place here.

It was the only time throughout the entire day that the jug was mentioned – and that obliquely.

He pointed to a door at the very end of the corridor. 'Through there,' he finished, 'are Maria's rooms. And that, my dear, is that.'

At some point while we sauntered along the panelled corridors of the old house, I like to think that I saw beyond the beauty of the place. I like to think that I recognised the burden of responsibility which must sit on the owner's shoulders and weigh him down.

We heard a gong sounding from the hallway and were summoned to lunch in the long dining room. It was a simple meal, a small salad with fruit and cheese to finish. It was the food I had been reared on. Simple, good, homely food. I commented as such to Maria and she beamed. 'He told me something simple for lunch.' Then she smiled. 'Ah, but, Susie,' she promised, 'tonight you will eat. Such a feast I will prepare. You will have to go for a long walk this afternoon to make your appetite.'

The entire day passed as in a wonderful dream. I remember wandering the long passageways again and noting more and still more, tapestries worked by the women of the family, the samplers by the children, toys in the attic rooms – a rocking horse, a doll's house, a Noah's ark, an oak crib, skittles and a top and whip. A Hornby train set, packed away in its box. 'And your son?' I asked. 'Does he live with you?'

Richard's arm was around my shoulders. 'No,' he said, 'Michael moved out a few years ago. He needed his space,' he added dryly, 'as I needed mine. We do work together but he lives a few miles away.'

'Is he married?'

'Not so far.' I felt his hand on my shoulder tighten and he stared very hard into my face as though wishing to read my thoughts. Not only current but past as well. 'And you, Susie Paris, have you ever come close to being married yourself?'

I shook my head. 'Not even close.'

I wanted to tell him that what I remembered of my parents' marriage was that it had been idyllic, loving, sharing and perfect. Of course I could only look at it through a child's eyes but my aunt had nurtured this belief and I clung on to it, that they had died together, happy. I wanted no less from my own marriage.

* * *

Later we strolled through woods carpeted with bluebells, down the bark path and the hundred steps to the lake at the bottom. We walked right round its perimeter, well over a mile of muddy paths, the water bright blue in the afternoon sunshine, its still waters reflecting the fluffy, white clouds and we watched, silent and motionless, as a heron speared a fish with its beak. We turned to look back at the house and watched the sun drop behind its roof while Maria switched the lights on one by one. It was getting cold. I shivered. And still I did not want to leave but to hold this image in my mind for ever. He kissed me then, hard on the mouth and I knew this was where I wanted to stay for all time. 'You love it too, don't you?'

There was no mistaking the enthusiasm in Richard's face and I remember that I wondered whether it was possible that a man could love a house too much. Perhaps the reason he had never married again was because all his love was caught up in Hall o'th'Wood leaving him none to squander on a woman. I remember too that when he kissed me I wanted him to keep going. I opened my mouth to him, remembering my aunt's words. I was still drowning.

I shivered again. Perhaps I knew that this was not real life. There was too much. 'You love it here, don't you?' I said.

'I do,' he answered. 'I do. My ex-wife said too much.' He gave a dry little laugh. 'She said it took over my life.'

He was frowning abstractedly and the spell was

broken. I wished he had not mentioned Julia Oliver.

I felt a compulsion then to lighten the heaviness in his face by teasing him a little. 'It's a good job some of my colleagues aren't with me here, today, Richard,' I said smiling. 'They'd be falling over themselves, bidding you on some of the pieces here.'

I swear he shuddered. 'Don't even mention it,' he said. 'The thought of this being broken up and squabbled over, picked over like carrion by vultures after it's been in my family for three hundred years.' He shivered again. 'Don't even mention it, Susie. It is my worst nightmare.'

'I hope you're not calling me a vulture,' I said briskly. 'It's an honourable profession.'

His face still looked strained and unhappy and so I continued in the same light vein. 'Have you heard the old joke about four antique dealers stranded on a desert island with a Chippendale chair? They all make a living out of it until a boat comes along.'

He snapped out of his reverie. 'Is it really like that?'

'Oh yes,' I said.

He had lightened up completely. He drew me to him and kissed me again and I put all rogue ideas far from my mind.

We walked back up the steps. Lights were sparkling all over the house as though it too was in party mood. Two glasses of sherry stood on a silver tray and we picked them up.

'Come,' he said. 'I want to show you something.'

He led me again along the corridor lined with

portraits, which led to a much smaller dining room and a library. It was shabby and lived-in. There were two Queen Anne armchairs either side of a fireplace, a television, a desk and shelves of books.

'This is my inner sanctum,' he said. 'My own private world. Welcome to it.'

He drew me to him and kissed me, his mouth open, urging and I responded.

I felt alive with this man.

'Come,' he said, only minutes later. 'Maria only allows me fifteen minutes at most to take my sherry.'

I glanced back at the room.

One day, I thought, I shall know. Records exist in churches and family Bibles. I would learn what I needed to know about this family.

Maria served dinner in the great hall, a saddle of lamb, vegetables and a bottle of claret then some fruit to finish. Instead of sitting us at either end of the table she put us across the top corner so we were intimate and close. I spoke to her again in Spanish and she bent and kissed me on the cheek with real affection. 'Come again, my Susie,' she said, 'before too long. You make this place home. He—'

'That's enough, Maria.' Richard dismissed her abruptly.

This was something I was to learn about him. It was not my nature to accept that people serve. I was egalitarian. To me anything done for me was a favour but to Richard it was a simple right.

Maria did not attend our table again but left dessert and coffee on the side table and walked out. I promised I would see her in the kitchen before I left.

We talked until late, finished the bottle of wine and I found myself relaxed and comfortable in his presence. He asked me about my day-to-day existence in Majorca, the people I'd met there, about my sister and my aunt's house, even about my boarding school and what I recalled of my parents. He asked me a question or two about pieces of furniture which had become damaged. I recommended a furniture restorer, knowing he would like Trevor, who dressed like King Charles I complete with pointed beard and shoulder-length curls. We spoke about woodworm and damp rot, about picture cleaning and pottery restoration. I promised to return and oversee some renovations of the antiques and in turn he told me about his life, about stocks and shares, financial management, his business in Newcastle. He frequently touched my hand as he spoke, stroked my cheek, kept his gaze on my face. I didn't want the evening to end. I wanted it to go on for ever and ever because the minutes were all charmed. The truth is that I didn't want to go home but to stay here and never re-enter the outside world. How different would events have been if this had happened? But Richard did not invite me to stay so at a little after midnight I stood up. I had planned an early start in the morning to attend an antiques fair near Preston before going to see Sara. The fair was a good two hours' drive away and it started at 5 a.m. I would get little sleep.

Less sleep than I thought.

I put my head round the kitchen door but the lights were off and the room tidied up. Maria must have gone to bed hours ago. Richard saw me to my car and wished me goodnight. He kissed me again then closed my car door. 'Goodnight, Susie,' he said.

I wished him goodnight too.

'Until we meet again then,' he said and I drove away, back down the long drive and onto the A525. I was home forty-five minutes later.

I reflected on the words most of the way home. He hadn't said he'd ring me or made any definite arrangement to see me again. Only until we meet again. What if we never did? But surely the day had gone well, I told myself uncertainly.

I was back in my teenage years when a first date could lead to a second or a second to a third – or not – and felt disappointed. I had thought we had been close. Had it all been my imagination?

Until we meet again? What did that mean? Exactly?

I pondered the question right up until I turned into my own drive. And saw the front door swinging open.

It was splintered. Someone had kicked it in.

I ran inside and the first thing I noticed was that the jug had gone.

Then I noticed something else. Nothing else was missing. Nothing. My paintings, my pottery, my television set, my stereo were all in place. Nothing else was gone. Only the jug. And gradually the significance of everything sank in. It all fell into place perfectly. The jug had been stolen to order.

I didn't need to think who by.

'Rychard Oliver,' I whispered. 'Hys jug.' And now he'd got it back.

I should have paid more attention to those words. They had been a warning and I had caught a glimpse of the steeliness that lay beneath his charm. What could he possibly have wanted from me except…? I felt so silly.

The jug was not mine. Never had really been mine. Never would be. Who could possibly possess it except the owner of Hall o'th'Wood?

I felt my resolve strengthen.

He wouldn't get away with it.

I was calm as I rang the police who promised to come round first thing in the morning, still calm as I nailed a panel over the splintered wood, but when I sat up in bed that night I felt hot tears drip through my fingers and wasn't sure whether they were tears of fury or grief at the glimpse of something so beautiful and yet so far out of my reach. I felt a fool.

CHAPTER SIX

Dawn always comes, doesn't it, stealing in like a thief on the unwary, expecting to find them still asleep?

I wasn't. I had watched the pale light move across the field towards me with only one thought in my head. What a fool I'd been. How could I ever have thought I meant anything to him? It was all his precious house. That was what he cared about.

Only that. And while I'd been distracted he'd sent someone over to steal the jug.

My thoughts were as bitter as aloes as I ran through every moment spent in Hall o'th'Wood, every single glance or gesture – and interpreted them differently. Patronising, a superficial interest and, above all, get her away from the house. Leave the coast clear. Even the kisses I now saw as a way of binding me to him so I would not report the burglary. I could not help thinking how like his ancestors Richard Oliver was. Flawed. A felon, a gambler. Who knew what other faults came to the fore in old, wealthy families?

At six o'clock I finally rose, wrapped my dressing gown around me, made some coffee and sat on my sofa while the Tudor woman's eyes mocked me for being naive and trusting. She would have seen through him.

A small voice inside me ran through the arguments against Richard having been involved but I swept them all aside. Surely the man I had judged him to be would not have stooped so low? The most significant fact, to me, was that while there were far more saleable or valuable items in my home – my eyes rested on my Tudor painting and then on an Obadiah Sherratt figure of Polito's Menagerie worth thousands – nothing else in the entire cottage had been taken. Not paintings or silver, television or stereo. Not cash or jewellery. Nothing was missing but this one piece of pottery. But that would be his downfall because the jug was not only distinctive. It was unique. And one day I would find it again. Of that I was sure.

The facts were staring me in the face. I had been lured away from the cottage purely so Richard Oliver could reclaim what he saw as his own.

The police came at eight-thirty.

They did their best, examining the cottage and its surrounds for evidence. After an hour they said they had found nothing. They asked me if I had a photograph of it and I produced the Sotheby's catalogue, almost crying when I saw it pictured. Then they asked me if I had any idea who might have taken it and I gritted my teeth and told them all.

I didn't go to my antiques fair that morning but sat in my cottage, almost as though I was frightened to leave it.

At ten the telephone rang and I picked it up, expecting it to be my sister but it wasn't.

I don't remember what words I screamed down the line to Richard, only the shocked silence that greeted them.

At eleven the phone rang again and this time it was Sara. I told her the cottage had been burgled and she offered to come round. My dramatic news distracted her from asking how my Saturday had gone so in one way I was let off the hook. I had the door mended and new locks fitted and on the Monday I flew to Majorca. I needed to be with my aunt.

She met me at the airport in her battered Ford, her face wrinkled with concern.

'Susie,' she said. 'What on earth has happened? What is going on? I've never known you like this. What is it?'

I simply dumped my case on the tarmac and flung myself into her arms, sobbing.

'Wait, wait, wait.' She stroked my hair. 'Susie. Please wait at least until we're back home and then we can sit down in a civilised fashion and talk about this. You say you've been burgled, that only one thing has gone? I don't understand.'

Aunt Eleanor was my father's sister, my sole living relative apart from Sara; my mother had been an only child. Eleanor looked nothing like how I remembered my father. He had been tall and muscular, with thick, black hair, whereas she was tiny, skinny – almost bird-like, with quick, jerky movements. She tended to wear brightly coloured, hippy skirts and T-shirts and generally looked the archetypal bohemian artist. She had a warm, generous character and spoke quickly in a clear, decisive voice. She was a person who always seemed to know what to do. An obvious choice in my dilemma. I trusted her judgement implicitly.

My aunt had been younger than my father by only one short year. They had been close and she had been our natural guardian when my parents were killed. She had accepted the responsibility without demur. She might not resemble my father physically but she was like him in character in that she was adventurous, unexpected, unusual and unfailingly loyal. During the long winter evenings in Casa Rosada she had told me endless stories about themselves when they were children, about her and my father's mischief, the scrapes they got into which their parents told them had turned their hair prematurely grey. Hers was henna tinted. She often told me that I resembled our father – muscular and sporty whereas Sara was like our mother, very slim, sharp-featured with an angular body and almost white, blonde hair whereas I was swarthy. I had olive skin and hair which was almost black. I could easily have been mistaken for a native Majorcan.

My aunt had lived in Majorca since the late 1950s. Her bohemian lifestyle had delighted me and appalled the conventional Sara. I had loved our upbringing surrounded by artists and sunshine. It had been a very, very happy childhood and I loved my aunt for her sacrifice. Sara, on the other hand, minced her way around the Casa Rosada and was heartily glad to return to school, whereas I loved our wild holidays and I was very close to my aunt.

In fact, she was never tired of telling us that it had not been a sacrifice to bring us up but a bonus, that rather than cramping her lifestyle we had brought light and perspective into her life. Aunt Eleanor had been thrilled when I had finally opened the antiques shop. At one point she had tried to teach me to paint, hoping that I would have inherited her talent and that she could nurture me as her pupil. But it was not to be. I was hopeless with a paintbrush. It didn't take a genius to spot that and no genius could ever give me the skills I so obviously lacked. But my aunt was a genius. Maybe, so far, an unrecognised one, but I firmly believed that one day she would be recognised. That people would step back in some great art gallery somewhere in this great, wonderful world of ours and say in whispered tones, 'That, of course, is an Eleanor Paris, you know. You can recognise them from right across the room. The distinctive use of movement and colour. Such a talented woman.'

I would overhear them and smile.

Or my other daydream would be to sit in an art sale and watch one of her paintings fetch thousands of pounds, to watch bidders fall over themselves to possess an Eleanor Paris. One day her fame would be such that her name would be a descriptive noun in popular English vocabulary, like an Agatha Christie or a Ruth Rendell, a Vermeer or a Renoir. Her paintings would hang in the Guggenheim or the Tate or the Getty Museum.

She was my stability. My rock.

She lived on the north-west coast of Majorca, near the town of Soller, cut off then by rocky mountains, reached only by sea or a narrow mountain pass. Now a road carves its way through the mountain and it has opened up to the outside world. But then it was traditional Majorca, beloved of artists and bohemians alike, full of traditional crafts – lacemaking, net making and others and safe from the tourists who had started trickling into the island in the early Sixties but now were pouring in on their cheap package deals. Luckily for us most of those hugged Palma and didn't venture anywhere near the Casa Rosada. Eleanor had built the pink-washed cottage high on the cliffs, a hundred and forty-one rocky steps up from the sea.

My aunt told me that the first thing she had done when she had heard of her brother and sister-in-law's deaths had been to extend the tiny house so Sara and I had our own bedrooms with balconies overlooking the sea which crashed against the rocks when the wind was in a certain direction as it was today.

Apart from the sea it was as quiet a place as can exist in this world, sealed off from the road by a track so narrow you could barely drive a car up it and which led to the Casa Rosada and nowhere else. A local couple, Carmina and her husband, Ramon, helped her around the house, doing the washing, some of the shopping and most of the cooking. My aunt was no great cook.

That afternoon as soon as I had showered the dust of the airport away and changed into shorts and T-shirt we sat on the veranda and she opened a bottle of Rioja Particular and waited for me to speak. I stared down at the stormy white crests and knew they matched my mood.

As usual she was in the middle of a painting, a swirling seascape in bright colours which clashed and screamed around each other. Had I had the job of giving this painting a title I would have called it Turmoil. And that too matched my mood.

She saw me eyeing the canvas and threw a cloth over it. 'And that was before you rang,' she said dryly. 'I dread to think how it will develop. Now will you please tell me what's going on?'

I didn't know where to start so it all came out in a jumble – the jug – the house – the names – the man hanging. I left Richard until last but as she asked me about him I felt my face burn with humiliation.

'And then,' I said, 'when I got home...'

I threw myself into her lap, crying as I hadn't cried since my parents had died. Then it had been sobs muffled into a pillow. Now I allowed myself the luxury of loud, sniffing tears and felt the better for it.

At first she said nothing. Then she looked troubled. 'It

doesn't sound right to me, Susie. Are you sure it was him?'

'It's surely too much of a coincidence? That one piece taken when I've items worth far more? If it was a small-time, opportunistic burglar why take just that? Jewellery is far easier to transport, easier to sell – less distinctive. There are pieces of silver too. The jug was the wrong thing to take for a sneak thief. It's distinctive, unique, fragile and would be difficult to sell on. The police have a photograph of it. If it turned up at one of the antiques markets they'd be on to it like a shot. It's too easily recognisable – not the sort of item a burglar would take at all – unless it is intended it never is for sale.'

My aunt opened her mouth to speak but I continued, relieved to be voicing all the arguments that had rolled around in my head. 'He would have known that I was away for the day and that the coast was clear. That's the final point.'

She tried to speak again but I had not finished.

'There are pieces in that house worth far more than the jug,' I repeated, sobbing again. 'And it's so distinctive.' I stood up, agitated. 'Maybe if you had seen Hall o'th'Wood and knew how fiercely he clings on to everything about it you would understand and agree with me. If you'd seen the way he was with the cashier at Sotheby's you'd believe anything of him.'

She still looked doubtful. 'It still doesn't sound right to me, Susie. Are you sure you're not being over-imaginative?'

'What else?' I said, warming to my conviction. 'Who else? He has an obsession – a pride – a feeling of destiny for that place. In his weird way he believed the jug belonged to him anyway and he almost sucked me into thinking that. I don't even know whether he'd recognise it as stealing. He sees himself as a custodian for his family fortune. He was merely reverting to what was proper.' Anger was taking over my grief now. 'The bugger of it is that I had practically decided to sell it to him anyway. He could have bought it.'

Eleanor gave an annoyed sigh, pulled the cloth off her painting and daubed some paint in the centre then exclaimed and wiped it off. I knew I'd upset her. She never could paint while troubled. 'Well you've met him,' she said, exasperated, 'and I haven't so...'

'He took it,' I said viciously. 'Or at least he asked someone to return it to him. I was wrong about him. I thought...' I couldn't finish the sentence. Too many tears were spilling out. I had woken from the dream and I still wanted to return to it, however foolish.

She was looking at me. 'There's more to this, isn't there?'

My tears started again.

'Well – I'm not going to be able to paint until I've sorted this one out,' she said crossly and put the cloth back on the painting.

Majorca was having something of a heatwave that late spring. I spent days sailing and swimming out to the rocky island where Sara and I had built our secret dens with pieces of driftwood. They had always been washed away when the storms had come but we still built them. I found small shells and a few treasures we'd squirrelled away, knowing we would be back. My rock seemed timeless and I spent hours sunning myself on its flat top, looking back to the cottage and wishing I had never met Richard Oliver, never bought the wretched jug and never clapped eyes on Hall o'th'Wood.

At least that was what I pretended I wished.

One morning, very early, when the mist was still clinging to the water's surface, I swam out to the rock. I had packed a paperback and some food in a waterproof bag and planned to bask on the rock for most of the day, leaving my aunt in peace to try and recapture her painting. I sat, mermaid-like, on the top of the rock and stared back at the pink walls of my aunt's home – my home – the only home I had really known well – until I had bought my own house. Through the haze I imagined I saw the shape of a man standing on the balcony. I peered through the haze that was heralding another hot day. He was not tall – I could make out square shoulders and what looked like a grey suit. Not one of my aunt's painter friends then – perhaps a gallery owner or even a buyer. I shielded my eyes from the sun and squinted, trying to make out more but I could only see a general shape which was keeping very still. Another puzzle. All of my aunt's friends were lively people, gesticulating and talking with their hands, restless and noisy. But all was stillness from the Casa Rosada. As the mist cleared I looked again – and saw no one on the balcony – not even my aunt and I could not even make out the shape of her easel. I must have been mistaken and I felt angry with myself for trying to conjure him up here. When I returned to the house my aunt said nothing about a visitor. But I noticed that she spent the early evening painting ferociously.

After two weeks I knew I must return home and run my shop again. Joanne had been selling steadily since I'd been away and I needed to replenish my stock. It is the constant juggle of an antiques dealer, the everlasting search for fine new pieces. I must not neglect my business.

On my last night Carmina grilled us some sardines and we sat on the balcony, watching the moonlight sparkle across the sea, drinking yet another bottle of Rioja Particular. I was thinking how very much I loved this place when my aunt cleared her throat and I waited for the inevitable judgement. 'Susie,' she said. 'Please listen to me and don't interrupt. Don't be pig-headed and don't be angry. I rang your Richard Oliver. I spoke to him and he came over here.'

'So it was him,' I said. 'He was on the balcony, wasn't he?'

She nodded and took my hand. 'He had nothing to do with the theft of your jug and the break-in at your cottage. It was a wicked and cruel coincidence. Now I've met him I can't believe you thought that of him. Even for a moment. Susie,' she said, 'what were you thinking of? He's perfectly charming. An absolutely lovely man and he's quite bowled over by you.'

So she had been taken in by his charm too.

She was frowning at me. 'I thought I'd always taught you to trust your instincts. I trust him. He wouldn't do you any harm. He wouldn't steal from you. What were you thinking of, child?'

It was the way she had always spoken to me, part mother, part friend.

I couldn't believe that Richard's influence had persuaded her to turn the table on me, making me feel defensive when I had presented all the arguments to her. I said nothing but stared at her mutinously, knowing she would interpret the look. She sipped her wine slowly, looking at me over the rim. Then she reached across and cradled my face with her hands. 'You're a daughter to me,' she said. 'You must go onwards into your life and face your future whatever it is but don't misjudge him.'

And suddenly all my arguments seemed foolish and blown away in a puff of the sea breeze.

I had one last question. 'Who took the jug then?'

She shook her head sadly. 'I don't know. You may never know. Some things are never explained but remain mysteries throughout our lives. You may never know the full story of the jug's creation. Then again your friend David might have found something out from archives or church records. One day you may know the full story of the unfortunate people. But they are all dead and you are alive and have your future in front of you. The theft of your jug and your accusation of Richard Oliver is one of those cruel twists of fate that can so easily send us hurtling down the wrong road in our lives.'

I watched her and knew she spoke of something in her own life.

For one second a shadow passed across her face, making it look sad and tired. Then she looked at me and brightened. 'Oh Susie.' She kissed my cheek. 'It wasn't Richard.' She stood up. 'I know that. And now,' she said, rising, 'it's late.' She yawned. 'You've got an early start in the morning. Ramón will drive us to the airport.' I studied her sunburnt face and felt overwhelmed by love of her. What would have happened if she had not stepped forward to become our guardian? Where would Sara and I have gone? To an orphanage? To be fostered? What would I ever do without her?

I stayed out late on the veranda for a while, alone. I thought and I made my choice. I picked one thread of my destiny and decided I would follow it through – to its end. Whatever.

I flew back to the UK the next day and the first thing I did was to pick up the phone and ring Richard.

CHAPTER SEVEN

He was around within half an hour. No slow Jenkins in the Rolls this time but Richard skidding to a halt outside in a small, black Mercedes. I heard his car door slam and opened my door to him still wondering. Then I read the expression in his eyes and I couldn't think how I could ever have doubted him. 'Susie,' he said reproachfully. 'How could you…?'

'I'm sorry,' I said stiffly. 'It seemed a logical conclusion. I was at your house while the jug was… Did the police…?' I couldn't finish.

A wry smile crossed his face. 'I did have a visit,' he said, humour warming his eyes, 'but I don't think they took the allegation that seriously. They didn't take a lot of convincing.' His lips twitched. 'They didn't even have a search warrant to search Hall o'th'Wood.'

'I'm sorry,' I said again. Then I saw that he was laughing at me and I joined him.

'It's a shame about the jug though.'

He drew my face to his and brushed my lips with his own. 'It'll turn up again.'

'I hope so.'

He hesitated. 'In a way,' he said tentatively, 'I'm not sorry it's gone. It was a tragic episode in our family history.' Then he met my eyes. 'It's done its job,' he said. 'It brought us together.'

'And nearly parted us too,' I said.

He nodded, his expression heavy. Then – just as suddenly – it lightened again. 'Aren't you going to invite me in?'

'Yes – yes. Of course.'

I offered him coffee but he produced a bottle of wine. 'Rioja,' he said. 'Particular. I bought it while I was in Majorca, seeing your aunt. She's given me a taste for it. I hoped we might drink it together.'

I fished a corkscrew out of a kitchen drawer and returned with two wine glasses. He half-filled them both then held his glass up. 'To us,' he said, 'and to your aunt. As you said. She's a very remarkable woman. You were right and I'm glad I've met her.' He smiled. 'I only have your sister to brave and then I've met the family.'

I giggled, heady not from the wine but from his company.

We sat together on the sofa, drinking the wine, until he took my glass from me and set it with his on the hearth. He kissed me lightly on the cheek then searched my face. 'So, Susie,' he said. 'Where do we go from here?'

Richard didn't go home that night nor any night after

that. He rang Maria and muttered some excuse down the phone. I could hear her sceptical chuckles from the other side of the room. From then on we were barely apart except for our work.

We were married six months later, on a blustery October day, at the tiny, stone church in Horton. It was a small wedding with only fifty guests. My brother-in-law, John, gave me away. Sara's daughter, Samantha, was my bridesmaid, in claret while I wore white, a fitted dress with a train and a long veil. Michael, Richard's son, was his best man and we mumbled our responses in front of another stained-glass window, Christ crucified. As we walked outside the wind whipped my veil around my face and set my skirts dancing around my legs. Richard kissed me and told me again and again that he loved me and would always love me. We posed for pictures, beneath the lychgate, as Sara and my aunt threw confetti at us and we laughed together, the cold hardly touching us in our happiness.

It was a whirlwind romance but sometimes the first, full flush of love is the time to consolidate it.

They were still throwing confetti at us as we climbed into the back of the Rolls Royce. Even Jenkins threw a handful in before he too wished us happiness and closed the door to head the long cavalcade to the wedding reception at Hall o'th'Wood. The entire house was festooned with flowers and the scent of lilies was heavy in the air, mingled with the aroma of the log fires. There are photographs of us standing in front of the house but the day was blustery and cold and we were glad to enter the hall, mount the stairs and pose in front of the stained-glass crusader. We kissed and had our pictures taken again and again.

For once Maria had accepted help with the food and it was set out on the long dining-room table, fresh salmon garnished with lemons, slices of beef, dishes of tiny potatoes, steaming vegetables. And, I noticed, with a smile, that Maria had not been able to resist adding a couple of dishes of olives.

The centrepiece was a three-tiered wedding cake with a porcelain bride and groom on the top, posing underneath an archway.

As the evening wore on I changed into a dress and jacket, Jenkins brought the car around and we slipped away to the airport to honeymoon in Vienna.

It was the perfect city for us, even in the rain, a city of romantics and aesthetes.

We spent evenings at the Grand Opera and coffee houses, attended concerts and museums and the puppet theatre. We watched the Viennese ballet perform Giselle and almost wept at her final descent into madness. We spent an evening spinning dizzily to Strauss at the Viennese Ball and even watched the Lippizaner horses at the Spanish Riding School.

So I fell deeper in love with Richard than I would have thought possible and, I believe, he with me. It was a magical, charmed two weeks.

* * *

A week after our wedding we visited the sad hunting lodge of Mayerling where, in 1889, Crown Prince Rudolf murdered Mary Vetsera before killing himself. Maybe it was the visit to a place where love had entwined itself so completely with tragedy which planted seeds in my brain, seeds of apprehension, seeds of a conviction that all this, like the love story of my parents, was too good to last. I do remember that in the huge hallway of Mayerling Richard and I clung to each other, affected by the doomed atmosphere of the place.

Had Rudolf not died it is possible the First World War would not have happened. All that tragedy down to one murder, one suicide. I mentioned this thought to Richard and he looked at me strangely. I thought briefly about the jug before tucking the moment away. I had already learnt to be selective in my memories.

But the climax was the last night. We had planned to dine quietly at our hotel on the Kaerntner Strasse but when we wandered outside we found a small gathering queuing up to listen to a young Japanese girl playing Chopin. The last piece she played that night was the haunting 'Nocturne in E flat major' and I listened, feeling tears of pure joy rolling down my face. I couldn't believe that I was to spend my life at Hall o'th'Wood, with Richard. I turned to my husband and caught the same emotion mirrored in his face. His arm tightened around me. I rested my head on his shoulder and wanted this moment to remain with me for ever, throughout my entire life. 'Don't ever leave me, Susie,' he murmured and

I shook my head and promised him that I never would.

We flew back the next day and I became mistress of Hall o'th'Wood.

And the jug? Tucked away in the darkest recess of my mind. Possibly I would never see it again. But then maybe I would. Who could know? For now it had played its part in my destiny and would slip away. Maybe for ever.

CHAPTER EIGHT

1970

For a period my life was charmed and privileged. I appreciate that more now although I was aware of it then. I loved living in the old house. I never tired of walking its corridors, staring at the portraits, discovering oddities and features even Richard was unaware of. But most of all I grew to love Richard even more as I got to know his character. He was always an enigma. I never quite reached his core – or – more truthfully there was always a part of him that was beyond anything I could understand – a room locked away like the secret of the jug. He was, in a way, a fairy tale husband, thoughtful, generous, exacting, deeply passionate. Our life together was very happy. We loved nothing more than simply sharing our lives, being together. It was all we wanted or needed. We were enough for each other.

Perhaps I was aware that the clock was ticking away steadily in the background.

I became very friendly with Michael, Richard's son. He was, as Richard had mentioned on our first 'date', about my age and we became as close as brother and sister, sharing intimacies and secrets, even teasing each other. He had the same, strong family resemblance, the same basic face, clear, grey eyes, full lips, a classical straight nose. He was a couple of inches taller than Richard, still slim, with light brown hair and a certain merriment in his personality which was unlike my husband. I liked Michael very much but was aware that Richard had some extra quality. He was deeper and it was this depth which made me love him so very much.

When wandering the corridors of the old house did I ever catch the rustle of a silk skirt, hear a muffled scream, breathe in the acrid scent of fear, feel the chill touch of a dead hand? Perhaps. Was I aware of the story which lay behind its panelled walls and had led to that terrible face staring from the gallows? Did I sense dark secrets within its walls? A potential threat to our happiness? Again 'perhaps' but instinct warned me not to ask questions if I might be afraid of the answers.

My antiques business flourished so Bottle Kiln became even better known and a stopping point for dealers from all over the world. I spent days at salerooms, returning with more and more beautiful pieces and selling them easily. I was gaining a reputation for stocking the finest of antiques, the rarest of pottery, the most beautiful of paintings and the oldest and most genuine furniture. A business like this snowballs so when a person does have a fine piece they are thinking of parting with, who else would they approach but Susanna Oliver of Bottle Kiln Antiques? I knew that living in such a house surrounded by so many authenticated pieces of art had increased my expertise and that was one reason why my 'eye' was well respected. My new home was as famous as my business to those who appreciated antiquity.

I had not forgotten my jug. Sometimes I dreamt about it, seeing it in the finest detail, and each time I woke after one of these visions I felt the stab of disappointment that my hands were empty and not holding the lovely piece. Whenever I entered a saleroom or visited another shop I would look around and wonder whether it would be sitting on a shelf or standing on some item of furniture but it remained elusive for now. It was somewhere else – hidden from me, with another owner, possibly not even still in the country. Sometimes for weeks I would forget about it; I had many other things to occupy my mind. But always, just when I thought it had been finally banished from my mind, I would fall asleep one night and hold it again in my hands and waken to the disappointment afresh.

But no business runs completely smoothly. I had a few hiccups. Early in the January of 1970, on a day muffled by swirls of freezing fog, a day when we expected no one in the shop, a blue Bedford van pulled up and a swarthy man of around thirty climbed out.

I opened the door to him. He was not someone I knew but a stranger.

He brought the damp chill of the fog trapped in his clothes so I felt the temperature of the shop drop a few degrees.

I quickly realised he was not a browser.

'What can I do for you?'

He jerked his head towards his van. 'I got a collection of Staffordshire wares in the back,' he said. 'It's all first-quality stuff.'

I pulled on my sheepskin coat and followed him outside.

He swung the van doors open and pulled the first of the boxes towards him, lifting the lid. He pulled out the first piece, unwrapping the newspaper with great care.

It was a model of Neptune, complete with sea creatures, multi-coloured shells and a trident. Instead of a flat base it was raised on four 'feet' and I knew this was an Obadiah Sherratt piece dating from the 1820s. My pulse rate quickened. I set it to one side.

I unwrapped the second – another beautiful thing – this time a Martha Gunn toby jug, the woman sitting, proudly bearing the three plumes of the Prince of Wales – a tribute to the bathing attendant who had been brave enough (it was reputed) to throw His Majesty, the Prince Regent or 'Prinnie', into the sea at Brighton.

I looked at the man with new respect. He was eyeing me very carefully, taking stock, measuring me up. As I was him.

He had spoken the truth. The pieces I was pulling from the boxes were top-quality Staffordshire. Valuable and desirable.

'Dave,' he said. 'My name's Dave Weston. I got more than forty pieces here. All of them as good as these.'

I could see Joanne watching me through the shop window and studied the man's face. There was something shifty about him. Something here which did not quite hang together.

'How much are you looking for for the entire lot?'

'Two thousand,' he said.

This worked out low – fifty pounds apiece.

It is a well-known scam to display the only good pieces of a collection and lure the dealer to bid blind, trusting them all to be of equally fine quality. Maybe that was his trick.

'I'll have to see every single piece unpacked in my shop to even consider bidding for them,' I said, watching his face for signs of disappointment but he agreed readily.

Together we shifted the boxes into the showroom of Bottle Kiln and Joanne and I and Dave Weston started to unwrap them. Soon we were surrounded by a sea of pottery.

I immediately realised I had misjudged Weston. His scam was not to mislead me about the quality of the purchase. Every piece was unusual, rare, in good condition and genuine. As I unwrapped the pottery I revised my opinion. Now this put me in even more of a dilemma. I wanted the collection. Badly. All dealers chase after the same pieces and I could make a good profit from these. I knew it. But there was still something wrong.

I thought and quickly realised I'd inadvertently put my finger on it. This was a collection. I glanced again at the van driver.

'Where did these come from?'

'A private collector, Mrs Oliver.'

I didn't need to ask how he'd known about me. I spent a lot of money advertising Bottle Kiln Antiques and anyone in the trade would have known that I paid cash for good Staffordshire.

'I'm sorry,' I said. 'I need to know the collector's name.'

Weston's eyes flickered. 'Look, ' he said. 'The collector doesn't want you to know his name.' He grinned. 'Inland Revenue. Understand?'

He had a Bristol drawl.

I chewed my lip. It is hard, as an antiques dealer, to remain perfectly on the right side of the law and I had bought pieces before when the vendor wanted cash and to sell anonymously. But this was too big and too valuable a collection. Besides I did not know this man. I'd never seen him before. He wasn't a regular caller.

I also realised that he was being evasive.

I didn't trust him; but I wanted these pieces. A dealer's dilemma.

Joanne bustled off to make some coffee. She knew the format.

'Sit down,' I invited.

'I still need to know where the pieces come from.'

'Lancaster,' he said, 'at least – just outside.'

'I'd like to buy your collection,' I said, 'but I really need to know a bit more about them.'

'Nineteen hundred,' he said quickly. 'I'll take nineteen hundred.'

I waited. Nothing flushes out a suspect story as fast as silence. Liars can't stand it. 'It belonged to an old guy, see,' he said, waving his palms around. 'He's died and his son don't want to pay death duties on his old man's collection.'

'Understandable,' I sympathised.

Weston's eyes met mine and wavered. He wanted that cash just as much as I wanted his goods.

Badly.

And now he changed his story. 'Actually,' he said, leaning forward conspiratorially, 'it's a collector who has fallen on hard times and needs cash quickly. Really quickly. He owes a very nasty set of people money and they've threatened him. He suggested I came to you, knowing you'd have the readies.' He grinned.

Every time he trotted out a story I was well aware that it could be the truth and just as aware that it could be a lie. The law is that stolen goods, which is what my nose was sniffing out, belong to the rightful owner. I have known many antiques dealers watch the police clear their displays with no chance of recompense. You can try and catch your vendor to demand redress but they are notoriously elusive.

And as I have already said, with antiques, provenance is all.

I looked again at the van driver and decided to stall.

'Can you leave the collection with me overnight?' I asked. 'I need to do a little research into one or two figures which I'm unfamiliar with. If I decide to buy I'll have the cash ready for you at ten tomorrow morning.'

Weston's eyes gleamed. He was sensing the 'readies' in his hot little hand. He argued a bit but the pull of the money was always going to win.

'OK,' he said grumpily and finally he left the shop and drove off. I watched him go then put two of the best figures up on the shelf and looked carefully over them with an ultraviolet light. It didn't surprise me to find a name. I rang the police.

They returned my call an hour later and confirmed what I had suspected – the goods were stolen – the result of an armed robbery in not Lancaster but Leicestershire. The next morning they staked out the shop, their squad cars out of sight, and waited for the van to pull on to my car park, pulled Dave Weston in for questioning and confiscated the entire collection. I watched them carry the boxes out ruefully. I'd probably never get the chance to buy such a good, entire collection again. Collections of this uniform quality were rare, and even when the owners die are more often left to museums than put in the local saleroom.

There were three results from this: I was well aware that I had made myself an enemy. Weston was sentenced to three years – it had been a violent robbery – but he would soon be out and I could be a target.

The second result was that after the vicious assault, the owner decided he no longer wanted his collection and so I did finally get to buy all the pieces, though not for two thousand.

The third result was that I had now made the acquaintance of Detective Inspector Robert Stallwood, of the Staffordshire Police, stolen goods, Fine Art department. I asked him to look into the theft of my jug three years ago and to see if there had been any reported sightings.

It was a month or so later that I made one of my 'discoveries' at Hall o'th'Wood. During a particularly vicious bout of flu I spent a couple of days in bed. On my marriage I had moved into Richard's room and we slept in his carved-oak four-poster. It was a huge thing with thick balusters at each corner, a carved wooden ceiling and heavy, embroidered drapes. Halfway through a dreary afternoon I felt suddenly awake and lay, still aching in every joint, staring up at the carving over my head. The panels were plain – except for one which had been carved with a name. Rebekah Grindall, I read.

It had been done amateurishly. By her?

I realised then that I had never done anything about finding out the provenance of the jug which had led me here. David had promised to look into it for me. But David had proved an unexpected casualty of my marriage. He had met Richard once – when he had walked into my shop a month after my return from Majorca and subsequent engagement. When I had introduced Richard to him David had shaken hands stiffly, made some excuse and walked out. I had not seen him since. He no longer came to my shop at all and on the two occasions when I had visited the museum hoping to see him he had been 'out' or 'busy' and I knew when I had gained a husband I had lost a friend. I missed our easy chats and his fount of knowledge but it was a small price to pay for my new, charmed life. Because of our estrangement David had never had the chance to tell me what, if anything, he had found out about my jug. But now, stimulated by my discovery of Rebekah Grindall's name carved into the roof of our bed, I was burning with a need to find out more of the secrets of Hall o'th'Wood. I made a decision then that as soon as I was back on my feet one of the first things I would do would be to call on David at the museum.

One of the other changes that had happened since my marriage was that I had rented out my cottage in Horton to a young couple who enjoyed living in the Staffordshire Moorlands village as much as I had. They had asked me to sell Horton Cottage to them but I had resisted. It was a superstition of mine that one day I would have to leave Hall o'th'Wood and return there. In that way living at Hall o'th'Wood always seemed an interlude, a beautiful dream from which I would, one day, waken.

* * *

July was hot that year and we spent a couple of weeks at the Casa Rosada with my aunt, swimming, sailing or simply lazing on the terraces, reading paperbacks through the day and finding tiny restaurants and cafés in the nearby towns in the evenings. Richard enjoyed being at our island hideaway almost as much as his own home and I loved to watch him truly relax in the sunshine. He loved my aunt too and they would exchange friendly banter – often centred around one of her more modernistic paintings. He appreciated her art as well as the fact that she had been kind to her orphaned niece and given me the childhood, as he said, which had formed the woman. Richard was a romantic and could be quite silver-tongued. But it was sincerely said and meant. He was a man of frequent, thoughtful gifts and a courtesy that marked out his character. But he was also prone to long, brooding silences when he retreated into this secret place where I could not follow. And occasionally displays of bad temper, as I had witnessed on our first meeting. But in those weeks in Majorca, away with my aunt, his silences were shorter and less frequent and I felt the ghosts of the past were banished in the bright, hot sunshine. I had noticed, with amusement, that my aunt had fallen under his spell and I occasionally found her sketching his face, glancing frequently at him then down on her pad, to mark out the straight nose, the fine eyes, the full sensuality of his mouth which I could not look at without wanting to brush it with my own. Perhaps it was through her that I came to appreciate the beauty of his features. She called him her Michelangelo's David.

But by August the island had filled up to capacity and the weather was too hot to do anything – even sit out in it – so Richard and I returned to Hall o'th'Wood. We had both felt a sudden lust for its cool rooms, the damp grass and the shade of its trees.

Besides – I had an ulterior motive. There was a country-house sale I wanted to attend. It was at a Queen Anne mansion in the middle of acres of parkland in Gloucestershire and the duke, who was now being forced to sell up, had been an avid collector of Staffordshire portrait figures. I could not afford to miss this sale. It was so full of rare pieces – more than three hundred lots of pottery alone. I suppose at the back of my mind I was always thinking there was always a slight chance that my jug would turn up again. When the catalogue arrived the quality was even better than I had anticipated and I decided to attend for the entire two days. The first day was viewing; the second the sale.

Country house sales are a push-me-pull-you sort of affair. They attract all sorts – from the wealthy, local landowners to foreign millionaires, 'A' list celebrities, genuine collectors, the penniless pretending to be millionaires, millionaires masquerading as the poverty-struck, dealers and not a few thieves watching out for unguarded lots or carelessly left handbags or wallets.

Sometimes the prices are unrealistically high – particularly for the star lots, the pieces on the front of the catalogue and photographed inside. These are the prestige pieces which will be boasted about at grand houses over dinners to come. 'Darling, I bought it at the duke's house, you know. Picked it up for an absolute song. Rumour has it that...' And so on. But for all that there are also, for the careful dealer, 'sleepers', bargains. Unrecognised and genuine rarities.

There is always a frisson at these sales, a sense of excitement which is rarely present at provincial auctions. There are fun lots and lots for serious bidders.

The two-day sale would be a welcome break. We had returned from Majorca because we had felt claustrophobic there but the truth was I felt exactly the same back at home. There was an atmosphere. I sensed that something was not right, that my Elysium was threatened and I did not know from what direction. Richard seemed distracted. I often wandered into his study to find him frowning over bills or on the telephone, his voice raised. When he looked up at me I would catch an expression almost of panic in his eyes. I didn't question him. Whatever it was, I reasoned, he would tell me in his own time. I did not pry except for one thing. I had always realised that Hall o'th'Wood was expensive to maintain. Any repairs had to be carried out using traditional materials and we always needed the services of master craftsmen. Nothing was ever cheap or simple. Because Richard had lived there before our marriage he had never expected me to contribute to what he considered his house, his ancestral home and I respected that stance. I constantly offered him money or to pay some expenses – even Maria and Jenkins's wages – but he always refused although I suspected that the money would have been useful. Like many men of that generation Richard expected to support his wife. But it was not the way of my age. I had grown up expecting to support myself. It was yet another manifestation of the difference in our ages and generation.

But this problem put a strain between us. What could have been so bonding, a shared responsibility, instead became a missed opportunity.

The result was that I was, for the first time since my marriage, glad to escape the house and its secrets, glad to leave the air of tension, which pervaded every corner of it, reflecting from its glossy panelling, high ceilings and crooked walls, peering at me through the leaded casement windows. So, early on a Tuesday morning in late August, I caught a train down to Gloucester planning to return with my carrier.

I booked myself into a local hotel and was reunited with two of my colleagues, John Carpenter and Eric Goodwood – the very same dealers who had been at Sotheby's on the day that I had first met Richard. They knew my story from beginning to end, had sympathised with the theft of my jug and promised to keep an eye out for it. 'It'll surface one day, Susie,' they'd said. 'It'll be somewhere and one day you'll have it again.'

But it never had.

We three antiques dealers spent a happy day marking down lots, discussing the finer pieces and arguing over their authenticity. It felt good to be amongst old friends again. I had neglected them since my marriage. I no longer tarried at the back of salerooms or joined them for protracted dinners after the sales but hurried back to my home and my husband. Now I realised that it was fun to be back in the thick of it. We worked out which lots we would be bidding for, enjoyed pointing out restoration work, new handles, poor-quality pieces and trying to spot which would be the 'sleepers' in the sale. It was all good fun and the day brought perfect English summer weather with a cool breeze freshening the proceedings.

We picnicked on strawberries and smoked-salmon sandwiches, sitting on the lawn, and spent the afternoon wandering through the house, admiring the furniture, paintings, porcelain and pottery. The auctioneers had piped string-quartet music playing softly in the background, which gave the proceedings a glamorous, classy atmosphere.

We dined well at the small, Cotswold stone hotel and sat gossiping and drinking until the small hours. I went to bed, leaving my companions at the bar.

The next day stands out in my memories as one of the happiest of my life.

My two colleagues were suffering from hangovers the next morning but I felt clear-headed and joyful. The day was blisteringly hot; the breeze had dropped and I dressed in a halter-neck minidress and some wedge-heeled, white sandals. I wore little make-up. A touch of mascara, a slick of lipstick. No more. As I brushed my hair I felt the familiar swell of anticipation that had never quite left me. A sale is such unknown territory. Fortunes and reputations are made and lost at such places. It is the thrill of the chase.

At the back of my mind a small voice argued that hot days and country-house sales can be a magnet for the wealthy who enjoy nothing more than buying up from the dispersal sale of a duke. But I tucked that voice away. Surely I was canny enough to buy the right pieces with confidence – and sell them again? So I finished brushing my hair, grimaced at my reflection then hitched a lift to the sale in Eric's Volvo.

I felt lucky today. Even more so as I arrived at the marquee early and the first thing I saw was a pair of square shoulders disappearing through the flaps. It is always a double joy to see someone you love unexpectedly. I ran up to him. 'Richard,' I called. 'Richard.' He turned around and gave me a wide grin. 'Susie.' His eyes rested on me with affection.

I linked my arm through his. 'What are you doing here? You hate country-house sales. "All that sitting through lot numbers..."' I quoted, kissing his cheek, fondling the smooth skin, brushing his mouth with my own and taking mischievous pleasure in the smear of lipstick which had transferred to his face.

'It was so warm,' he said. 'I couldn't concentrate on work. The office was stifling and I thought of you out here, nibbling strawberries.' He kissed me back. 'Honestly it was just too nice to stay in and I fancied a drive out.' He drew me to him. 'To be with you, if I'm honest.' He smiled. 'The sale was the price I had to pay.' His eyes crinkled at the corners. 'The necessary evil.'

I challenged him then. 'And will you sit right through it?'

'I think so.'

'It'll be awfully hot in the marquee,' I warned.

'I don't care.'

'Oh,' I said suddenly, putting my hands either side of his face. 'It is so good to see you.'

I took a good look at him. He had abandoned his grey suit, white shirt and sober ties for khaki chinos with a short-sleeved, open-necked white polo shirt. Usually a formal dresser, even his shoes were casual loafers. He looked relaxed and happy in his holiday clothes.

We filed into the tent together.

They were selling the furniture and paintings in the morning and the pottery in the afternoon. I bought two or three pieces of period oak which neither the general public nor the other dealers seemed to want and a fine pair of Georgian portraits which were the subject of some frenzied bidding. I had to fight off stiff opposition but emerged the victor and felt very pleased with myself. We sat right through the morning's lots and broke off for lunch, sitting on the grass and feeding each other strawberries. Richard lay back and closed his eyes. He was almost asleep and the lines on his face softened so he looked youthful and content. It struck me then how strained he'd been looking lately. I touched his brow, smoothing it with my fingers and almost asking him what the matter was but I didn't. Instead we talked about other subjects, to do with Michael and Maria, and the house. I reflected that perhaps even Richard realised he was better away from it for a change. Lovely though it was I was beginning to realise that Hall o'th'Wood wound its tendrils around you, binding you to it just that little bit too tightly. Its air might be rarefied but that could make it difficult to breathe.

I can recall almost everything about that day. It has impressed itself into my mind so deeply. The sweet taste of the strawberries, the cold of the ice cubes in our Pimm's, the mingled perfume of lavender and roses, the scent of newly mown grass, the drone of the auctioneer's voice selling lot after lot, the rhythmic bang of his gavel as another piece was sold. The haze of dust in the marquee, floating in the air, even the shifting and whisperings of people arriving and leaving the tent, the simultaneous crackle as another page of the catalogue was turned in unison. The flaps of the marquee had been bound open so the tiniest of breezes just about made the temperature bearable. Bees buzzed in and out uninterested in the proceedings. A few people swatted, impotently, at bluebottles. Once or twice a sparrow or a swallow swooped in accidentally and flew to the top of the tent before flying out again.

The afternoon lots were to begin at two o'clock and we sat near the front. I wanted to have the chance to inspect some of the items again. My customers were becoming ever more discerning and I didn't want to miss any restoration, however well done. Sitting near the pieces can make you revise your estimates. Sometimes up, sometimes down. I was well aware that labelling an item part of a duke's collection would appeal to some customers' snobbery. And there is much of that in the antiques world.

As I had realised when I had bought the jug, provenance is everything.

The piece I really prized above all else was quite small but it was also rare. A tiny rabbit nibbling a piece of enamelled green lettuce. In my years of dealing I had never sold a rabbit. Horses and cats, plenty of dogs and even an elephant or two but rabbits were rare and I suspected this one came from the Alpha pottery firm which had made the very finest of pieces. First out of the mould, prized by collectors, sharp-featured and beautifully painted on a whiter than normal body. I badly wanted to put it in the showroom of Bottle Kiln. In fact I could almost see Joanne dusting it off and draping a label around its neck. As I had expected the bidding was steep and I held my breath as it reached two hundred pounds, breathing only when the auctioneer's gavel slammed on his podium and the piece knocked down to me for two hundred and ten pounds. I turned to

Richard, excited. 'I have it,' I said. I think I was laughing with the pleasure and grazed his cheek with my mouth. I seem to remember that we exchanged a look as long and loving as at our wedding. He laughed too and tucked his arm around me, stroking my hair, whispering a tease in my ear – 'I'd have thought a hardened dealer like you would have been immune from such pleasure at buying a little rabbit.' I laughed with him. 'Never,' I vowed, whispering back. 'If I lose my joy at acquiring a beautiful piece I shall retire.'

Those words would return one day to haunt me; 'joy' – not a word to be used so carelessly.

If I search the most obscure consciousness of my mind I believe I can drag something else out of that moment. Right behind me I might have heard a small commotion, perhaps a gasp, certainly a movement but I did not turn around.

Richard, as I had anticipated, did get bored and wandered towards the back of the tent then went outside but I stayed on till the bitter end. I would not need to return with the carrier now but could travel straight back to Hall o'th'Wood with Richard and Jenkins in the Rolls.

It was as we left that the incident occurred.

Jenkins had brought the car around to meet us at the side of the marquee and Richard and I were sitting in the back. I had my head on his shoulder, tired now, with the excitement of the day and the heat. There was a throng of people milling around so Jenkins was driving even more slowly than usual to avoid them. Quite suddenly someone approached the car and banged very hard on the window, startling me. I sat up. It was a tall, slim youth with yellow-blonde hair. His mouth was open. He was shouting something – at me, it seemed. I assumed that we must have driven too close to him and leant forward, meaning to open the window and apologise. I saw his palm slap on the glass again and met some sort of mute appeal in his face. Richard leant forward. 'Drive on, Jenkins,' he urged furiously. 'Drive on.'

We left the youth standing in the middle of the drive, staring after us. His mouth was still open. He was still shouting but I could not distinguish the words. I turned around and watched him until we rounded a corner and he vanished from sight. The entire incident must have taken less than two minutes.

'Well,' I said, leaning back in my seat. 'What was all that about?'

'Young buck.' Richard's face was still flushed and furious. 'Bloody arrogant young buck. Who does he think he is?'

I was none the wiser. 'Richard?'

His face was livid. 'He's been watching you all day. I saw him. Sitting behind us. Never took his eyes off you. What does he want?'

I tried to reassure him. 'I don't know,' I said. 'I didn't notice him. I didn't see him at the sale. I don't know him, Richard.'

But Richard's face was still hard and angry. 'Who is he?' he said.

'I don't know.' I leant my head back against his shoulder. 'And I don't care either.' I said no more until we stopped at a hotel to have dinner. And then Richard relaxed again.

He apologised as we climbed out of the car. 'I'm sorry,' he said. 'I just hate it when young studs like that pay attention to you. It makes me feel...'

How could he possibly think I would have any interest in some callow young man with a passing fancy? 'You don't have to worry,' I replied. 'I'm not interested.'

'Sure?'

I linked my arm in his, still struggling to reassure him. 'Perfectly sure.'

The incident was forgotten by the time we had ordered our dinner but something of it, some bitter taste, remained.

CHAPTER NINE

And then, slowly, as the summer started to die, the charmed, magical period of my life began to unravel.

Imperceptibly at first. I did not recognise what was happening. I was given such small clues – the door to Richard's study would be closed when he was on the phone. He was secretive and distracted. Occasionally I would come upon him speaking to workmen and he would look at me, almost distantly. I know that he was upset when some woodworm was discovered in the panelling in our bedroom. He spent hours on the phone to the company who had guaranteed their work. I heard him shouting frequently. He wasn't sleeping either but spent hours tossing around in bed, finally giving an exasperated sigh and padding downstairs to make a drink. Sometimes Maria and I would exchange glances and I wondered when all this would settle down.

It was impossible not to listen when the experts came

round, stroked their chins and looked grave at the extent of the infestation. We moved out of our bedroom. The room was sprayed again and the affected panelling removed and replaced. To my relief our four-poster bed had been properly treated years before so did not have active woodworm but more than half of the panelling of the bedroom had to be removed and the other half sprayed. Richard was muttering about it all being his fault, that he should have inspected the wood more frequently. He seemed to feel guilty.

It was during this time that one of the workmen sought me out. I was in the smallest bedroom, converted now into a study. He was a rough man, from the Meir, but honest and a good worker. He handed me fragments of yellowed parchment.

'Look at this, Mrs Oliver,' he said. 'We found it tucked behind the panelling. I can't even begin to think how old it must be.'

I took it from him. Only part of the missive was here. The rest had simply flaked away. But I made out the words. '*Please, Rychard I beg of you. Do not do this wicked thing. My troth was plighted. I cannot be yours.*'

Here the paper had fragmented but the signature on the bottom was clear:

Rebekah Grindall.

I felt a shiver. Not only because of the name which recalled such vivid memories of my jug and the image of the hanged man or even because of the desperation which lay behind the words. I was shocked because there was no mistaking the rusty colour of the 'ink'. It had been written in blood.

I stood up then. 'Thank you,' I said. 'If you find anything more don't bother my husband with it. Bring it to me.'

I would not concern Richard with the past when the present was so troublesome. But it was the past which beckoned me now. I would go to the museum and speak to David. I had vowed to do it years before and then done nothing. I did not want to delay any longer. I felt suddenly that time was terribly precious.

We had a problem with the roof too. Maria found a patch of damp in her bathroom ceiling. Scaffolding was erected outside the house. I only minded because it shrouded our bedroom window and tore up the knot garden which lay beneath it. I was worried that the lavender, roses and herbs would not flourish next spring and aware that I would miss their fragrance. One afternoon after watching workmen shin up the ladders and listening to the banging over our heads I tried again to offer my help to my husband. 'Richard,' I said. 'Please listen to me.' His gaze rested on me and for those few minutes I could see again the man I loved. His forehead uncreased. 'Susie,' he said, glancing at the scaffolding and wincing at the banging. 'Hardly Arcadia, is it?' He grimaced.

'I didn't marry you for some fantasy world, Richard,' I said. 'I came here to be part of this.' I looked around the room, at the portraits of his ancestors, the samplers and needlework done by the women of the Oliver clan. 'And if what the house needs is a bit of attention – well – so be it. It hasn't disappointed me.' I took his hand, kissed the fingers. 'And neither have you.'

His smile was so sad I wanted to put my arms around him but I didn't. Instead I ploughed on.

'I have more money than I need, with the rent for Horton Cottage, the shop.' He opened his mouth to protest. 'Please – let me contribute to all these repairs.'

He gave me an odd look. 'You mean that, Susie? You really mean that?'

'Of course,' I said. 'I'll do anything to preserve Hall o'th'Wood to pass on to your descendants.' I eyed him sneakily. 'Possibly our descendants.'

He didn't take me up on my hint but put his arm around me and kissed me with a warmth that had recently been lacking. 'I believe you would do anything,' he said. 'You're a bit of a daredevil really.' Then he smiled. 'Come,' he said. 'Let's walk.'

It was a damp, mild day. Leaves lay slippery on the floor. We descended the hundred steps along the bark path and walked towards the lake. The ducks were noisily gabbling and squabbling and took no notice as we passed. We sat on a fallen log and looked back at the great house. Richard gave a long sigh. 'It is a heavy responsibility,' he said. 'But...' He put his arm round me and drew me to him. 'I could wish,' he said, 'that it was just a little less beautiful – a little less perfect. It would break my heart less.' He smiled at some far-off point in the distance and I studied his familiar, well-loved profile. 'Although it is heresy to say it I could even wish that Hall o'th'Wood was a little less old. A little less decrepit.' He looked back at me. 'Like an elderly parent I feel the burden of its age sometimes outweighs the pleasure.'

'That's a shame,' I said, 'when it should give you happiness.'

'It does,' he said abstractedly. 'And at the same time it is a painful happiness. I worry all the time that I will not live up to it, that it will be during my custodianship that Hall o'th'Wood will have to be sold.'

I felt a sharp pain. 'Surely,' I said, 'things aren't that bad?'

He shook his head. 'Nowhere near,' he said and I was reassured.

I laid my head on his shoulder and we sat still, watching the clouds' reflections chase the ripples along the water's surface, watched the afternoon turn to evening and still sat until we knew Maria would scold us for being late for dinner. Dinner was at eight. Always at the same time. Things didn't vary in this shrine to time warp.

Richard was thoughtful throughout dinner, looking sad and again preoccupied. My brief glimpse of the adoring man I had married had hidden again behind this impenetrable mask.

The next day I called at the museum early and spoke to David. He was very stiff with me at first, asking formally how I was, how business went. Of Richard he made not a mention.

I asked him what he had found out about the jug.

'As you'd lost it anyway, Susie,' he said, 'I didn't think you'd want me to trouble you with details.'

'No.' I agreed. 'I sort of lost interest.'

He looked at me keenly. 'So why now?'

'I don't know,' I said.

He was offended. 'OK,' he said. 'It's hard to believe you once confided in me about everything. Then you go to a sale, meet someone else and bingo! Exit David.'

I felt guilty then. It was true. I had dropped friends. But – 'Wait a minute,' I said. 'It isn't just me. You haven't called in the shop. I've come up to the museum a few times and I've been told you're out or busy or in a meeting. It's you who have been avoiding me.'

'OK,' he conceded grumpily.

I gave him one of my most radiant smiles. 'Come on, David,' I said. 'Give me the dirt. What's the story behind my bit of gruesome pottery?'

He pulled a sheaf of papers from the bottom drawer of his desk. 'I don't know the full story,' he said. 'Only the bald facts. Fact one – that a woman was found dead at Hall o'th'Wood late in 1787. Her name was...'

'Rebekah Grindall,' I supplied.

'Correct. The circumstances appeared suspicious. She was only eighteen. Records say only that she was found *lyeing in the gardens in a sore and sorry state and dyed four days later.*'

'Ugh,' I said. 'Horrible.'

David ignored my squeamishness.

'This Rebekah had a brother...'

'Matthew Grindall.'

David flashed me a grin. 'You don't know everything,' he mocked. 'This Matthew was a master potter for one of the smaller potbanks. But his talent was huge. The story has it that he did *'lock himself in one of the kilnhouses and threw a wondrous large pot.'* He then proceeded to fire the kiln and went on to paint the pot. By the time it had cooled down from the enamelling kiln Grindall had been hanged for the murder of one...'

'Rychard Oliver,' I said, 'of Hall o'th'Wood.'

David nodded.

'I don't know anything more,' he said. 'Sorry.'

'But I do,' I said, and produced my piece of paper.

He read it through. 'I would guess at false imprisonment,' he said and I recalled the carving in the roof of our four-poster bed and something else – the huge key in the lock of our bedroom. We had never used it but surely if it could lock the door from the inside it could also lock from the outside?

I had one last question. 'Do we have any idea of provenance?' I asked.

'It must have belonged to the potbank owner,' David said. 'Sotheby's finally told me that a man called Cridman actually put it in the sale. According to records someone called Cridman was foreman in the potbank.

'Where's he from?'

'The current Mr Cridman is a local farmer near Nantwich,' David said. 'And that, Susie, is the sum total of absolutely everything I know about your jug.' He grinned. 'That's it. Time for a drink?'

'Not today, David,' I said, 'but stay in touch. Please?'

He promised he would and I left.

Something struck me as I drove home.

'Lyeing in the gardens.'

The knot garden of which I was so proud. Had the poor child jumped from the window and died four days later from her injuries? I would never look with such pleasure at the view from my bedroom window again but imagine a young woman, mortally wounded, desperate and in pain. *'Dyed four days later.'*

They were terrible words.

Richard had refused my financial help towards the house so I invested my money instead.

But underneath I resented the fact that he did not include me in our joint expenses. It seemed almost patronising to one who'd been brought up by an independent aunt to expect a bohemian existence. Yet when I considered it later I realised it was part of Richard's traditional outlook and attitude. Part of his breeding and his old-fashioned values. How then could I criticise him for the very reason I had fallen in love with him?

But I was not one to give up. When a second team of

workmen started arriving I tackled him again, only to meet with the same brick-wall response. 'It's all in hand,' he said abruptly. 'There are just a few repairs that need to be done or the house will deteriorate.'

'Are they expensive, Richard? Because,' I continued doggedly, linking my arm in his, 'I have money from the rental of the cottage and plenty of money of my own. The shop is doing well. I am your wife. Richard,' I appealed, 'let me help. Include me in this – please. Don't shut me out.' I held his face in my hands to stop him from either moving or looking away but his eyes dropped from mine and I knew that I had lost the argument. He was intransigent and it would prove our downfall.

I can never pretend to understand why Richard made the decisions he did. I simply have to live with the consequences.

He looked strangely at me and didn't reply but pressed his lips together and retreated into a long, moody silence that lasted the entire evening.

It was almost bedtime before he looked across at me and his face had softened. Whatever the problem he had worked his way through it. He drew in a deep breath, as though about to dive into deep water. 'Susie,' he said, watching me for my reaction. 'I have to go to London for the weekend. I'll be back on Monday evening.'

I didn't argue but it made me realise that his business trips had become more frequent since the beginning of the year. Majorca had been a brief respite but again I wondered what was going on in his private world that he needed to shut me out of. I already knew, instinctively, that he would continue to exclude me. And that made me feel lonely.

I argued the point with my aunt and she reiterated what I had already worked out for myself – that Richard had been divorced for many years and had grown used to running his own life without considering another person. It was not selfishness but the behaviour of someone used to solitude. It was something I had realised about him early in our marriage, that he resented interference or intrusion. So I had learnt to step back.

I could respect his desire for privacy but underneath I wanted to share everything with him. I was greedy for his attention, his love, his company and his confidence.

However as I was to have an entire weekend to myself I planned it all, right down to the very last detail. I would spend the whole of Saturday with Joanne, at the shop. We would clean it, stocktake, reorganise and perhaps weed out a few pieces which should be entered in Louis Taylor's, the local saleroom in Hanley. I would have an early night, with supper in front of the television and on Sunday I would, for the first time since my marriage, rise at 4 a.m. and drive up the M6 to the Sunday morning antiques fair at Charnock Richard services. I felt quite excited.

And that is exactly what I did. Joanne and I had a Saturday together at the shop, eating fish and chips for lunch and serving customers, rearranging the windows and adjusting the lighting. It felt quite like old times.

I ate supper alone then watched an old film in the night. And on the Sunday morning, to Maria's disapproval, I put my alarm on for 4 a.m., drank two strong cups of coffee, showered and brushed my hair then set out in the fog, driving north up the M6 and exiting illegally through the services.

It was a practice frowned on by the police but it was rumoured that somebody slipped them cash to turn a blind eye to the procession of Volvos and vans who passed through the back exit.

The fair was a huge, eclectic, disorganised free-for-all with cars, lorries, trailers full of every type of goods you could imagine – some second-hand but always there were the lovely antiques hiding away in boxes, under tarpaulins or behind some monstrosity. I worked quickly, moving through the car park, shifting stuff and peering into the dim interiors of estate cars with my flashlight. I found a Tudor coffer hiding beneath a tarpaulin sheet, covering it from the damp. I loaded it into the Volvo, which had replaced my old Ford, and made my way into the main halls.

There were four of these, each one stuffed full of stalls. There was only one way to assimilate everything and that was to walk up and down, quickly, stopping at each stall for a few minutes to see what was on offer.

I found a pair of bow puttees, some copper lustre jugs – just right to hang on a Welsh dresser I had in the shop. I found an Obadiah Sherratt figure of Christ in the

Garden of Gethsemane and countless other pieces. Every time I walked the corridors of antiques fairs I always wondered whether my jug would turn up today, here. Scanning the room I saw two or three policemen also treading the walkways. They were also on the lookout for stolen goods and, at a bet, they would find some.

My jug?

Maybe.

I used up all my cash and suddenly the early start caught up with me. I felt shattered. I made my way to the coffee stall and to my delight found David there. He greeted me with kisses on both cheeks. Obviously the awkwardness was completely over. 'Susie,' he said. 'What a treat. How's married life?'

Only a month ago I would have said, a dream. Now I was more circumspect.

'Interesting,' I said. 'We're settling down.'

He gave me a sharp look. 'Starting to find out what sort of a man you've married?'

'Sorry?'

'Nothing,' he said. 'Just rumours.'

'What rumours?'

'They're probably not true.'

'What are you talking about?'

'Susie,' he said awkwardly. 'I've heard he's made some dirty business dealings – that's all.'

I was silent. As with the jug there was always that sniff of scandal around the Oliver name. The uneasiness, that small hint that something was wrong.

We chatted easily for a while, drinking coffee and gossiping and then I sensed a change in him. 'How is your husband?' he asked.

'Fine.' I was wary now. 'He's away on business for the weekend.'

He grabbed my hand. 'I never thought you would sell your soul...' he said.

I stared at him. 'David,' I said, 'what are you on about?'

'...for a house, wealth, social position.'

I took my hand away. 'Is that what you think?'

He said nothing.

'Because you've got it wrong, you know. I didn't marry Richard because of the house or wealth or social position.'

He simply raised his eyebrows and I felt angry.

'I married him because I love him,' I said.

'I loved you once, Susie.'

The dismay I felt cancelled out all the pleasure I'd experienced at seeing him again. He'd spoilt it now. I felt I'd had to defend my marriage and at the same time I'd lost a friend. I stood up.

'I'm going home,' I said and knew I had alienated him. Probably for ever.

I loaded up my pieces and drove home.

But in spite of my successful buying, David had cast a sour note over my day. I felt tired and, for the first time since I'd lived in Hall o'th'Wood, a little depressed as I let myself in through the front door and walked into the hall.

I was aware of all the eyes of the Oliver clan watching me from the gallery. I walked along until I reached the eighteenth century portrait of Richard's namesake and studied his face. I had always felt there was something wasted and dissolute about the arrogant features. Deny it as I might I could see some of my husband there. In the straight, angry gaze of the grey eyes. There was something direct and clear – and uncompromising. The question was what had Rychard Oliver done in the eighteenth century that had led the potter to portray not only the house but also a set of gallows? What part had Matthew played in the story and what had Rebekah, his sister, been to the master of the house? I felt a sudden lust to see the jug again and wished I had been able to keep it and find out its history. Rightly or wrongly I believed that to know its story would be to know something of my own.

I moved away from the portrait and reflected then that Richard, my husband, should sit for one of these portraits. I would suggest it to him.

Maria had lit a fire in the library and set out the Sunday papers. The room was cosy and warm and I alternatively dozed and read. At five she brought me a meal on a tray, thin slices of beef and vegetables, and I sat back in the leather library chair and ate it before turning again to the news of the day: Arab terrorists in Jordan, complaints about the noise of Concorde, Mary Wilson's poems. I fell asleep.

I was wakened by the telephone ringing. No one was answering it. Maria would be having a late siesta, a habit she had never quite dropped. I picked it up.

'Susie.'

It was Richard. 'Susie.' There was something urgent in his voice which should have alerted me.

'Richard?'

He asked me what I had been doing and I told him without telling him anything about bumping into David. I described some of the pieces I had bought and realised he wasn't really listening but distracted. 'And now I have a fit of the lazies,' I said, smiling to myself as though he would be able to see it. 'You'll be ashamed of me. I started to read the papers and dropped asleep in the chair.'

'It doesn't sound like you.' His voice was abrupt, strained.

'How is your business trip?'

'Good.' Suddenly he sounded excited. 'Actually, Susie, I think I can say very good. Darling, I believe I can see a light at the end of the tunnel.'

What tunnel? The tunnel you have been fumbling along alone, and in the dark?

'Are you going to tell me any more?'

'No need for you to know, my darling.' It felt like the pat on the head you give a child. ' Except that everything – everything,' he repeated,' is fine.'

I wanted to believe him. It is one of my faults that I believe what I want to believe, sometimes ignoring facts to the contrary, facts which may be staring me in the face. As a child I had the superstition that if I told myself enough times that something was right it would be so. I did this when my parents had died but I could not have repeated it enough times. How many more?

Underneath that choice veneer Richard was presenting to me I was perfectly aware that everything was not fine.

'I am so looking forward to coming home,' he said next. 'I shall tell Jenkins to put his foot on the accelerator.'

We both laughed. Jenkins's slow and cautious driving was one of our shared amusements.

'Wear your best dress, Susie, we have plenty to celebrate and tell Maria we are to have a special dinner tomorrow night. A very special dinner. Tell her to kill the fatted calf.'

'I will.'

'Have a good evening, my darling, and I'll see you tomorrow.'

'What time?'

'Tell Maria to have dinner ready for eight and to uncork the wine. I'll be back before then. Susie,' he added, 'I love you so very much.'

I told him I loved him too and replaced the receiver with an uncomfortable feeling. Richard sounded almost drunk with excitement after his subdued behaviour since the beginning of the year. Something had been worrying my husband. And now? Whatever it was he was not going to share it with me. Perhaps in my heart of hearts I already knew that the clouds were gathering over our heads. Perhaps I even accepted it.

Wonderful times are not meant to last.

*   *   *

I did not go to Bottle Kiln on the Monday but spent the day catching up with paperwork and chores around the house, helping Maria wax the furniture and prepare the meal. We had always enjoyed working together in the kitchen though I knew Richard didn't quite approve of this fraternisation with his housekeeper. But she cooked in the same way as did my aunt, with garlic and olive oil and tomatoes, chattering all the time and sipping the cooking wine. I felt comfortable with her. As she chattered and tossed the vegetables in the inevitable olive oil I ironed a few of Richard's shirts and at six went upstairs to change.

My skin was still tanned from the holiday in Majorca so I creamed my legs and wore a pink dress with high-heeled sandals, took time and trouble over my make-up and hair. The dining room would be warm, with a log fire in the grate, and I wanted to feel close to Richard.

Skin to skin.

I hoped he would learn that I was a grown woman and that he would confide in me.

At a quarter past seven I heard the car rumble across the courtyard cobbles. I ran downstairs and out through the front door into the chilly night. Richard was just climbing out of the back seat and I flung my arms around him – terribly – abnormally – glad to see him, to hold him. 'Richard,' I said, breathing in the tang of his tobacco. He must have smoked a cigar in the car, something Jenkins disapproved of. 'Richard. You're back.'

He held me to him, speaking into my hair. 'What a welcome,' he said. 'What a homecoming.' He held me at arm's length. 'Better than a puppy,' he said, laughing.

I spoke briefly to Jenkins and Richard dropped his arm around my shoulders and together we walked into the great hall. He looked at me fondly. 'What have you been up to today?'

I related all the mundane things I had done – including the shirts. All six of them. He laughed and I knew he wasn't really that interested.

Jenkins took his case upstairs and he followed him up. 'I need a shower,' he said. 'Pour me a drink, my darling, and I'll be right down.'

There was a special atmosphere in the dining room that night. Maria had made a great effort. The meal was good, beef stroganoff with creamed potatoes and dishes of miniature vegetables. And she had had the sense to use fillet steak and not skimp on the quality of the meat, I noticed. Candles flickered down the polished length of the table and that was the only light – apart from the flames licking the logs in the hearth. The room was warm – stuffy almost. Intimate. We drank two bottles of wine which went to my head. Maria was watching me with an almost sentimental expression in her dark eyes. She produced the tarte aux pommes with a flourish and Richard dismissed her then drew me to him. 'Sit nearer to me,' he said. 'I want to talk to you.'

I was excited and a little drunk because I believed he was about to confide in me. But instead he asked me questions about my business, about doing something illegal which would bring in a great deal of money. I related the story of the stolen goods. His eyes were shuttered then and I wondered whether the moment had passed but he spoke again about Hall o'th'Wood and what it meant to him. He followed that up with questions about what it meant to me and I enthused, as I always had, over the beauty and tradition of the place. He seized on the word 'tradition' and told me that when he had noted my enthusiasm for preserving the past, in the form of antiques, he had known I was the wife he had been waiting for. I was flattered and, as I said before, a little drunk. I felt that Richard was celebrating something but he was celebrating it alone because I did not know what it was. I could not share it.

We made love that night on the rug in front of the fire. I remember I was naked and Richard was above me. I recall seeing his face and our complete abandonment to pleasure. I believe it was in that moment that my child was conceived. Afterwards we tumbled into the four-poster bed and slept instantly.

I had thought I would sleep until morning but perhaps we had drunk too much wine for normal sleep. Or perhaps I was disturbed. I awoke at some time in the middle of the night and became aware of the footsteps pacing over my head.

In Elizabethan times, when Hall o'th'Wood was built, in inclement weather the ladies and children had taken their exercise in the long gallery on the top floor which stretched the entire length of the house. It was a light room with windows facing all directions overlooking the Cheshire Plain. Oak floorboards and wainscoting were the only decoration, apart from four plush sofas which stood back against the walls, giving a clear run to the energetic. But the lack of carpeting meant that if anyone did walk the boards you could hear it. Every hollow footstep.

I am not a superstitious person but I wondered then if the dead could walk.

I stretched out my hand to rouse Richard and found that his side of the bed was empty. He had pulled the covers back over me so I would not feel the cold and wake. I sat up and reached for my dressing gown from the bottom of the bed.

I could hear footsteps echoing above me, walking the length of the room, pausing, turning and walking back again. I imagined I could hear long skirts rustling and children calling to each other.

Then I told myself not to be so silly. It must be Richard.

I tied the sash around my waist, pushed open the door that led to the twisted stairs up to the long gallery, and climbed. Though logic told me it would only be Richard, unable to sleep, my heart was pounding as I rounded the corner and raised my head to peer along the length of the room. There was enough moonlight to make out the entire length of the room, blue pools creating an unreal, almost frightening effect. I saw at once it was Richard who was pacing up and down. But for a moment or two I wished it had been some ancient ghost. I watched him, unseen, for a few minutes, more frightened by what I saw than I would have been of a headless, medieval spectre or even Rebekah Grindall's broken body. My husband looked old and shrunken. Already one of his ancestors. Frozen to the spot I stifled a scream because I had glimpsed my future. Then he turned his head in my direction and saw me watching him. 'Hello, Suse,' he said, in a voice which struggled to be normal. 'Couldn't you sleep?'

'Couldn't you sleep, you mean?' I walked towards him, desperate to recognise him again, to watch him become, once more, the man I loved. 'Richard,' I appealed. 'What is going on?'

He didn't speak at first. He said nothing while minutes stretched silently between us but stared at me as though, like me, he was seeing something not quite of our time and I became even more frightened. 'What on earth is it?'

He walked right up to me, very slowly. I could pick out his features now in the moonlight. I don't know why but I found his stare quite horrible. 'Susie,' he said with difficulty, gripping me by the shoulders. 'You do know, don't you, that you can't inherit the house? When I die Hall o'th'Wood must go to Michael?'

I panicked then. 'Are you ill?'

'No. No.' He spoke quickly. 'I'm not ill at all but I wouldn't want you to misunderstand anything. I love you more than I can ever say. I love you more than my life. From the day I found you I have loved you more than anything in this universe but this is something different. Michael must inherit Hall o'th'Wood.'

I wondered if he was more perceptive than I had realised, that he knew how I yearned for a son and that he was preparing me for my future, warning me that any son he and I had would not live here.

I didn't give voice to these thoughts but kept silent. Most people would think it fanciful that I could possibly know that the cells of my child were already multiplying inside me. What if that child should be a son?

I said nothing of these things but reassured him with a smile. 'Of course. I've always understood that.' I put my hand on his arm. 'I know, Richard.'

He looked more normal then, nodding, as though he had always known this would be my response and as though he was relieved he had got it off his chest.

'Come now, darling,' he said. 'Let's go back to bed.'

He made love to me for a second time that night.

To make sure, I told myself, that I would have my son. But there was a desperation, a ferocity, almost a cruelty in his love making that I had never known before. His climax was urgent, felt like unfinished business, and when he had finished he lay back, spent, with his arm around me and my head on his chest. He slept quickly and deeply but I did not. I stared at the canopy of our bed and knew that Rebekah Grindall had lain after just such love making and made her decision to commit suicide. Finally I did sleep until the sun woke us in the morning and we heard Maria clattering about in the kitchen.

All these were portents of a future I had no knowledge of. If I had I would have screamed for the rest of that night.

Perhaps, in some terrible way, I still scream.

CHAPTER TEN

I'm not exactly sure how I met Julius Isaacs, whether he came first into the shop or whether he knew Richard before me. I only know that at some point in the autumn of 1970 he was there, in our lives and part of our lives. He was an odd man with a whispering, soft voice, oversized features – a huge nose and ears and large, bony hands. His eyes were very black, topped by thick, long eyebrows which badly needed a trim. Whatever the weather he always dressed like an undertaker, in loose-fitting, black, shiny suits with white shirts and a dark tie. I never saw him wear anything else. He had been a customer of mine for a few months, always buying strange pieces, the very items I worried over because they were not quite what they seemed: a bureau which was commonplace or had more than an acceptable percentage of restoration, a piece of pottery which was later than I had first thought, a painting which had been clumsily relined. It is odd but I was always glad to see the pieces he bought leave the shop. He never bought my prize items, never haggled for the trade price, always paying the full price and sending a van around to collect the pieces. He was, in a way, my rescuer, the ideal customer. He bought a wide variety of items, right across the board. I could never predict what piece would catch his eyes. And yet – to always buy the 'wrong' thing was, in its way, a skill. He became a part of my business which I grew to depend on.

Somehow, I was never quite sure how, he knew Richard too. I assumed it was through Richard's financial dealings but I had no confirmation of this. Richard never told me and I never asked. In those days I didn't ask enough questions.

He came to Hall o'th'Wood, to dinner, late in the September and somehow the conversation drifted towards the political situation in China which Mr Isaacs seemed to know something about. He asked me my opinion of the Mao communist regime and I muttered something superficial about the 'Little Red Book'. The truth was that I knew very little about China or what it was like to live under Chairman Mao.

Isaacs then mentioned a collection of Chinese porcelain which had been smuggled out of the People's Republic into Hong Kong and subsequently bought by a British collector. I listened, interested and intrigued by stories which came from a land which kept itself so hidden and separate from the outside world. The collection, he claimed, needed cataloguing and valuing and finally shipping back to the UK. He asked me if I would consider flying out to Hong Kong and organising the project myself.

I remember I demurred, saying there were plenty of dealers who would undertake the trip who were far better qualified than I: that I was a dealer in English pottery – not Chinese porcelain – but Julius Isaacs told me that the collector, who always, always, remained nameless, had insisted that I do the work. I didn't work out why until later – until it was too late. What clinched it for me was Richard saying that he would love to take a trip out to the Far East as he and Michael were considering expanding their dealings out there. I remember staring at him across the table, knowing this was the first I had heard of it, but Richard's face was firm. Impassive. I studied him across the dinner table and read nothing there – no duplicity, nothing except his gaze on me, waiting for me to answer. I remained quiet. But as Julius Isaac was a dinner guest I could not discuss the subject then. He was clever, witty, amusing and I couldn't work out why he gave me such a feeling of disquiet. Even so, before Maria brought in the port and cheeseboard, I found myself agreeing to fly to Hong Kong in the November to undertake the work and Richard was to come with me.

Hong Kong was not a place I would have chosen to visit but I was promised a very generous fee for my trouble and all business people learn to seize the opportunity to make money. One never knew when one would hit lean years; the antiques business was notoriously fickle. The trip was finally settled for the second week in November.

10th October 1970 was our third wedding anniversary and Richard and I had decided to celebrate with an evening at a local hotel with our families – my sister Sara and her husband John, Aunt Eleanor who had become a frequent visitor to Hall o'th'Wood (she had struck up a friendship with Richard and besides she insisted that the house aided her creative painting instinct) and Michael, Richard's son. I was excited because after we had invited him to the anniversary dinner Michael had asked if he could bring someone along, a physiotherapist called Linda. As we were dressing that night Richard and I discussed it. I was of the opinion that this was a serious relationship and was trying to persuade him to my point of view. But men are slow at recognising blossoming relationships. I was cleaning my teeth and pressed my point, wandering into the bedroom. 'I think Michael's serious about her. He's never brought anyone here before. And,' I added meaningfully, 'to such an important occasion too.'

Richard was having trouble tying his bow tie. 'No, I don't agree, Susie. Michael won't settle down for years yet. He's a rover.' He turned around to give me a grin. 'Just like his dad.'

I finished my teeth and emerged from the bathroom.

'Not as much of a rover as you think,' I said darkly. 'I tell you. He wouldn't have invited her unless she meant something to him.'

Richard made a face and vanished into the dressing room to use the mirror.

I said nothing back. I had missed a period and wondered how Richard would respond if he was to be a father again after so long. I dropped my dressing gown and struggled into my underwear then held my dress up. It was new and had been very expensive. Long, black, stiff taffeta, off the shoulder with a floor-length, full skirt. Tight over my breasts and waist. I can remember sliding it down over my body and wondering how long it would fit me so snugly. My breasts were already two sizes larger and scarcely fitted in the tight bodice. Richard wandered back into the bedroom, the bow tie hanging still, and simply stared. 'You look...' he began. He moved close to me, ran his hands over my breasts and pressed his mouth to them, each in turn. I felt both maternal and aroused.

'Words fail me,' he said huskily. 'Susie – you are so beautiful. So beautiful I want to stare at you all evening.'

They say that when a woman is pregnant she assumes a mantle of beauty.

I felt pleased and happy and not a little smug. I had everything, didn't I? A charming husband who adored me, I lived in a beautiful house, I had a successful business and a loving family. My fingers slipped down over my stomach. And now I had my son, growing inside me and I would have him beside me forever. I never doubted that this child was a tiny boy and already I had a name for him. A superstition was growing inside me with the child. Richard's son was called Michael – not Richard. I, then, could call my son by the family name.

I tied Richard's bow tie and together we descended the staircase.

Richard had arranged for a photographer to take some pictures of us and though I hated the posing I realised this was important to him. I felt I was getting off lightly. For months now he'd been persuading me to sit for a portrait and I'd been evasive.

When I was painted I wanted to have my son in my arms. I saw him in my mind's eye, with Richard's clear, grey eyes and direct gaze, with his smooth hands and long fingers, my husband's face and body, sitting erect on a horse; his portrait would hang beside the others. He would be the next generation. Proud, erect and strong, with the clear, grey eyes that marked the family. I would play my part in this family's history. When Richard was old, I told myself, I would have his son beside me.

So neither of us had had our portraits painted. Perhaps a photograph is the medium of the twentieth century anyway.

I sat in the library chair, Richard behind me, his hand draped across my shoulder while we posed this way and that, joined by various members of the family. I might have smiled. I know now that for some of them I did

smile because I have the photographs with me today. I
see them now. For others I simply stared, as had the
subjects of the portraits of the upper gallery, and looked
haughty, as though I wished the session was over, which
was partly the truth.

I have all the photographs now. Later I demanded the
prints from the entire film – not simply the selected
poses. This is the talent of inanimate objects. I can pick
the photographs up today, look at them and read all
that was to come. All that I did not know then. I see my
ignorance, all my misunderstandings, Richard's pride,
my soft expression, the secret I was nursing in my
breast. We were a family very sure of ourselves, proud
and certain. Michael, Richard, Aunt Eleanor and even
Sara.

That was the life mapped out for me. I was certain of
it.

Only it wasn't.

My aunt wandered across to me, speaking very softly
in my ear so no one else could hear. 'And does he know
you're pregnant, Susie?'

I met her eyes and shook my head. 'No. I don't want
him to know. I don't want him to worry. Not until we
return from Hong Kong.'

She gave me a knowing, sharing look. 'As you wish,'
she said, still very softly. 'Though how he can miss that
maternal glow you're wrapping yourself up in I don't
know, Susie. But then men are blind, aren't they?' She
brushed my cheek with her lips. I felt my love for her

well up inside me and spill into my heart.

I wondered then what had been her life? When Sara and I had been children, growing up. What chances had she missed because of us? What love had she eschewed? I watched her and realised how little I knew about her past. When she spoke to us it was more often about our father and their bohemian childhood. Richard wandered over and made some comment about my appearance. Then he bent and nuzzled the back of my neck and told me that I had changed my perfume.

I hadn't but I have heard that perfumes can smell different on the body of a pregnant woman. Perhaps it is something to do with the hormones. I don't know except that I felt intimate, as though I wanted the room to empty and for us to be alone. My aunt was watching us, her eyes misty and difficult to read. I realised then that she was an ageing spinster and that bringing up my sister and me had cost her dear. The thought stopped me. Then she produced a flat parcel, about two feet square, wrapped in brown paper. 'Sorry,' she said, 'I forgot to get wrapping paper. I have a gift for you.

'Here…' She handed it to Richard. Not to me, I noticed. 'Happy anniversary, both.'

He was as excited as a young boy at Christmas. In fact, I thought, watching him tearing the paper, ever since he had returned from his London business trip he had been on a permanent high. Had I not known better I would have accused him of being on a cocaine high. It was too bright, too sparkly. Not really him at all.

And yet...

He drew the paper away from the gift and held it up.

It was a painting, recognisably of Hall o'th'Wood but executed in surrealist style. The house swirled and spun and the walls were even more crooked than in real life. It was distorted Chagall. Spinning around the house were myself and Richard, both helplessly in its power, I in a long, white nightdress, eyes staring, mouth open, he in his sober grey suit, figure stiff, grey tie, grey hair but with fiery red eyes which burnt towards us. I opened my mouth to speak and stared at the canvas. Never in my entire life have I ever seen a painting so powerful as the one my aunt, Eleanor Paris, painted of Hall o'th'Wood. Because she had captured not only its crooked walls and crooked roof but also the way the house sucked in all who came within its vortex. In some ways the painting did not reassure me but frightened me because it was the truth.

I looked at the artist and caught some infinite wisdom in her face. She looked like a sage, a wise woman, someone who foresaw the future.

What did she see?

I glanced across at Richard and saw that he was as overwhelmed by the painting as I was. His hands were gripping the frame. I wondered then whether he understood its meaning as well as I did.

I kissed my aunt's cheek. 'So that's what you were doing on the top floor, was it?'

She nodded and looked pleased with our response.

I linked my arm in Richard's. 'Well it's saved us from having to sit for a portrait.'

He laughed. We drank champagne and toasted each other and our future years together.

Michael arrived then with a small, dark-haired girl he introduced as Linda. Richard and I exchanged glances at his proprietary pride. She was neat and pretty with a beautiful smile. 'I've heard so much about you all,' she gushed. 'I feel I already know you. And this house,' she added, looking around. 'It's so lovely. I can't believe it's for real.'

I remember thinking then, don't you realise, Linda? It isn't for real. My eyes moved across to the painting.

Michael gave me a huge hug and complimented me on my dress. I teased him about turning up in a dinner suit when we were more used to seeing him in jeans and sweaters. I reflected on our friendship in the three years we had known each other. He felt like the brother I had never had. From the first he had been open and friendly, quickly affectionate towards his stepmother. He was generous and boisterous, honest and kind. He was like his father yet in some ways so very different. He was far more circumspect about the house and more of a realist. He might have become my brother but I was equally aware that I had become, in some ways, a sister to him. He had more than once told me how much more content his father was since our marriage and how glad he was that I had come into their lives, and for that reassurance

I was eternally grateful. Michael had some of the warmth Richard could occasionally seem to lack and he had a talent for putting people at their ease, something else his father could be short on. I had noticed frequently people stiffening in Richard's presence. Perhaps these differences between father and son were Michael's mother's gifts. I also believed that Michael would not have excluded me from either business or family secrets.

Father and son were very close. They not only worked together but were the best of friends. Michael always greeted his father with an almost continental bear hug while Richard's face lit up when his eyes alighted on his son.

Sara and John turned up late, saying their babysitter had been delayed. Sara looked like an ice queen that night, in a sparkling, long, pale blue evening dress. She had pinned her long, blonde hair up and dressed it in curls. She wore drop pearl earrings and silver shoes. She greeted Richard with a warm embrace, kissing his cheek and laughing. The truth was that my older sister had a penchant for Richard and never stopped telling me how lucky I was to have such a life. John, her husband, paid me some compliment about my appearance and my dress and we all toasted each other in dry champagne.

At some point during the early part of the evening Richard and Michael must have slipped away from the library because I missed them. I wandered off to find them and found the dining-room door closed. I pushed it open.

They were facing each other, Richard frowning, Michael obviously angry. I caught only one phrase. 'Does Susie know?'

I interrupted lightly. 'Does Susie know what?'

Neither of them spoke and I spoke again. 'Does Susie know what?'

Michael shot a swift glance at his father, licked dry lips and said nothing. I searched Richard's face and knew, whatever it was, he didn't want me to know and he wasn't going to tell me. 'Nothing,' he said shortly. 'It's to do with the business. Come along now. It's time to go. Jenkins will have the car round.'

I could have let it spoil the evening but I didn't. I pushed the incident from my mind.

Oh yes. Hall o'th'Wood was a house of uneasy secrets that night as well as a house of celebration.

The faithful Jenkins drove us to the restaurant, Churches Mansion in Nantwich, another Cheshire black-and-white house, almost as beautiful as our own. The two other cars followed behind. Aunt Eleanor travelled with Sara, and Michael drove Linda, leaving Richard and myself in the Rolls.

The maître d'hôtel was sweating as we arrived, nervous as we entered, rubbing his palms together. I felt some sympathy for him. Richard could be an exacting client. I had heard him on the phone, ordering the meal, the room, directing the wine and stipulating the seating arrangements – almost, I had thought at the time, as though he was organising a second wedding. He had made no bones about it that tonight was to be – perfect. Special and memorable. But this was an added burden on an already agitated restaurateur.

I sat next to Richard at the head of the table, Sara on the other side. My sister missed no opportunity of flirting outrageously with my husband. She called him dangerous and sexy until I pointed out that she was confusing my husband with James Bond. It made no difference. Sara was drinking a lot of wine that night. John was driving and more than once Richard fended off her kisses. I knew that underneath his stiffness he actually enjoyed her attention. I watched her, feeling the strongest affection for my normally prim sister. We could be a close family, I reflected, if an unconventional one – sister, aunt, husband, stepson, his girlfriend. Since my marriage we had spent all our Christmases and New Years together at Hall o'th'Wood and many, many weekends, birthdays and dinners. Hall o'th'Wood was a house built for entertaining. For a family.

Dreaming, I brushed my stomach with my fingers and when I looked down the long table I caught my Aunt Eleanor's eye and smiled at her, sharing our secret.

Next Christmas, I thought, would be the most special of all because it would be complete. I would have my son in my arms.

How dangerous are dreams.

We had smoked salmon and asparagus for starters and the main meal was just being brought – chicken in soured-cream sauce – when I heard my aunt discussing a case which had made the headlines recently. She had a very clear voice and her words dropped into one of those lulls in the conversation. 'They can't hang him, surely?'

We all knew what she was talking about. It was a case of a British drugs smuggler in the Far East who had been sentenced to hang. As an example, surely, to other would-be drugs traffickers. John and Sara started to join in the discussion. I turned my head to the side and looked at Richard. His face was grey, his breath loud rasps, his eyes unfocused. He was about to drop onto the table.

'Richard,' I said. He tried to stand up and collapsed, in a heap, on the floor.

I bent over him. He gripped my hand. 'Get me home, Susie,' he said hoarsely. 'Take me home.'

My instinct was to call an ambulance but Richard gripped my wrist. 'Home,' he said again, struggling to sit up. 'I'll be all right if I can only get back.'

I summoned Jenkins and left the others to their meal, knowing the evening was ruined. Richard and I returned to Hall o'th'Wood.

CHAPTER ELEVEN

I called a doctor as soon as we arrived home. The trouble was that Richard's doctor was an old school pal, Doctor Irving Combermere, a plump, ex-public schoolboy who was in private practice in Nantwich. I had met him on a number of occasions and had disliked him intensely from the first time he had patted my bottom and told me that 'Oliver' and he wanted a bit of boy-talk. Oddly enough, although he often made what were probably meant to be flattering comments about me, I had the instinct that my feelings were reciprocated. Fully. Combermere had a patronising attitude to women that I couldn't stand. But Richard insisted he would see no other doctor.

Combermere was red-faced, overweight and a letch; it was nearly midnight when I opened the door to him and told him that Richard had collapsed at the restaurant. His eyes lingered on my low-cut dress (I hadn't bothered to change). He raised his eyebrows and went straight upstairs, I beside him, but halfway up he stopped me short. 'Absolutely not,' he said. 'I shall see the patient alone, if you don't mind.'

I kept my temper – and my dignity. 'I'm his wife,' I said. 'I have a right to—'

'I'll see the patient alone,' he repeated.

I argued. 'Shall we ask Richard?'

As I had half expected Richard agreed with Combermere and banished me from the bedroom. He wanted to speak to his 'old mate' alone, he said, so I was left, like an expectant father, to wait downstairs with Maria who kept wringing her hands and saying that she'd known he'd been doing too much lately.

She gripped my hand. 'All that worry,' she said. 'Not good for him.'

So I had her to comfort as well.

Fifteen minutes later I heard Combermere's heavy footsteps descending the staircase and came out into the hall to meet him.

'As I thought,' he said. 'It's nothing. Nothing wrong with the old chap at all. Just a heavy meal plus a couple of drinks. Indigestion. Oh – and I've told him he should really stop those cigars.'

I didn't believe him. 'Is that all?' I started to describe the episode to him but he stopped me with the usual pat on my bottom.

'Absolutely, Susie.' He leered at me. 'If you want my opinion I think it's having a nice young filly like you in the stable. Not good for we older men, you know.'

You have to hand it to Combermere. He really knew how to rile me. And to put me off the scent.

I watched him go with a feeling of fury mixed with anxiety. He was lying. But whether through his own misguided sense of confidentiality, or on Richard's instruction, I didn't know. And I had no way of finding out either. If Richard was determined to shut me out what could I do? Nothing? I climbed the staircase and entered the bedroom, told him he wasn't to stir for the whole of the next day and ignored his protestations.

'Punishment,' I said lightly, 'for spoiling our wedding anniversary dinner.'

We did spend the following day quietly, at home. Richard slept for much of the time and I watched as he gradually returned to the man I knew.

Once, when I was trying to tiptoe away, thinking he was asleep, he opened his eyes and I found him staring at me.

'Perhaps I did a selfish thing,' he said.

I stared at him.

'Marrying you.'

I shook my head. I would have none of it.

But he turned his head on the pillow. 'I knew our life together would not be uncomplicated,' he said. 'Susie, I'm so sorry.'

I lay across him then and put my head on his shoulder. We lay like that for a long time without speaking. There seemed nothing to say.

* * *

Three weeks later we flew to Hong Kong.

It was not my sort of place. I knew that as soon as I set foot inside the airport terminal. Modern, brisk, crowded. Humid and hot. Noisy for twenty-four hours a day. It was a climate to sweat in.

We checked into a hotel which had all the character of the Tardis and the next morning a car arrived to take me across the harbour to Kowloon and one of the warehouses or godowns, as they called them, where the Chinese porcelain was being held.

The political situation in China then meant that ancient pieces of porcelain were being destroyed by the people, my driver explained. So, 'Bobby' Liu told me that smuggling pieces of Ming or T'ang out of the People's Republic was a 'good thing'.

'Otherwise', he continued, 'there will be nothing left of our heritage. It will all be destroyed. You are helping the China of the future, Mrs Oliver.'

I didn't realise how much or what it would cost me.

Bobby Liu leant back in his driver's seat to speak more to me. 'Terrible things are happening in China today,' he said. 'We hear rumours, speak to people and we don't like what we hear. It seems to me, Mrs Oliver, that someone needs to take action.'

It is typical of the Chinese that even here, in Hong Kong, under British rule, Bobby Liu would not specify either what action should be taken and by whom.

The warehouse was an interesting building in traditional Chinese style, bustling with helpful porters trotting around with sometimes huge burdens. In the corner were shelves of Chinese porcelain. I knew little about the delights of the T'ang and Ming, Song or Kangxi periods but I could work it out. The Chinese potters had thoughtfully provided symbols to give the uneducated an idea of precise dates for their pieces. In fact as I warmed to my subject I discovered that absorption which always took me unawares. The thrill of the chase to a huntsman, the throw of a dice to a gambler, the thrill of discovery to a ceramics dealer. So for the next few days I spent my time checking up on pieces, cataloguing them and doing some rough valuations but I could not help wondering why it was that they had selected me. English pottery was my subject and surely there were plenty of experts over here on Oriental porcelain. It was all a puzzle. Each evening I supervised as the pieces were packed in sawdust, put into tea chests, labelled and transported to the airfreight terminal. We were to accompany them to Heathrow from where they would be picked up and transported to the collector, who, we understood, lived in Surrey. Payment was arranged for the other end.

There were odd little factors which I did not then understand. Richard seemed so eager for me to complete the transaction when he usually showed little more than a passing interest in my work. I could not understand his accompanying me here either. Hong Kong was not his sort of place any more than it was mine and he had little to do during the day. He told me he met various businessmen but he appeared deliberately vague and usually when I returned home he would be in our hotel room. I noticed that none of his business acquaintances rang him; neither did I meet any of them.

But he seemed anxious for the trip to be successful and for the deal to be completed.

I returned one evening to find him lying on the bed, his hands behind his head, staring moodily up at the ceiling. I stood in the doorway and watched him for a moment, wondering what was going on in his mind. He turned his head.

'Michael's just rung.'

'Oh?'

'He's got engaged.'

'Wonderful,' I enthused. 'I liked her.' I looked at Richard. He was looking very disgruntled.

'See,' I teased, sitting down beside him on the bed, 'I told you so.' I kissed him. 'You mark my words,' I said, watching for his reaction. 'You'll be a grandfather before long. So,' I stroked his forehead to iron out the scowl. 'How will you feel about that, my darling?'

His eyes looked suddenly forlorn. 'I don't know,' he said. 'How will you feel about being married to a grandfather?'

I lay down then beside him. 'I think I'll feel pretty good,' I answered.

He touched me then, knowing I would respond and we both drew breath.

'Dinner can wait,' he murmured.

* * *

It was a strange evening. In a foreign city we made love, toasted Michael and Linda and finally ate, not in one of the smart hotels but in a little café which cooked our food quickly over an open flame.

Finally all the crates were hammered down and I supervised the last one's transport to the airfreight terminal. We checked out of the hotel and Bobby Liu waited to pick us up. I felt quite sad at saying goodbye to my cheerful Chinese driver but he pressed my hand in a quick gesture. 'You are helping Chinese people more than you know,' he said. 'We salute you and thank you.'

I didn't understand any of it – then.

We spent the usual time in the first-class lounge, browsing through the newspapers. There were strikes in the public sector. Ted Heath was 'negotiating'. I was anticipating seeing Jenkins waiting for us at the terminal at Heathrow, supervising the handover of the crates, accepting our money for the job and returning to Hall o'th'Wood.

Finally our flight was called and we settled down into the aeroplane.

I remember I asked Richard whether he had got bored in those few days in the Far East and he answered no, that he'd enjoyed the break from normal life, and that he was looking forward to consolidating his business interests over there.

I settled back in my seat. Not quite satisfied.

We were both quiet for most of the flight, saying little. In all our lives we were never so silent as in those final strange hours returning from Hong Kong. I was suspended in a dreamworld which lay over the real universe, unconnected with any country we might happen to be passing over. In this sky-world Richard and I watched our son playing in the knot garden at Hall o'th'Wood, finally banishing the tragic ghost of Rebekah Grindall. The sun shone down on the crooked walls, the leaden panes of glass throwing the reflections this way and that. Maria was standing at the window, watching over us. I remember putting my hands out to touch this dreamworld, wanting to enter now, this very minute. Hall o'th'Wood could keep its secrets, I bargained, as long as I could live my dream.

As our descent began Richard grew agitated. He checked our passports three or four times, kept pulling at his seat belt, tightening it up. As we taxied towards the terminal I watched him grow even more anxious and put my hand in his. 'What's the matter?' I said.

'Nothing.' I knew it was a lie. 'I just hope Jenkins is there. That's all.'

I tried to reassure him. 'Of course he'll be there,' I said, 'standing at the barrier waiting to take us home. We'll be home soon,' I said. 'Back in Hall o'th'Wood with Maria and Jenkins and we'll see Michael tomorrow and congratulate him. We'll organise an engagement supper for the happy couple.'

Two happy couples, I thought, I shall take that opportunity to announce our child to our families.

He closed his eyes.

I watched him and worried again about his health, what he was hiding from me. I worried too about my child. I wanted to feel it move. But, of course, it was too early. Richard gripped my hand and I left it there. I take comfort from this.

As soon as they opened the hatch doors we knew something was wrong.

There was an armed guard to greet us as we left the plane and at the terminal two men came towards us. They were plainly dressed, of insignificant appearance, and in this there was something ominous about them. 'Mrs Oliver?' It sounded like an arrest.

'Mr Oliver. Would you come with us please?'

Officialdom is at its most threatening when it is at its most polite. Then you know.

We walked with them along the terminal corridor. I glanced at Richard and read something terrible in his eyes. 'Susie,' he said urgently. 'Susie.'

He dropped to the floor like a stone.

I watched him go with a sense of unreality because at the same time I felt a suffocating panic and a sharp cramp in my stomach. Not my stomach. My womb.

I saw one of the men bend over Richard, shout to his companions, thump his chest, blow into his mouth. I struggled to stand up. But in the end I dropped too.

Medics, police, all the dignity and organisation that is this country descended on us. I was aware of little except a voice which was insistent. 'Where is the pain?'

'Where is the pain?'

Other voices spoke to me. A woman this time. 'Mrs Oliver. I'm sorry. I have bad news.'

I lost consciousness and did not find a lucid mind again until...

The cases had been full of porcelain – yes. But they had also contained 'sensitive' Chinese documents designed to bring down the Mao government. I had never seen the letters which had been written by Madam Mao or Jiang Qing, as she had been then, denouncing the Communist Party. I knew nothing of this but it lit a diplomatic row. I became the sacrificial lamb to peace – of a sort – between the two countries. The lawyers could argue that I had been an innocent victim but it wasn't going to wash with anyone; least of all me.

How could I ever have thought that the hundreds of thousands of pounds Hall o'th'Wood needed in repairs could be supplied by one trip to China bringing back porcelain? Oh no, this had had money behind it. Money poured in by anyone who wanted to see Mao and the Communist government toppled. As is usual with me I had believed my own version of events, only what I wanted to believe.

They were more cynical. I was, after all, a well-known antiques dealer with a flourishing international business. It didn't take a great stretch of the imagination to picture me dealing in secret letters as well as Chinese porcelain. In the end no one really cared. They couldn't even decide what to charge me with – this Foreign Office hot potato.

Stolen goods? Where was the proof? But once China got wind of the story they insisted I be dealt with. In the end, almost apologetically, I was sent to prison with the trumped-up charge of endangering state security.

In fact I had lost all, my child and my husband in the same hour, my freedom and my future, because in those dreadful days doctors told me that I never would bear a child.

I faced a long court case and a prison sentence. I buried my husband flanked by two prison officers. My charmed life was over.

Now the nightmares began.

CHAPTER TWELVE

May 1973

Three years later

I was lying on my bed, in my cottage in Horton, watching a spider's web float in the breeze. The curtains were drawn. I did not know whether it was night or day and I did not care.

Way below someone was knocking on my door. Banging. Hammering.

'For he suddenly smote on the door, even louder and lifted his head

"Tell them I came and no one answered, That I kept my word," he said.

I continued watching the spider weaving his web. Sooner or later it would catch his prey. A fly was crawling towards it even now. Very slowly. Soon he would be stuck. He might struggle but what did it matter? A spider, a fly? We are all either spiders weaving webs or flies waiting to be caught.

I closed my eyes.

Knock knock knock. I wished it would go away.

'Susie!' A voice, shouting through the letter box. 'I know you're there. Open the door. NOW!'

I sighed. It was my sister and she would not go away.

Bang bang bang.

'Open this bloody door!'

I went downstairs and pulled it open.

She stared at me. 'Why haven't you answered the phone?'

I felt my face tighten.

She scrutinised me, her face twisted with concern. 'Susie. Oh Susie. Look at you.' She hugged me but I stood away from her, rigid.

Sara came inside and closed the door behind her. 'Oh, Susie,' she said again, her face creased with pain. 'How could you have let yourself come to this? Richard wouldn't have wanted this.' She hugged me tighter then moved back, still frowning. 'How much weight have you lost?'

I didn't know and I didn't care. I simply shrugged. It didn't matter to me.

She peered at me again. 'When did you last eat?'

I shrugged again. I didn't know. And I didn't care either.

She stepped back. 'John said we should leave you alone to have some time here alone in the cottage to readjust.' Her frown deepened. 'But he was wrong.' She hugged me again. 'I should have stuck to my guns, followed my instinct. I should have come before. You're my sister. I'm sorry.'

I shrugged. 'What difference would it have made?'

She sighed loudly. 'Come on,' she said suddenly. 'Get something decent on and I'll take you out to lunch.'

'No.' I didn't want to run the gauntlet of curious stares.

'Susie,' she said, her face loaded with concern. 'You've got to face the world again some time. Bury your ghosts. Move on.'

It was pointless arguing with her.

I came back down in some dark trousers and a white shirt and again she gave me a concerned look. 'How much weight have you lost, little sister?'

I didn't know and I didn't care either. Life was something to be endured. Not to enjoy any more.

Wisely she avoided the city but drove out towards Leek and the Mermaid Inn, a pub set high in the Moorlands, far away from civilisation, where it was wild and raw, yet quiet, peaceful, isolated – and private.

We ordered food and I played with mine while she scolded me.

Sara had very blonde hair – almost white – a throwback to our mother's Icelandic origins and today she had pinned it up in a French plait. She was a classic beauty with small, regular features and blue-grey eyes, unlike her swarthy little sister. But one strand of pale hair had escaped her severe hairstyle and as she talked and moved her head I focused on it. It bobbed and danced around, free and random. I concentrated on that bouncing curl. It had more spirit than I did. I might have had some once but now I had lost it. It had gone.

We finished our meal. I had eaten little of mine. Sara located the strand of hair and tucked it in with the others. I felt some sympathy for it. We ordered coffee and she took my hand. 'Susie,' she said, very gently, and I knew I was about to learn the true purpose of her visit. 'Susie.'

I stopped concentrating on her hair and met her eyes instead.

'Michael asked me to come.' She spoke very softly, her voice heavy with sympathy.

Michael and Linda had married quietly in 1971, two months after I had been sent to prison. While I had been allowed to attend my husband's funeral, flanked by two prison officers, I had not even asked to attend their wedding. My request would probably have been refused anyway. Michael was not a relative in the eyes of the law. I had lost even my 'brother'.

Both Michael and Linda had written to me frequently while I had been 'inside' but I had neither read the letters nor responded to them. I was not sure whether I wanted any contact with them again particularly now they lived in Hall o'th'Wood. I could never go back there. It was better that they carried on with their lives and forgot me, better for them to pretend that I did not exist, had never existed. In the three weeks since I had been released I had not picked up the phone nor, until now, answered the door.

I watched my sister warily.

'Linda's just had a baby.'

She waited for me to absorb this fact.

Then took a deep breath and ploughed on.

'They asked me to ask you if you would be the child's godmother.'

I stared at her and swallowed, feeling tears roll down my cheeks. I did not even try to brush them away. They were a relief. A baby? Richard's grandson? A child who would be a few years younger than my own would have been. The children might have played together in the Long Room, rocking the horses, spinning the tops, winding up the clockwork trains. The pain was as physical as a knife stuck between the ribs.

I sat motionless. They could not have asked anything harder from me.

Sara tried again. 'I think,' she said gently, 'that Richard would have wanted it.' And I knew this was the truth. He would have wanted it.

I nodded, then wiped the tears away with a handkerchief. 'I'll do it,' I said.

I would do it for Michael whom I had always loved – and for Richard too. He would have wanted it. I knew that. He would have smiled that tender, soft smile and asked me, knowing I would do it. I would have done anything for him. I had done anything for him.

I squeezed the tears away.

I chose a silk suit for my role as godmother. Cinnamon with grey piping and a grey hat with a net veil which covered my face. It was a convenient veil to hide me from prying eyes. They had chosen the local church at Balterley for the ceremony. It was the same church where Richard was buried and I drove myself – alone – to spend a few minutes communing with him at his graveside before seeing Michael, Linda and their son. I bent over the grey-stone headstone and traced the words with my fingers:

Here lies Richard Oliver 1916–1970 of Hall o'th'Wood

Beloved husband of Susanna, father of Michael

Thy will be done

'Oh, Richard,' I said softly. 'If only you could have confided in me, treated me as a woman rather than a child who needs a treat.' I touched the rough stone and knew I still loved him as I had on that first day when I had met him six years ago. I ached to have him back, to see that tender smile he reserved for me. I felt a terrible anguish that I would never see him again, never touch him, never speak to him. Then I stood up. I had a duty to perform.

I had not seen Michael or Linda since the night before we had set out for Hong Kong. At my request Michael had not attended any of the court hearings. They had taken up residence at Hall o'th'Wood immediately after Richard's death.

I tried to slip into the church incognito but they must have been watching out for me. Linda stepped towards me, a tiny, silk bundle in her arms. 'Meet Richard,' she said, her dark eyes speaking volumes, 'and take your vows seriously. You are his godmother and you will be his legal guardian. Remember this, Susie.'

I stared down at the tiny face and the child opened his eyes and stared back at me. I had a shock because they were Richard's eyes. My Richard. I stared at the baby and felt a yearning for the child I should have had, for the life that would have been mine, for the past that had never been and the future that seemed to open out into a desert expanse.

I felt a great swell of love for the child and met his parents' eyes. Michael was standing, motionless, behind his wife and baby son, watching me, gauging my reaction. 'Thank you,' I whispered. 'Thank you.' It was the best thing they could have done for me.

The christening was a brief affair and afterwards we travelled in a long, slow cavalcade back to Hall o'th'Wood. It was a dull day, cool too and the crooked walls seemed almost forbidding as I made my way up the drive and studied it. It seemed different now that Richard was not here. Less of a dream; more of a reality. It was still a majestic house but less a shrine and more a home.

Inside the house was festooned with flowers. They were everywhere, lilies and roses, the scent wafting from room to room. As the day was cool Maria had lit fires and put candles on the long, oak table. I breathed in the scent of beeswax polish and missed the scent of a cigar. Unlike his father Michael never touched them. I wandered from room to room, remembering – vignettes of our lives, a word spoken here, a touch there, an event in this place or that. A kiss, a hug. I eyed the rug in front of the fire in the dining room and remembered. I looked up at the people who peered down at me from the walls and saw with fresh eyes this flaw in their character. I had not been here since I had been mistress of the house but I still looked at it with a mistress's eyes, noted objects in other places, new books, an up-to-date television set. The scent of baby powder and washing. I moved on to stand in the doorway of the dining room. The table groaned with a buffet meal – sausage rolls, quiche, olives, bread rolls, cheese, a joint of ham. In the centre was the cake, topped by a tiny porcelain child in a crib. I moved forward, reached out and touched it. It seemed to represent all that I had lost. It was almost cruel. I studied the porcelain baby in the crib, its plump, rosy cheeks. Pink lips, chubby limbs. What would my child have been like? I could not know, only dream.

Most of the guests had clustered in the two main rooms but I let myself into what I still considered Richard's study and I was touched. On the mantelpiece, in a silver frame, was the photograph taken of us on the night of our third wedding anniversary. I picked it up and studied it in great detail, seeing now all I had not seen then, everything, the black sheen of my satin dress, my happy expression and full breasts, Richard's tender face as he stared down at me, but I saw too the lines of anxiety criss-crossing his forehead and I felt overwhelmed with grief. I wanted him to walk in, brush my shoulders with his hands, speak to me. 'Hello, Susie.'

I knew then, it had been a mistake to come back here. It made me too conscious of it all, my love, my life, this house. I leant against the mantelpiece and covered my face with my hands, overwhelmed by grief. I could not believe that I would never hold him again, never speak to him, never touch him, never see him. We would never again make love. He would never kiss me. I could never look up and see that tender expression on his face. I gave a cry.

'You must be Susie.' A brisk voice.

I turned around. A short, slim, middle-aged woman in a coral suit was watching me from the doorway. I didn't know her.

'I'm Julia,' she said, holding out a gloved hand.

Julia. Of course. Richard's first wife. The child's grandmother. What more natural than that she would be here for her grandson's christening?

I opened my mouth to speak but nothing came out.

'I hadn't thought you would be so young,' she said frankly and perfectly at ease. 'My dear,' she said – not without kindness. 'I'm so sorry about everything that happened.' She looked around her. 'I blame this bloody place,' she said with sudden viciousness. 'Gloomy and forbidding. Never liked it. I'm a glass-and-plastics girl myself. But then there's no accounting for taste, is there? I always said it would be the death of him, you know. And I was right.'

I said nothing. I could not imagine her with Richard.

'Anyway,' she said, moving away with a smile. 'I'm so glad I've met you.'

People move in and out of our lives. Some become part of it – but others are a fleeting contact. Nothing more.

I was more than ever glad of that net veil which hid my face.

I knew I must leave then but before I could I must see Maria. I found her in the kitchen, busily spooning tiny amounts of caviar onto small, round biscuits.

'Maria,' I said.

She turned around with a cry, dropping the spoon on the floor.

'I did not think you would come,' she said. 'They said you would but I did not believe them. I thought you would never come here again – not back to the place where you were so happy. So happy,' she repeated. 'But for all that it is good to see you.' She hugged me tightly then, as my sister had done, and peered into my face. 'He is dead,' she said. 'You are a young woman. You must move on. Don't forget that. Please,' she said, releasing me, 'come again.'

'Perhaps,' I said.

She wiped her hands on her apron and gave a sly smile. 'But you have a duty here now. You are his godmother. You must care for him. The new child.'

I nodded, hardly knowing what the role would mean.

I left quietly then, slipping away after saying goodbye to Michael and Linda. I knew Maria was probably right, that I would be back soon now I had a responsibility there.

Maybe it was fate that on that very day, when I returned to my cottage, a letter was lying on the mat with a foreign stamp. Airmail. It was from America, from someone in Long Island, New York, called Wernier-King IV who claimed to have a 'unique and extensive' collection of Staffordshire figures which he wanted cataloguing, photographing and valuing. He had heard that I might be willing to do the work for him. He estimated the work would take roughly three months and he named a sum which seemed exorbitant for a mere three months' work. I read through the letter twice, noticing the gold coronet heading and decided that if he could afford to pay the money then I would go.

What else did I have to do?

Without changing out of my christening suit I sat down at the table and penned out my reply to Mr Wernier-King of Tacoma, East Hampton, Long Island, New York.

CHAPTER THIRTEEN

I had arranged to arrive at Tacoma in early June which gave me two weeks spare to spend with my aunt in Majorca. Faithful Joanne would keep the shop ticking over during my absence, as she and David had done for the three years I had spent awaiting Her Majesty's pleasure. The truth was I had no stomach for the business any more.

'If I lose my joy at acquiring a beautiful piece I shall retire.'

Those words haunted me.

As soon as I arrived at Palma airport I knew I had done the right thing. Early summer in Majorca is a time for flowers and greenery, warmth rather than heat, for fresh, clean days and my aunt was a balm – the perfect person to spend time with.

She picked me up at the airport, making no reference to my appearance or saying anything, apart from observations about the weather, or the new road they were building through the mountain. She worried that Soller, no longer isolated by narrow mountain roads, would open up to mass tourism, like some other parts of the island. She didn't seem to mind my quietness. She was always sensitive to my moods and knew I was happier silent.

It was not her way to fuss over me, to worry about my mental state, nag about my weight or try to intrude on my suffering. She had not contacted me all the time I had been in prison, instinctively knowing I must fight that battle alone. She was one to shoulder burdens and accept what life threw at her without complaint and she expected me to be the same. She knew I needed time to heal and was content to allow me to recover in my own time. We talked a lot about Richard in those weeks. I found it better that she referred to him with the affection she had always shown him in life and did not blame him for my plight after he had died.

Every night when I opened my window to the stars I communed with my husband. He seemed close – some of our happiest moments had been on this holiday isle. I told him how much I still loved him, that I would not stop. I told him that Michael and Linda now lived in his beloved house, that it looked as proud and beautiful as ever, that he had a grandson. Some nights I missed him so much I almost imagined I could smell the smoke from his cigar wafting in through the open window. Those nights I would cry myself to sleep as I had cried in mourning for my parents.

One night when the weather was cool and damp we lit the log fire and sat by it, holding out our hands to its warmth and I confided in my aunt my greatest sadness.

'I didn't tell him about the baby,' I said. 'I should have done. I shouldn't have held it back from him. More than anything I wish he had known that we would have a son or a daughter. We could have shared that happiness.'

My aunt looked at me with a strange look. 'He knew,' she said. 'Of course he knew. Look at the photograph of the pair of you taken that evening. I've studied it. Just look at the way he is watching over you. He knew you were carrying his child. I never saw him look at you quite like that before. So caring and loving.'

'But if he knew that I was pregnant then he must have known too that he was putting not only me but his own child at risk.'

Her eyes clouded. 'We don't know exactly what he believed was happening. Susie – we'll never know.' She put her hand on my arm. 'Don't carry that burden with you. You must learn to live again.'

But I remembered his collapse at the table on the night of our wedding anniversary when she had brought up the subject of the hanging in the Far East and the dubious human rights and I doubted him. While I didn't want to believe that Richard had wilfully put me and his child at risk neither could I believe that he had been a dupe. And he must have been one or the other. It was a problem that rolled round and round in my head all the time.

I could find no answer and I never would now. I could not ask him so I fell silent.

'I did try to warn you, Susie,' she said softly. 'The painting, you know. It was my warning to you. Hall o'th'Wood influenced you both in your different ways. You saw only its beauty; Richard only its responsibility.'

She fell silent.

A night or two later she broached the subject of the job I was about to undertake. I showed her the letter with its gold coronet heading.

'Do you know anything about him, this Wernier-King?'

I shook my head.

'Is he even bona fide?'

'His secretaries have been very efficient at organising my flights,' I said. 'There was a problem with my visa because...' I felt my face crumple. I was, it seemed, persona non grata, as far as entry to the United States of America was concerned. I suspected that Mr Wernier-King, or rather his minions, had had to do much arranging and palm-greasing to facilitate my visit.

'They seem to have ironed everything out,' I said. 'I have no reason to have any concerns about him. I suspect he's an ageing millionaire – probably bald and fat and obsessed with his collection.' I smiled. 'I shall be safe enough.'

'Well – ' she still looked dubious. 'If things don't work out too well you can always come back here. Use it as a bolt-hole. The only thing is I won't be here.'

'What?' I looked at her, suddenly ashamed. I had been so wrapped up in my own emotions that we had not really talked about her. Something was different. She was excited about something. 'What is it?'

'I've been asked to have an exhibition in Paris, Susie,' she said excitedly, 'in one of the bigger art galleries near to the Louvre for the next six months.' She couldn't hide her joy. 'It's my big chance, Susie. I'm to do some lectures and teaching and most of all I have the gallery walls on which to hang my paintings. So I'm going to live there for a while.' She looked around her. 'Shut up this place. I'll be back at some point but this is my chance. I have to take it.'

'Of course,' I said. 'Of course. You must. Why – it's wonderful.'

I did feel happy for her.

I hugged her, suddenly very proud of her talent. I had always known that one day her art would be discovered and this was it. She was right. Opportunities should be grasped with both hands. They do not swing around for a second time.

We spent a few days in Palma, shopping for clothes, she for Paris and I for America. We bought casual and smart. I did not know how I would be expected to dress so bought trousers and shirts, a couple of miniskirts and two suits. We wandered into one of the more expensive salons and I bought an off-the-shoulder, red evening dress, full-skirted, with a fur stole for my shoulders. I teamed it with strappy, black, high-heeled shoes and at last met with my aunt's approval; even my own to some extent. As I looked at myself in the long mirror I reflected that I had changed beyond recognition since Richard had died. He would not have known me. I was much thinner than when I had married him. Sara was right, I was bordering on bony. I had lost all the curves Richard had so adored, the full breasts, the curving hips, the shapely legs. I had cut my hair shorter so it reached my shoulders. But the biggest and most awful change was in my face. Deep in my eyes. They stared back at me, world-weary. Cynical. Dull. Dead. I had lost all my sparkle.

My aunt, for her part, bought smart suits but she also bought baggy trousers and flashy tops which made her look like a tiny Pablo Picasso. We laughed and joked over our purchases and came home with a car full of carrier bags.

The next morning my aunt drove me to the airport and kissed me goodbye. I wished her luck and flew to Newark airport.

I had trouble with my green form and it took an age to pass through customs. My suitcase was opened twice but once I had passed through into the arrivals lounge I was spotted by a uniformed chauffeur who was holding up a placard with my name on it. Mrs Susanna Oliver.

Another example of my employer's efficiency. After the long flights, time difference and baggage protocol this end I was pleased.

The chauffeur dealt deftly with my luggage and within minutes we were speeding along the freeway, heading towards Long Island, in a black Chevrolet.

For the first time I was curious about my employer and leant forward. 'What is Mr Wernier-King like?'

The chauffeur half-turned. 'Best you make up your own mind, Mrs Oliver.'

A cockney accent. 'You're English.'

He gave a smile into the rear-view mirror. 'Mr Wernier-King is something of an Anglophile,' he said. 'He was at university in England and became fond of the place. There are a few Brits at Tacoma. You'll find out.'

'And Tacoma,' I said. 'What is it like?'

'You'll see.' There was something almost ominous about the statement.

I had my own visions of some rustic, rambling, ranch-like place, a clapboard house, with horses in surrounding fields kept in by post-and-rail fencing. I had never been to America before so my images were from the movies or TV. It turned out I could not have been more wrong. We drove for almost an hour before turning in front of an enormous pair of gilded gates which swung open as we reached them.

Someone must have been watching out for us.

Tacoma was an enormous mock-Palladian mansion. Pale pink, with a fountain in the front, white stone, a man driving a chariot through the waters which splashed over him. I thought it gross. In fact I hated the place on sight. For the first time since I had accepted the invitation to come to Tacoma I was frankly worried. This did not look like the home of a man who collected Staffordshire Pottery, which was – after all – a cottage-dweller's taste. This was about as far from a cottage as Buckingham Palace.

The chauffeur was watching for my reaction as we slid to a halt in front of the pillared portico. I said nothing but he met my eyes and nodded, understanding. Then the door was opened by a black maid wearing a black dress over which was a spotless, white apron. A manservant took my bags from the car and the Chevrolet slid away. The maid held the door open and I walked inside.

I was led into a huge hall with a domed ceiling three floors up. The floor was of black-and-white tiles on which stood white, marble statues, many of them copies of classical statues that I recognised. Rodin's The Kiss, Michelangelo's David. Even a Rosetta Stone. A staircase swept up the centre, splitting in front of an enormous window which blazed in the evening sun, the subject a huge still life. I was reminded of Richard's window in Hall o'th'Wood and felt my familiar twinge of pain almost like an old friend. Overhead blazed a huge, crystal chandelier. I stood still and felt dwarfed.

I remember my dual impressions. The first was that the whole thing seemed theatrical, a stage set designed to awe and impress. And my second thought was that this was my first brush with such ostentatious wealth. I stood in the hall, feeling tiny and insignificant then a door opened to my left and an older woman, also wearing a black dress, came hurrying up to me. There was a swift discussion between the two maids and all that I was conscious of was that I wanted to have a wash, brush my hair, clean my teeth – and sleep after the long flight.

It was not to be.

The older woman finally spoke to me. 'Mrs Oliver?' she said. Another English accent. 'Mr Wernier-King insists that you be brought to him straight away. So if you'll follow me please.'

There was to be no argument.

She led me along a long corridor, passing several polished, mahogany doors, until the passage narrowed and we stopped outside the door at the end. She knocked, pressed her ear to it, listened for a second, knocked again and held the door open for me to pass her.

'Mrs Oliver, sir,' she announced, closing the door behind her. I listened to her footsteps recede along the hall.

The room was small and dim – the curtains were drawn. In the corner a television was spewing out Disney cartoons. Draped across a sofa, watching them, was a young man – twenty-something at a guess. He had blonde hair which flopped over his brow and was wearing a pale blue sweater and white jeans. His feet were bare and on the floor was a pair of slippers. He glanced across at me then stood up, switched the television off and walked right up to me, standing very close. He was tall – a little over six feet and very slim. 'Mrs Oliver?' he said uncertainly.

'Yes?' I was wondering where my elderly millionaire was. And who this was.

'Mrs Susanna Oliver?' He seemed confused.

'Yes,' I said again with a tinge of impatience.

He relaxed then, gave a disarmingly wide grin and held his hand out. 'Hi,' he said. 'I'm Paul.'

I was confused now. I felt my jaw drop.

'Paul Wernier-King,' he said quickly. 'I wrote you about my collection?'

I had had my comfortable picture of a portly, middle-aged man, a collector. Not this callow youth. For a moment I didn't know what to say. I simply couldn't reconcile my idea with this reality. Neither could I imagine this youth collecting Staffordshire figures. Maybe I greeted him back, shook his proffered hand, said something. I'm sure I did. It would have been rude not to but I don't remember the details now. I only remember my utter confusion on that first evening.

I do recall taking stock of him. He was tall and slim. He had a shock of blonde hair and very bright blue eyes. He had regular, straight, white teeth and wore a casual air which seemed at odds with the formality of Tacoma. I was intrigued.

'I can't wait for you to see the pieces,' he said, enthusiastically. 'But I've decided we should hang on until tomorrow. I guess you're tired.'

I said yes, that I was.

'So I'll just show you around the rest of the house so as you don't get lost.' He laughed. 'Then we'll have something to eat and you can take a bath and retire. Your bags will already be in your room and unpacked.'

Again I knew I had no choice. For all his casual, friendly manner, this youth did not seem used to being argued with and I was aware that in this huge, horrible house I was no more than a servant. A paid employee.

He walked quickly from the room and I followed him.

That night Paul Wernier-King displayed his great home and his wealth. He led me from room to room to room and I quickly realised that his family had a great deal of money. I wondered how they had made so much.

I recognised many original paintings that night, a Vermeer, a Titian, Picasso. I saw Sèvres porcelain, Chinese cabinets, a Chippendale table of the highest quality. The house was a perfect, soulless storehouse of the world's treasures and as I watched Paul Wernier-King point out all that he owned I wondered what pleasure they really gave him and how he owned so much when he was still so young. A year or two younger than me, I supposed.

We must have spent an hour walking through the house on this guided tour, finally returning to the hall where the trim, black maid was standing.

'This is Jemima,' my employer said. 'She will be your personal maid while you are here. She'll do your laundry and your shopping. Wash your hair.' He shrugged and laughed again. 'I don't know. Anything you want she'll sort you. Her room is next to yours so she'll hear if you want anything in the night. We eat in a half-hour. I guess you'll want to wash up.'

He waited, politely, in the hall, while Jemima led me up the stairs, turning right, along a long corridor, pushing open a door at the end.

It was an enormous bedroom; cream-carpeted, with tall windows which overlooked miles of garden – manicured lawns and maple trees and at the bottom, the sea.

'You're on the East Coast here,' Jemima said. She was an attractive light-skinned Negress with sparkling, mischievous eyes and a pert figure. 'It's one of the prime positions on Long Island. East Hampton, ma'am.' There was a touch of Southern twang in her accent.

I stared through the window.

Jemima slid open the wardrobe doors. 'Your stuff is all unpacked, ma'am.'

'Thank you, Jemima.'

She pulled open the top of the chest of drawers, looking nervous. 'Is there anything else, ma'am? Would you like me to lay your dinner clothes out?'

I disliked the attention. 'No. Thanks. I'll just have a quick shower.'

'I'll come back for you then in twenty-five minutes. Mr Wernier-King doesn't like to be kept waiting.'

The bathroom was as big as an entire floor of my cottage with a walk-in shower and a huge, roll-top bath complete with taps in the shape of dolphins. The bath would have to wait. Tonight I opted for the shower. It was good to stand under the warm water and wash the day's grime away. I felt much better, cleaner, spraying perfume on, scrubbing my teeth until they felt shiny again, putting on a short dress and brushing the tangles out of my hair. I applied some make-up and listened for the soft knock on the door. I would never find my way down to the dining room alone.

We ate in a small room somewhere along the miles of corridor and I saw, to my embarrassment, that Paul Wernier-King had dressed for dinner in a black dinner jacket.

Even then I sensed that some uncomfortable evenings lay ahead during my months at Tacoma then I reassured myself that I had just arrived. He was simply being polite. I would, in future, be eating alone.

Although Mr Wernier-King tried to put me at my ease it was a stilted evening. I was very tired and made little conversation and I knew that he was disappointed in me. He had expected someone with more scintillating conversation. More sparkle.

After an hour and a half of trying to make conversation he gave up. 'It's OK, Mrs Oliver,' he said ruefully. 'I guess you're just tired. Get some sleep. We breakfast at eight-thirty and then I'll show you my collection.' He gave another of his wide, toothy grins. 'I think I can promise you some surprises. You'll just love them.'

I wished him goodnight. Jemima was standing outside the door. Without a word she led me back up the stairs and into my bedroom.

I was tired but I could not sleep straight away. Jet lag had caught up with me and now I felt more awake than during dinner. I pushed open one of the windows and stared up at the sky. I sometimes did this, tried to imagine that Richard was one of those stars and that if I only found the right one I would be able to communicate with him and he with me. On that night some of the stars were hidden by clouds but I sensed his presence, felt his arm around my shoulders, leant in towards him and cried out of sheer loneliness.

CHAPTER FOURTEEN

The next morning I felt different.

Jemima woke me with coffee, at seven-thirty. I had finally slept deeply without dreams in the four-poster draped with muslin curtains and for a moment I was confused and stared up at her.

'Ma'am,' she said, waited for me to sit up and handed me the coffee.

I had expected to wake up in my own bedroom in my aunt's house but the sunshine pouring in through the windows seemed too bright, the room too large and opulent. I cradled the coffee cup in my hands and looked around me. Cream-coloured, thick-pile carpet, mahogany furniture, sparkling mirrors all the way around. Wide bay windows. Jemima was hooking back the long curtains.

I drank the coffee and carried on staring around me, at the room. Only now did I start to realise that everything here had been designed for my comfort. Coffee in hand I stepped to the floor, slipped a wrap over my shoulders and walked around. New brushes were laid on the dressing table, boxes of lotions, still in their wrappers, set out neatly. A bottle of Chanel No 5 waiting, it seemed, for me to spray it on. A brand new box of cosmetics. Jemima watched me then handed me a white towel. 'You want me to run you a bath?'

'No. No. Thanks. I can manage myself.'

I had a shower and when I returned to the bedroom Jemima had laid out some clothes on the bed, a short, cream, linen skirt, a blue blouse and some sandals.

'I hope that's OK, ma'am,' she said anxiously. 'I wasn't sure what you'd planned on wearing.' I told her it was and dressed, sat at the dressing table and brushed my hair. I supposed then that it must have been coincidence that many of the cosmetics were my favourite brands – Clarins and L'Oréal, Estée Lauder and Clinique. The bathroom was the same – well stocked with shampoos and luxury bath oils, even a new toothbrush and toothpaste. It felt as though a great deal of preparation and thought had gone into my visit. I couldn't imagine Paul Wernier-King doing the shopping himself so assumed it would have been the housekeeper.

'It's almost eight-thirty, ma'am.' Jemima was prompting me.

As I descended the staircase I heard my employer shouting at someone.

'The toast is burnt. Do it again.'

He was waiting for me at the breakfast table, no sign

of his ill humour. He looked very happy and as excited as a child on Christmas morning and greeted me with his wide grin. 'Good morning, Susanna. I hope you slept well.'

'I did, thank you.' I didn't know what to call him. 'Sir' would have seemed too deferential but 'Mr Wernier-King' too formal so I called him nothing. 'The bed was very comfortable.'

He looked pleased. 'Good. It's a new one and I haven't used that store before. Well,' he said with another of his wide grins. 'Today's the day.'

I nodded.

I had my usual fruit and yoghurt, more coffee and some freshly squeezed orange juice, Mr Wernier-King watching my every move. Whenever I looked up his bright eyes were on me. The second I had drained my cup he stood up.

'I've been so looking forward to showing you this.'

I knew he had. This was the truth.

He led me along the corridor into a room at the far corner of the house near the sitting room where I had first seen him watching cartoons. With a flourish he threw open a pair of double doors. I entered and was immediately in a different world. The room was beautiful, octagonal, cream-painted, with three long windows which overlooked the gardens. Between the windows were floor-to-ceiling, glazed cupboards and they were crammed with Staffordshire pottery. I gasped. I had expected figures but nothing like this. In my mind

I had hardly considered the pottery which would be here. Coming to Tacoma had merely been a device to escape.

I walked across to the first cabinet and opened the door, picking up the first piece to catch my eye.

'Polito's Menagerie,' I said. 'I have one of these at home.'

It was an Obadiah Sherratt figure, dating from around 1830, supported by four brown, rococo feet and swagged with colourful flowers. I cradled it in my hand and felt the first stirrings of a returning passion.

In the early nineteenth century Mr S Polito had owned a travelling menagerie.

'Polito's Menagerie of the Wonderfull Birds and beasts from Most Parts of the World, Lion and Giraffe.'

The figure was of circus performers, monkeys, a lion, a tiger and an elephant complete with a howdah on its back. It was one of the most famous and colourful Staffordshire figures ever made and one of the most collectable too. Everyone who collects Staffordshire aspires to own one of these but few do. They fetched thousands.

Crowned by the elephant, the title emblazoned across the top, queues of people in Regency dress, waiting to enter and see the wonderful spectacle, it was an excellent figure.

'The one I sold,' I said slowly, 'had some restoration work on it. The monkeys were missing.'

I recalled spending hours talking to Steve and Jules about the exact size and colour of the monkeys. David had finally produced a perfect museum specimen and we had taken moulds. I slid my fingers across the top and met Mr Wernier-King's eyes. 'Like this one.'

I replaced it on the shelf.

'This is it, isn't it? You bought it from me.'

He said nothing but gave me his awkward grin again.

I picked another figure from the shelf.

Years ago I had said to Richard that the reason that I loved these pieces was because all of humanity was represented. 'Mazeppa,' I said, turning around to speak to my host. 'It's one of my favourites.'

He looked pleased. 'Mine too,' he said and took the figure from me. 'Great story.'

So here he was, this Polish Cossack commander, strapped to the back of a wild horse, his punishment for having an affair with a nobleman's wife. I put Mazeppa down and picked up another – Victoria and Albert, and another – Romeo and Juliet.

'Oh, Mr—'

'My name is Paul,' he said impatiently. 'And I shall call you Susanna. You're going to be in my house for a coupla months. We may as well get acquainted and drop the formality right now.'

'Paul,' I said, turning to him. 'The pieces are beautiful. You must have haunted the salerooms,' I caught his eye, 'and antiques shops to buy them. It must have taken you years to amass such a collection.'

'Three,' he said. It was a clue to this young man's ferocious energy for the things he wanted. He put a hand on my shoulder. 'I couldn't wait for you to see them,' he said. 'I travelled all over the UK and the US. I wanted to have a very special collection for you to catalogue.'

I tried to pull away. What was he trying to say? I looked into his face. There was an intensity there that I could not understand. I moved back and his arm dropped. I should have asked many questions then – where exactly had he got my name from? How had he heard about me? What did he know about me? What was he up to?

I only know that I sensed some deep purpose in this man and eyed his face uncomfortably.

He moved back. 'I want you to be happy here, Susanna,' he said.

'I'm sure I shall be,' I answered crisply.

In the centre of the room was a large, round table covered with papers, a camera, pens, a typewriter. Also a telephone. I was ready to start.

'I guessed you'd prefer a working lunch most days,' he said slowly, 'so I asked Jemima to bring you sandwiches at one. Anything else you want like coffee or something just pick up the house phone. I do want you to be comfortable in my home.'

I started to thank him for his courtesy and for all the extra comforts in my room but he brushed my thanks aside with an airy wave of his hand. 'It's OK,' he said. 'My pleasure.' He stopped and I caught a sparkle in his eyes. 'I enjoyed guessing what beauty products you'd use. I'm glad if I got it right.'

I was startled. Surely he had not bought the cosmetics himself?

He looked a bit anxious. 'I was right, wasn't I, about the Chanel?'

I nodded and he looked pleased.

'We'll have dinner together at eight and you can tell me how the day's gone and if there are any problems. So for now, Susanna, I'll leave you to it.'

I had imagined that he would lead his own life during my stay here, at Tacoma. I wasn't sure how I'd feel about sharing every single evening with him for the next three months.

However I smiled and he left.

I soon settled into a routine at Tacoma. Sometimes Paul and I would have breakfast. At other times he was missing. At one, on the dot, Jemima would bring lunch – sandwiches, cheese, fruit and as the weather grew warmer I frequently stopped for an hour or two in the afternoon to wander the gardens and walk down to the shore. A couple of days when the weather was very hot I even donned my bikini and swam in the pool. Then I would return to the octagonal room and work through until six, sometimes seven. I never saw Paul in the day but our evenings grew lively as we got to know one another and argued over the pieces. I found one or two reproductions which he agreed to dispose of. They would spoil the rest of the collection. There was also some poor restoration work which I offered to take back to England to have my own ceramic restorers repair. I found great joy in discovering some pieces I had hitherto only seen in books and I became completely absorbed in the work. If I wasn't happy I was at least content.

And Richard? Richard was beside me all my waking hours, his grey eyes watching me whenever I closed my own. Sometimes I breathed in his scent– a hint of cigars, and the indefinable scent of the old house, of seasoned oak and beeswax polish, of crystal and glass and dusty corners. In Tacoma, alone and unwatched during the days, I allowed myself to grieve for him because in prison he had never been there. Prison was a place Richard could not enter. He would not have belonged so I had not been able to conjure him up however hard I had tried through my lonely years' sentence.

I had been at Tacoma for almost a month and sensed Paul Wernier-King was inching closer to me. He was always polite but there was something else – something deeper which he kept concealed. He would ask me personal questions about my home life. I was deliberately evasive but he did not back down until I confronted him and told him that my personal life was mine and mine alone.

One night we had drunk more good wine than usual. I was excited. I had found a beautiful model of Uncle Tom and Eva, the child putting a garland around Tom's head. I liked it so much I had brought it in to dinner with me and read out the rhyme.

Eva gaily laughing was hanging a wreath of roses round Tom's neck.

He stood up and moved behind me. I felt his hand touch my hair.

My hair was shorter now than it had been but still a little below my shoulders. I froze and did not move. I sensed an intent in him. I turned my head and his hand briefly brushed my lips then pulled away but I was nervous now and on my guard. I excused myself soon after, saying I was tired but it wasn't that. I was uncomfortable and sat in my room for a long while, wondering how to deal with him.

Of all the people I have ever known in my life Paul Wernier-King had the most unfortunate sense of timing. A few days later it was a warm Wednesday late in June and the room felt hot, the figures warm to my touch. I had thrown open the tall French windows which overlooked the garden and was working my way through the second shelf of the middle cabinet.

When I felt a wash of grief. I had reached my hand out without seeing what it would grasp. I had picked up a figure of a small, grey rabbit daintily nibbling a piece of lettuce. It wasn't the one I had bought at the country-house sale with Richard because I never had sold that piece. It was far too precious a memory and it lived at home with me, back in Horton Cottage. But it was a similar enough figure to conjure up his memory. I put it down on the table and felt the tears coursing down my cheeks, asking myself the tired, old question. Is it better never to have loved than to have loved and lost in that way?

I sank down in the chair, overwhelmed, covering my face with my hands, still asking unanswerable questions. Did I wish I had never met him, never been to Hall o'th'Wood? Never fallen in love? At that time and through that pain I almost thought so. Life had no meaning for me without Richard and Hall o'th'Wood.

And then the door opened and Paul Wernier-King was standing right in front of me.

'Hey, Susanna,' he said. 'What is it?'

I said nothing but tried to brush the tears from my cheeks but when I looked at my fingers they were black with mascara. I must have looked a wreck. His eyes rested on the figure of the rabbit and he seemed to understand. He picked it up and stared at it. 'I came in to say,' he spoke awkwardly, 'that I have tickets for a concert tomorrow night. I'd be very glad if you would accompany me.'

I had not been out at all since my arrival. I had never been to America let alone to New York, that great, famous city. 'Yes.' I managed a smile. 'Yes, Paul. I'd love to come. Thanks very much.'

He gave me a warm, friendly grin. 'That's settled then.' He made no reference to my tears. 'It's in the city,' he said. 'I'll drive us in. It'll take an hour. Be ready for six. Formal dress.'

Then he was gone.

* * *

I stopped work early the next evening, washed my hair and ran a hot, steaming bath. I soaked for ages in some of the expensive oils left for my use. I sat in front of the dressing table and took extra care over my toilette, finishing with red lipstick, Jemima hovering around, nervously. Then I stepped into the gown I had bought in Majorca. I sprayed the perfume across my neck and shoulders and made my way downstairs. It was almost six. Paul was already standing in the hall, in a white dinner jacket and bow tie. He looked what he was, a playboy togged up for the night.

Yet, I thought as I descended the stairs, I had no evidence that he was a playboy apart from Tacoma. It struck me then that I was being unfair, making superficial judgements. He'd been nothing but courteous and polite. And his invitation to work with his pottery had been a welcome, helping hand. What else would I have done?

His eyes were fastened on me as I descended, staring admiringly without trying to hide it and I realised how close we were in age. I had always thought of him as much younger but, I realised now, I simply felt older because of my life experiences. And we were worlds apart. As I reached the bottom he put his hand on my waist, drew me slowly towards him and gave me a light kiss on my cheek. 'You look,' he said, 'fantastic.'

I've never been very good with compliments. They are hard to accept without sounding coy, conceited or coquettish. I thanked him.

He drove at speed, in a little black Porsche, right into the heart of the city, to the Carnegie Hall, which was bustling with people. Everything in the States is built on a grand scale and this was no exception. We found our seats and settled down to listen. It was a good choice, a popular programme of well-known pieces, a violin soloist, a pianist and a Japanese harpist. I closed my eyes, dreaming.

During the interval we went to the bar for a drink. One was waiting on a bill as Paul had pre-ordered. I picked up a Martini and we clinked glasses. I felt young and almost gay at the beginning of that night. I was leaning against the wall, avoiding the crush. I realised that Paul had wanted me to enjoy the evening. And it was working. It was a treat. I smiled into his face and caught again that surprising gaucheness. He was blushing. 'Thank you, Paul,' I said, 'thank you so much for bringing me here. I haven't been to a concert for a long, long time. I'd forgotten how exciting they can be.' I looked around. 'And this is a wonderful place.' It was a mistake. He put his hand behind me, trapping me against the wall and stared at me with an intense gaze. He bent his head so his mouth was almost on mine. 'Susanna,' he said huskily. His body was pressed hard against mine. I sensed his arousal and knew he was about to kiss me.

'Paul. You naughty boy.'

He cursed and wheeled around.

A plump, overdressed, overmade-up woman was

poking him in the shoulder with her finger. Behind her stood a small, dark-haired girl of about twenty.

He recovered and good manners took over. 'Oh, hi, Mrs Swanson. Hello Frances.'

'Where have you been hiding yourself away, Paul? We haven't seen you for a month or so. What have you been doing with yourself? Have you been away?'

'No,' he said curtly. 'Just busy.'

The older woman was scrutinising me with undisguised hostility.

'Oh – this is Mrs Oliver,' Paul said quickly. 'She's doing some work for me at Tacoma.'

'Pleased to meet you,' the older woman said, taking in my dress, my shoes, my jewellery, my wedding ring and engagement solitaire.

'Likewise,' I responded politely.

Her attention flicked back to Paul. 'Well promise me you'll come over and see me and Frances before too long or I shan't forgive you.'

Paul dipped his head which they took as an assent and moved on. I heard Mrs Swanson's voice taking the same, loud, arch tone a little further along the bar. When they had gone Paul moved even closer. I could feel the pressure of his leg against mine. But I could not move backwards because of the wall. I stared up at him, very aware of the bright eyes and slack mouth.

He gave a short, cynical laugh and spoke in my ear. 'You don't know how very predatory New York mammas can be when they contemplate the Wernier-

King millions,' he said. 'It's a shame you don't seem to feel the same way.'

I felt chilled. 'What do you want of me, Paul?'

He didn't answer but continued watching me until the interval bell sounded and we all trooped back to our seats.

I knew for sure then that Paul Wernier-King had a hidden agenda and that the pottery had been simply an excuse to bring me here. I didn't understand the full story but I also knew that I should take the next flight home. Perhaps I would have done except that the very word home depressed me. I had only one home. And Michael and Linda lived there now with their son. There was no place for me there or here or anywhere where Richard was not.

So I didn't go. I stayed.

As I have said, Paul's sense of timing was unfortunate. He was not blessed with good luck.

The second half of the concert began well enough – with some piano playing, Schubert and Beethoven and some Dvořák 'Hungarian Dances' which were lively and happy. It was a varied selection – not highbrow but melodic and I knew almost all the tunes. In fact it was hard not to tap one's foot in time to the swift rhythms. I turned to Paul and laughed. I was enjoying myself. I believed that I was happy. I felt reckless.

Then the auditorium fell quiet and I heard the perfect sixth, the first few notes of the 'Chopin Nocturne in B flat'. I gasped. I was drawn back there, to Vienna, Richard at my side. I was back in that precious minute in my life when all had seemed so perfect. As the pianist played I stood up, tears pouring down my face. I had had my perfect time and now I had lost it all for ever. Richard, Hall o'th'Wood. My life was wasted. I never would be truly happy again. I had a desperation to escape. I struggled to my feet and ran from the concert hall. I could not listen to any more.

I ran down the steps, not even thinking where I was going. I reached the bottom. Then I felt a hand grab me from behind and Paul was there, his face flaming red. He stared at me, breathing heavily. Without a word he handed me my stole and we left the hall together. He was too angry to speak.

He drove like a maniac all the way back to Tacoma, still saying nothing except a few times he made a guttural sound in his throat, like a wounded animal. He hardly waited for the gates to open, threading the car through them. He skidded to a halt outside the front door, threw the car door open and stamped around to my side. He opened my door, pulled me to my feet and threw me back against the car. 'So what was all that about?'

All the time I had spent in prison I had not shed one tear. Now I had started crying I could not stop. The sluice gates were open and the water poured out. I put my hands in front of my face but he pulled them away. 'No. You tell me. I want to hear it from you. I want you to say it. I took you out on a date and you run off halfway through. You owe it to me to give me some explanation.'

His body was hard against mine. I could feel his breath on my face. He was too near for me to move.

I looked into his face and read lust and fury.

But he was right. I did owe him an explanation. 'It was the music,' I started. 'The Chopin 'Nocturne'. We heard it played on our honeymoon. I just—'

'Susanna.' He put his hands on my shoulders and pulled me towards him, his lips brushing my hair. 'Susanna. Put it all behind you. You're young. You're beautiful. It's time to move on.'

'And if I can't?'

'You can. I know it.' His lips were kissing my hair. He tilted my mouth towards his and kissed me long and hard. I knew he wanted to make love to me and I was frozen.

I pulled away. 'No,' I said. 'Please, no.'

His face changed then as I watched. Something hard and gritty entered it, a facet I had not seen before.

We all have another side.

'I know about you,' he said.

It was not a cold night. It was hot and balmy, a New York summer's night but I shivered then.

'I met you before,' he said softly. His hands slid down my back and he pulled me in towards him.

I turned my face to the side. I could see our reflections in the bodywork of the car. Elongated, the scarlet sheen of my dress, the white of his dinner jacket, his yellow hair – even his anger, tangible and hot. Even through the distortion I was afraid of that anger.

I struggled to return to normality. 'We haven't met before, Paul. I would have remembered.'

'Yep. We have.' His hand was brushing my cheek. 'You remember the little rabbit you were holding the other day and getting all upset about?'

I nodded.

'Do you remember the day when you bought your little rabbit?'

I nodded again. Like the Chopin 'Nocturne' that day was etched into my brain. Scarring it.

'I was sitting right behind you that day,' he said, 'in the marquee. I was close enough to smell your perfume. Close enough to breathe your air and identify your perfume. Close enough to touch you. I was watching you.' He gave a self-conscious, humourless laugh and he gathered a handful of my hair. 'The sunlight was flashing on your hair and I don't know...' His hands were holding me against him. 'You looked so kind of alive. So animated. I thought...'

He stopped. 'I decided the guy you were with was your father. He looked so much older than you.' He cleared his throat noisily. 'So I made a little plan that I would come over and introduce myself to you both and maybe we could share a drink. All through the sale I worked out what I was going to say and...' He shrugged. 'And then you bought your little rabbit and then you...'

'I kissed him,' I said. 'I kissed him.'

'And I realised that he had to be your husband.' His hands dropped to his side. 'It would have been OK but I'd been making up your life story. Fantasising, I guess.'

He was staring beyond me now.

'You were the young buck,' I said.

He watched me, not understanding.

The young buck whom Richard had found so threatening. I recalled the hands smacking on the car window, Richard's fury.

Do we see into the future? Had he?

'I went along to your shop,' he said. 'I bought some things and I found out what had happened to you. I wrote you in prison but you didn't write back.'

'I had a lot of letters in prison,' I said coldly. 'I was notorious for a while. It was a high-profile case and they managed to get hold of some very flattering pictures of me to go with the article.' I met his eyes. 'I got plenty of letters, Paul. Plenty of proposals of marriage. Plenty of gifts too,' I finished bitterly.

He folded me against him. 'Hey,' he said. 'Move on.'

I looked straight into the blue eyes then. 'I can't,' I said. 'And I don't want to.'

He looked angry again. 'How can you feel any loyalty towards a man who used you like that?'

I pushed him away. 'What do you know about it?'

'I read the papers. I read about the house. I went up to take a look.'

I felt an electric shock. 'You went to Hall o'th'Wood?'

'Sure,' he said. 'It's beautiful. I'm sure you loved living

there. But it doesn't justify him using you like a sacrificial lamb.'

I ducked under his arm, started to walk away then, back towards the house, knowing someone would be watching and open the door to me. 'How dare you!' I threw back. 'He didn't use me. He didn't.'

He caught up with me and grabbed me again. 'I read it all – he had an obsession with the house and he used you to smuggle stuff – to make some money knowing what would happen to you if you got caught. He risked your life. And your child's too if the papers are to be believed.'

I slapped his face then – hard.

He simply stared at me, breathing hard. But whether it was lust or temper I didn't know. I didn't care either.

I should have left Tacoma that very night but I didn't. I stayed.

CHAPTER FIFTEEN

I dreaded meeting Paul across the breakfast table the next morning but I needn't have worried. He didn't show. So I worked, as normal, through the day and put him from my mind. It was easy, surrounded by so many fascinating pieces, and I was absorbed for the entire day.

So the days passed. He didn't show either for breakfast or for dinner for almost a week. The weather had turned hot and humid but still I worked.

I had finished the second cabinet and opened the third. And as usual I was struck by the quality of the pieces. Paul had been a discerning buyer. It is all too easy to buy the wrong piece of Staffordshire – commonplace, poorly moulded, downright fakes or pieces with bad or too significant restoration. In general Paul Wernier-King had avoided these pitfalls and my respect for him as a collector grew. But then – he had had unlimited funds. It would have been tempting for him to have simply amassed quantity ignoring quality but he had, what is fondly and respectfully called in the trade, 'an eye' for a piece and I recognised this.

The first figure I took from the third cabinet was a good example of this. It was a famous piece, St Peter. Well modelled, in perfect condition and beautifully coloured. I'd always felt sorry for poor old Peter, denying Christ when put to such a cruel test. The Staffordshire figure of him draws attention not only to his failings but also to his forgiveness. A Christian trait.

There, at his feet, are the keys to Heaven while the cockerel is behind him, ready to crow.

I finished my text about St Peter, photographed the figure from all angles, inserted a valuation and returned it to the cupboard, taking out the next piece, one of the funniest.

The eloping bride, ladder standing at the open window while her swain stands beneath, waiting for her. The whole thing was terribly out of proportion – and it was that that always made me smile. The bride never could have fitted in the tiny house. And if the blunt face of the swain was true to form he was no handsome man but a freak with a flat nose and popping eyes.

I worked all day until seven that evening when I heard Jemima's footsteps approaching. She always reminded me of the time but as I had no need to attend dinner promptly I had fallen into the habit of working later. I stood up, switched my spotlight off and left the room, meeting her in the passage. I smiled at her. I couldn't really make her out. Sometimes she seemed almost a friend, at others, sly and deceitful. I had no doubt that she and Paul held private conversations about me and I always felt guarded in her presence. I sensed there was something between them. Well – I wanted nothing of it. I would finish my work here and go home.

Home?

Again that wave of bleakness washed over me. Where was my home? I had no home. No real home. I had loved living in my cottage before I had met Richard but compared to Hall o'th'Wood it had lost its charm. I had no great desire to return to it – in fact no homing instinct at all but felt peripatetic, loose, dangling free in my future. Majorca had been the only childhood home I really remembered but it was now just a place I visited. And even that was empty now. A couple, Carmina and Ramón Destida, looked after the place, visiting once a week to make sure all was well, but without my aunt it would seem a lonely house not a home. She had made it the home for myself and Sara.

'Dinner is at eight,' Jemima reminded me and led me along the corridor to the stairs and up to my bedroom.

I dressed for dinner that night with little enthusiasm. I felt embarrassed now I knew the design behind my invitation here. I had been lured by a love-sick, bored, rich youth who had some romantic vision of me as an ethereal beauty he had fantasised about in a country-house sale – as false and rarefied an environment as any – and when I had served my prison sentence I had become victim to his hero. Anyone who has been in this position will know that some people are drawn to such a situation. So I wore a plain, black dress and, recalling his words, pinned my hair up in a severe French knot.

I need not have worried.

Only one place was set for dinner. Paul Wernier-King had gone without a word. I realised then that he might not be back before I left. I had a week or two's work – no more.

Jemima served my dinner, an irritating, knowing look in her eyes as though she expected me to ask where he was but I deliberately didn't, thwarting what I perceived now as her malice. In fact I felt as though the whole of Tacoma was hostile and I decided I would be pleased to leave it. I simply hadn't decided where to return to so delayed booking my return flight.

Even though my evenings were now quiet and spent alone I had a happy week. Tacoma was not without its charms. I spent the evenings now studying the works of art scattered so carelessly and prolifically around the walls. I touched them, shone lights and magnifying glasses on them, learnt more than if I had visited many of the great galleries of the world. I wished Aunt Eleanor could have been at my side. She would have loved to be so surrounded by art and beauty. I wandered the grounds and found plants, flowers, trees, many recognisable but others I had never seen before.

Beyond the great lawn which almost begged for a garden party I found a lake and beyond that could see the spit of the sea. From my brief searches it seemed to me that the Hamptons consisted solely of mansions like these, built in vast swathes of parkland, and I was reminded of F Scott Fitzgerald. I found The Great Gatsby in the library together with other great American classics, Uncle Tom's Cabin, Moby Dick, To Kill A Mocking Bird. It was another room, apart from the octagonal china room, where I was completely happy. The house was so peaceful I could almost believe the world outside no longer existed.

But it didn't last.

He came back. It was about eleven in the morning and I was halfway through the last shelf in the fourth cabinet. Most of these pieces were not the nineteenth-century pieces of Victorian Staffordshire but more eighteenth-century figures, the works of such greats as Obadiah Sherratt, Colclough, Whieldon and more. Some of these figures were worth thousands of pounds – Christ in the Garden of Gethsemane, The Tythe Pig, A Bull-Baiting Group and the most gruesome figure of all – Munrow being carried off in the jaws of a tiger. Even the Staffordshire potters had managed to portray the poor man's agony. All the more terrible since it depicted an actual event. Calcutta, 1792.

Knowing their value I was handling them with extra care and absorption, noticing as I picked the first one up that it had had some clumsy restoration. I put it to one side, wishing I could discuss it with Paul. It seemed now that I might be gone before he returned. I was deciding I would leave him a note when the door opened and he was standing right beside me.

I started. He had been gone for more than a week. I had not seen him since our disastrous night at the Carnegie Hall.

I put the piece down. 'You gave me a shock,' I said. 'You're lucky I didn't drop it.'

He simply stared at me without speaking which gave me time to observe him. Wherever he had been it had been hot and he had been out of doors. He had a deep tan. That was my first observation. My second was that he was still in a temper with me.

'You've almost finished,' he observed.

I started to speak about the restoration needed but he held his hand up. 'Do what you want,' he said. 'I don't care anymore.'

He stayed in the room, looking at the way I had set out the pieces. His bad mood was making me nervous and I said little but took out the next figure. I was anxious now to be gone. I did not know where – simply elsewhere.

I glanced back at him uneasily. He was watching me with an odd expression, appraising me as if wondering something. I stared back at him uncomfortably.

'It's my birthday today.'

I said something trite, that he should have told me and that I would have bought him a birthday card but he brushed the comment away.

'We'll have dinner tonight,' he said. 'Wear something pretty, Susanna. That'll be better than a card or a gift.' He moved towards the door. 'Till eight then?'

And he was gone.

I clocked off early that night, planning my return to England. Jemima ran me a bath and shampooed my hair, drying it so it fell sleek and shining to my shoulders. She had laid clothes on the bed, a white, off-the-shoulder dress, high-heeled, white sandals, lace underwear. I couldn't be bothered to argue with her or to choose something else to wear. I simply slipped them on.

I put my own make-up on and sprayed perfume. But the face that stared back at me from the mirror looked apprehensive – not happy or excited or pretty but dull and flat. I was dreading this evening. I would be so glad when it was over.

I felt even more apprehensive as I took my seat opposite him. He was again wearing his dinner suit and was tense and quiet. Lola, the older housekeeper, served our dinner. I did not see Jemima again that evening. We ate the best of food that night, caviar and lobster, iced strawberries and chocolate sauce and drank the best of champagne and wine. It flowed and Paul's tongue loosened. He started telling me about his years in England, about his recent trip to the Everglades. I listened and said little but I knew, in his way, he was still trying to charm me.

He asked me about Richard, how I had met him, and

I told him the story of the jug. For a while he listened, his face interested and alert, his bad humour melting away as I told him about the carving I had found in the four-poster bed, the research David had done, and the huge key which fitted the bedroom door in Hall o'th'Wood.

He was as intrigued as I had been.

As the wine flowed Paul became a different man. His temper, unhappiness, awkwardness, were all gone. He laughed a lot, smiled that engaging, wide grin which showed big, white, straightened, American teeth. His hair caught the candlelight and shone almost like gold and his eyes stayed on me for the entire evening. He hardly looked at his food or at Lola while she served each dish. He was very charming. He told me about his family coming from Germany in the last century, about the pride he felt in being a fourth-generation American, about the banking business his grandfather had worked in – first as a clerk, later swallowing up the entire business. He told me about his mother who had abandoned him for an Argentinian meat millionaire when he had been two years old, about his father who had brought him up, tragically dying of cancer four years ago. He told me how he was, in name, head of the Wernier-King Bank but in reality it was run by a board of trustees and I caught a glimpse of his lonely, empty existence. When he spoke of his years at Oxford I understood his love for all things English. This had been where he had been the happiest – and where he had first set eyes on me. So I would always be associated with a period of happiness for him.

As I listened and watched I began to understand how the Wernier-King family had made their fortune. And I perceived the charisma that must have marked out his predecessors.

Like the Oliver family this was a dynasty of success.

I couldn't help reflecting how sad it was that I was incapable of returning even a passing romantic interest in him. Had I never met Richard and lived for those all too brief years in Hall o'th'Wood, Tacoma and Paul would not have measured up so inadequately. I put my hand on my chin, listened to his soft, American voice, watching his mouth move, lulled into a feeling of warmth and safety.

And he knew it.

The room was lit only by candles that reflected in the long, mahogany table.

He kept filling my wine glass and I knew I was drinking too much.

I excused myself to go to the bathroom and stumbled against the table. I put my hand over my mouth and giggled. Surely I hadn't drunk that much? I knocked over a wine glass and watched a thousand diamond pieces skid along the table.

No one came to clear it up and I giggled again.

The sound seemed to break into a thousand more dangerous fragments.

I tidied myself up in the washroom, again looked at myself in the mirror. I looked a wreck. When I returned to the room Paul had left the table and was sitting on one of the wide sofas. 'I was a little worried about the glass,' he said.

It seemed reasonable.

I moved towards the sofa and knew I had made a mistake.

My dress was fastened only at one shoulder by a small tie, easy enough to slip down and he was against me. I opened my mouth to say something but his lips were against mine. I felt dizzy and closed my eyes.

I could feel Richard touching me, pressing his mouth to mine, whispering, whispering. 'Let me close to you.'

I lay back and drank in his kisses, held his body close to mine and moved underneath him. I opened my mouth to his and tasted him. I felt his arms underneath pulling my hips beneath him and I opened my legs.

'Richard,' I murmured.

'Susanna.'

And I remember then that I screamed. Because Richard always called me Susie.

CHAPTER SIXTEEN

I remember nothing until the next morning when I awoke with a banging headache and a foul taste in my mouth. I lay perfectly still for a moment, trying to reconstruct what had actually happened. The truth was that I didn't know. I wasn't sure. I recalled that great lust at believing I was again with Richard, that coiling of our bodies together, those kisses when I breathed his air.

But it hadn't been Richard. It couldn't have been. In the cold light of day I knew that.

I stared up at the canopy over my bed and felt a terrible wash of pain. Why had I ever thought that I could carry on without him?

What was my life alone?

The more I thought the more obvious it seemed. I did not want to live my life without Richard, away from Hall o'th'Wood. There was no life for me without them. There was no life for me elsewhere, only pain and disappointment. It was over.

I sat up and slowly I began to work things out. My mind was not unhappy. It was accepting what must be and what never could be. Seeing things with a clarity I would never have achieved without Paul Wernier-King.

Jemima came in with a tray of coffee. She said nothing but placed it on the bedside table without a word, giving her sly, backwards glance. I drank the coffee and began to feel energised because now I had come to a realisation. Paul Wernier-King was irrelevant. Unimportant. He was nothing to me. He could slide out of my life because all he had achieved was to make me understand.

It was then that I noticed a white envelope on the tray and knew it must be from him.

'*Susanna,*' he had written, '*forgive me. I swear I believed. I really believed that I could make you love me. Now I guess I understand it is not possible. I am sorry but believe me all I did I did out of love. Maybe it was misguided and wrong but my only defence is this one. I love you. I wish I didn't but...*

You'll be through in a week. Lola will arrange your return journey.

Be happy with your life, please.

Yours for ever,

Paul.

PS If I can be of any assistance to you Lola knows how to get in touch with me.

PPS Don't worry about me. I'm heading off for one of my trips. I won't be back before you go.'

I read the note and dropped it in the waste-paper basket. I was making my plans already.

I asked Lola to book my flight – not to England but to Palma airport. I arranged to pick up a hire car and rang Carmina to tell her that I would be spending some time at Casa Rosada but would not need her to call in.

I worked furiously hard, late into the evenings for the next few days, and just after the weekend I was ready to finally leave Tacoma. As the car drew down the drive I turned around and looked back at it without affection. I did not believe I would ever return.

I was determined through the flight that I was doing the right thing. I was detached now from my entire life. At the airport I picked up a Fiat and drove to Casa Rosada. It was dark and deserted which suited my purpose well. Eleanor would still be in Paris.

I did not need to leave her a note. I believed she would understand.

Early the next morning I locked up the house, swam out to the rock and beyond, ignoring a few fishing smacks bobbing around on the horizon. As I grew tired I kept swimming out to sea. And then, finally, I emptied my lungs and dived down.

It was not a suicide but an acceptance of a life that was over, that could never, ever, be retrieved.

CHAPTER SEVENTEEN

I was retching into a smelly, black, plastic bucket, heaving up everything in my guts – gallons and gallons of seawater.

I was aware that I was on a boat and was sick again. I lay back and closed my eyes.

And was sick again.

Someone's hand was on my shoulder. 'Come on there. Fetch it up, honey. Come on, Susanna. Throw up.'

I looked up – 'What are you doing here?'

'I was worried,' he said. 'I didn't want you to be alone. I was frightened for you. Jemima told me you'd changed your ticket, that you'd asked your servants not to come in. I knew your aunt was away. I flew over and kept a watch on you. I had some field glasses and I saw you lock the door. There was a sort of...' He bit his lip. '...finality about it.'

I sat up, furious, and realised that under the sheet I was naked. I tucked it around me. 'How do you know these things? What spies do you have on me? What business is it of yours anyway? Why don't you leave me alone?'

He moved away, warily. 'You know the answer to that.'

'Oh – get out,' I said and was sick again. The wretched stuff sloshed around in the bucket, making me even more disgusted. He took it away and a new one was brought and eventually I stopped being sick.

For a couple of days Paul came and went and my hostility and resentment compounded towards him so I simply turned my face to the wall when he entered and refused to speak. I hated him.

By now, I thought, I could have been out of this, oblivious to life's struggle, wherever Richard was. Heaven or Hell or simply oblivion but not here.

I did not want to be here in this small boat, with him.

I don't know how long I lay in that tiny cabin, two or three days, I guess, before he came in with a glass of water and sat on the edge of my bunk. 'You should drink something,' he said. 'All that seawater's poisonous.' He gave that uncertain grin. 'Loaded with salt.'

I drank obediently and lay back weakly.

'Susanna,' he began.

I looked up at him and met the bright blue eyes, noted how his face looked young and eager. Once I had had a youthful, eager face too.

He put his hand over mine. 'Please. Tell me you're not

sorry you're not lying at the bottom of the ocean?'

I shook my head. I could not say this. Instead I challenged him.

'What have you done to my life, Paul? I don't want to be here.' I sat up. 'What have I got to live for? Why would I want to be alive? There's nothing here for me. Not in this big world. It's all gone. Lost.' I appealed to him. 'Don't you understand? My life was dear to me. Precious. I had everything I wanted. A husband I loved, a home I loved too. Now I have nothing.' He winced and I knew I was hurting him but I wanted him to understand how I felt. 'I can't see any place for me.'

'Oh.' It was a groan of real pain and I saw that his eyelashes were wet. His face was very pale as though he had had a shock. And still I ploughed on.

'Life holds nothing for me,' I said. 'I didn't take the decision to end it lightly. I don't want to be alive. I have no reason to want to extend my life. It's irksome to me.'

'Ssh,' he said, putting his finger over my lips. 'Be quiet and listen to me talk. When I've finished you can tell me then whether life holds anything for you. If it doesn't, well...' He blinked. 'But at least listen.'

I lay back and closed my eyes. I was so weary I didn't care now what happened. All my energy had drained away. My fight had gone.

Paul moved away, to sit in the corner on a small stool. He didn't look at me but fixed on a point over my head.

'I've been watching the antiques trade for some time now,' he said. 'You obviously understand it. I want to finance an import/export business. Some things fetch more in the States and others more in the UK. You have a good outlet in central England and I have an interest in an out-of-town warehouse near New York. Susanna,' he said eagerly, 'we could run it. Together. It would be great. We'll call it Wernier Oliver if you like.'

I looked at him suspiciously. 'This hasn't come out of the blue,' I said. 'You've been giving it a lot of thought.'

'Yep.' He was unabashed. Pleased with himself. 'When I went to sales in both the States and UK I could see that antiques are really quite fashion driven. I mean – period oak fetches much more money in England than it does back home. But it's the other way round when it comes to Victorian furniture and porcelain.' He waited while I thought – slowly at first and then my mind speeding up, as though a match had caught dry tinder.

I knew he was right. With his familial business acumen he had put his finger right on the pulse. The disparity between UK and US prices was something that could easily be exploited to great advantage. Shipping costs were not too high then. It would be an enormous amount of work but the opportunity to expand filled me with excitement – the first excitement I had felt for years. Three years. I sat up and opened my eyes wide. 'Are you sure you've got the time? Don't you have some work in the family business?'

He made a face. 'Unfortunately for me the board of trustees is just that mite too efficient. I haven't had contact with my mother since I was two. I wouldn't know her if I passed her in the street. No one needs me, Susanna.' He gave a rueful smile. 'I just get in the way.'

I thought for a brief moment – no more.

'OK,' I said. 'I'll give it a try for a year. If it prospers that'll be good. If not – well at least we'll have given it a try.'

His eyes lit up. 'You won't regret it, I promise.'

'But no more nights like–'

He grinned. I loved that grin, wide and somehow unguarded, gauche. It was the most natural thing about him.

It is strange but for many people, however sincere their wish to die, once their suicide attempt is foiled or unsuccessful they do not try again. They have reached the brink of life, peered over the edge and they move back. Their life moves on in an unpredicted and previously unsuspected direction.

So it was with me.

The small fishing smack took me to the bottom of the steps to the Casa Rosada and I climbed them, thinking I had not ever thought to do this. I watched the boat sail away until it rounded the headland. Paul would not come back with me. He had work to do, setting up carriers and shippers and drawing up legal documents.

I spent another day and a night at Casa Rosada and flew back to England on the following day. I arrived at lunchtime and the first thing I did was to drive to Hall o'th'Wood and tell Michael and Linda what I was doing.

Michael, so like his father, looked dubious and said he would have to do a little bit of finding out about this 'Wernier-King fellow'. He was as protective towards me as an older brother. But Linda linked her arm through mine. 'It's just what you need, Susie,' she said, 'as long as you don't neglect your duty.'

Richard was eight months old, a solemn child who regarded me with all the gravity of his grandfather. I picked him up and nestled him close to me, wishing above everything that he really was mine. I could feel my breasts ache with love for him. He was the son I had never had, the child I had lost, the child I now never would have. I stroked the soft down of his hair, closed my eyes and breathed in his Johnson's Baby Lotion scent while Linda watched me.

'Susie,' she said, with a quick glance at Michael. 'We know you love little Richard. If anything happens to us we want you to bring him up as your own. Here.' She smiled and looked around her. 'It would be unthinkable that an Oliver should live anywhere else. Darling, we know how you felt about Michael's dad. We know about the child you lost. Michael's father would have wanted it. Do you mind if we appoint you his legal guardian?'

It was a step even further than being a godparent. 'No,' I said. 'But it won't happen.' I laughed. 'You're young and healthy.'

'Please,' she said, 'promise.'

'Most solemnly,' I responded. 'If I am ever called on I will devote my life to him and...' I looked around at the portraits who were my witnesses, 'this beautiful house.'

Perhaps, at the back of my mind as I made these solemn promises, I was conscious of the sacrifice our aunt had made when Sara and I had been orphaned.

It was a delight setting up the business. A real excitement. Paul and I had long phone calls late into the night, planning and getting the details just right. We decided which types of furniture and ceramics we would concentrate on initially, who we would use as shippers, advertising budgets, retail outlets, target salerooms. It was a wonderful time.

Sara called round one evening when we were talking on the phone and listened in silently. 'What's he like?' she asked curiously. 'Was he the ageing, fat millionaire?'

'Mmm,' I said and moved on to another subject.

I did not want her interference.

Paul and I did not actually meet for some months but we talked almost every day. Not only about the business. I began to see into his life – as he did mine.

They were heady times for the antiques trade. It was before the real popularity of TV programmes exposing the worth of those attic oddments and there were bargains to be had. I scoured the salerooms up and down the country, finding the right pieces to ship across the Atlantic and finally sent the first shipload in January 1974.

It had taken me months to accumulate a container full. I was still unsure of American taste or what the items could sell for so it was a tense time, waiting for Paul to unload them in the warehouse and invite dealers and collectors to buy. He rang up late in March, elated. We had sold almost everything, covered our costs and made a healthy profit. More importantly we had learnt that the Wernier Oliver business could be a viable venture.

After that we grew more confident. We sent containers full of Victorian furniture straight into the heart of New York, arranged to have pieces polished and repaired and set out in the warehouses. In the meantime Paul found English period oak, travelling to the Southern States to buy. Sometimes he would unexpectedly discover early ceramics, pieces which were less to the American taste than the English and more importantly would fetch higher prices in England than in the United States. For three months we worked hard, talking three or four times a week on the telephone. Bottle Kiln Antiques was now buzzing, full of furniture and pottery and Joanne loved it. When the containers drew up she would be standing, waiting for it to be opened and unpacked. They were heady, happy times.

I had rediscovered my joie de vivre.

Almost all of my time off I spent with little Richard at Hall o'th'Wood, babysitting when Michael and Linda wanted an evening out or taking him for long walks in a little baby carrier I had bought. I adored the boy. Whenever he looked at me with Richard's grey eyes I felt a pang of recognition. It was as though he was mine. And Michael and Linda encouraged our close relationship.

It was the hottest day so far that summer, early in July. Too hot to do hardly anything. For once I had spent the entire month in Majorca and returned a few days before. The antiques trade can be notoriously quiet during the summer although another country-house sale, lasting over two days, was to take place the following week. So I felt justified in dragging the sunlounger out onto my small lawn and dozing in the heat in my bikini. Until I heard a car skid to a halt outside. Then saw Paul's blonde head peering round the corner of the house. 'Ha,' he said. 'I just knew I'd find you in the garden.'

I sat up. 'What are you doing here, Paul?'

He had never been to the cottage before. In fact I didn't know he even knew where it was. And I wasn't sure I was pleased that he had found it either.

'Why didn't you ring and say you were coming?'

'I was at Oxford anyhow,' he said grumpily, bending down and kissing my cheek.

'I just stayed on. Don't look so pleased to see me.'

He sat down on the low, stone wall which bordered the lawn. He was watching me, appraising me. I wished I had a wrap to cover myself up.

'I just didn't expect you, Paul. Why are you here?'

'The weather was so fine I thought I would visit Staffordshire,' he said. 'Call round, see you, see the shop, check out how things were going. Joanne said you were taking the day off and told me how to get here. Hey,' he said. 'Try look a bit pleased, Susanna. I've kept out of your hair for months.'

'I am pleased,' I said defensively. I felt very rude. 'Let me make you a drink.'

He eyed my bikini, his face almost breaking out into that well-remembered grin. 'So you can go put a wrap on over that nice body?'

I flushed. He'd read my mind.

He stood in the doorway, looking around him. 'Are you going to invite me in?'

'Yes sure.' I stood back.

'I never came in here before,' he said, prowling around. 'It's small, isn't it? How do you live in such a small house? Why do you live in such a small house?'

I smothered a grin at the memory of Tacoma – a house you could get lost in for a week. 'It suits,' I said shortly, tugging a T-shirt dress over my head. 'There's only me and I spend a lot of time either at the shop, at salerooms or at Hall o'th'Wood.'

'Wow,' he said. 'Now this is nice.' He'd stopped in front of my Tudor woman. She stared down haughtily at him while he admired her and I watched them both suspiciously.

'So whose is the Porsche?'

My sister Sara never waited to be invited in but always simply barged in – as she barged into my life, reorganised it and moved on.

'It's mine.' Paul stepped forward. I watched my sister's

eyes widen when they rested on Paul. And he, as always, rose to the occasion.

'Hi,' he said, extending his hand. 'I'm Paul – Paul Wernier-King – Susanna's partner in crime.' He grinned.

She looked furiously at me, her eyes narrowing. 'But I thought you said...'

I hadn't actually said that my partner was an elderly, paunchy millionaire. I merely hadn't corrected her assumption. We had surmised it before I had gone to Tacoma. And afterwards I had deliberately not corrected her image.

I waited for the inevitable sparks to fly.

She shook Paul's hand. 'I'm Sara, Susie's sister.' Her wide eyes were frankly flirtatious. 'I expect Susie's told you lots about me.'

Paul gave me a quick, enquiring glance. We both knew I'd never mentioned my family to him. 'Yeah,' he said.

I offered to mix them both a drink and vanished into the kitchen. When I returned with a jug of Pimm's, complete with cucumber, strawberry and lime slices, clinking ice cubes and three tall glasses, I could see the pair of them were as close as peas. The two blonde heads were together on the sofa and they were discussing me.

'She was so heartbroken when Richard died. You know, Paul, I think this business venture's been really good for her.'

'So do—'

I clinked the glasses loudly and they both turned around. I knew they didn't care that I had heard them.

Sara stayed till late and when Paul went to get his overnight bag from the car she launched in. 'You know, Susie. He's lovely. So charming.'

'Charming if you like,' I said. 'But he's not for me so leave it.'

'Oh, Susie,' she said disappointedly.

'Leave it,' I said. 'He's a good business partner but I don't love him and I wouldn't marry him if—'

I looked across to the doorway. Paul was standing in it and I knew from the disappointed expression in his eyes that he had heard all that I had said and understood all that I had not said.

Sara kissed him goodbye, hugging him far longer than was necessary and muttering something in his ear. I could guess what it was, that she'd work on me.

I went to bed as soon as my sister had left. Paul had the spare room.

I heard the Porsche roar away early the next morning. He hadn't even said goodbye.

CHAPTER EIGHTEEN

1975

I thought I was beginning to reconcile myself to this new life. It was exciting and glamorous. I had my stepgrandson to visit whenever I liked at Hall o'th'Wood, an international business to run. And while we were apart I had a good business partner. It was only uncomfortable when we were physically together – which was rare. I believed that nothing could rock my new-found stability.

And then, quite suddenly and without warning, the jug was back.

I'd been in Glasgow, attending a sale, having been tipped off about some good pieces of Staffordshire in a small, provincial saleroom. While I was there one of the Scottish dealers told me about some fine ware in an antiques shop in Aberdeen and I determined to travel up. I drove up to Glasgow on the Thursday and spent most of the morning studying lots and marking my catalogue. I was excited because none of my usual rivals had travelled so far north and I believed I would be able to buy plenty of good items. Sometimes it was well worth travelling out of area.

I was very successful at the saleroom, buying pieces – some of them very cheaply – and the exhilaration fired me to drive the extra miles to Aberdeen. I bought the lots and stayed overnight in a small bed and breakfast just north of Dundee. The next morning I arrived at Aberdeen. I found the shop easily, a lovely double-fronted place in the old town. And then I saw it. Standing on top of a poor quality mahogany bureau. My jug, looking so familiar I could have cried. I picked it up, cradled it in my hands, felt the same warm, light, soapy body.

The dealer was watching me. 'Fabulous piece isn't it?'

I couldn't disagree. 'Yes it is. Where did you get it from?'

He had a think about it. 'It came in with a whole load of other pieces,' he said finally. 'It was the travelling Gypsies.'

'I suppose you bought it for cash?'

He nodded.

'I owned this,' I said, 'many years ago.'

It was only eight. It felt more like eighty.

I could have brought in the police, proved that the jug

once had belonged to me. I still had the catalogue and the bill of sale. The police would have records of its reported theft, within days of my purchase. But I did not want the delay.

I wanted it back now. So much time had been wasted.

The jug was one of the few threads I still had to bind me to Richard. I felt its smooth, warm body in my hands, closed my eyes and recalled the last time I had held it. Before so much happiness and unhappiness.

Rychard Oliver. Hys jug. I looked at Hall o'th'Wood again, so familiar now. Remembering the time when I had not known which would be his bedroom window. I knew every strut of its walls, every angle of its structure, every pane of glass in its casement windows. I turned the jug around to look at the back, studied the hanged man and knew. Matthew Grindall had portrayed himself. This was no one of the Oliver clan. Even distorted as the man's face was, there was no sign of the straight nose, the regular features. The face was coarse – not refined. It was no one of the Oliver family. Matthew Grindall had portrayed his own death. The jug had been his confession to, and reason for, the crime he had committed. Why? In revenge for his sister's end.

I held it up to my face and wondered, as though I could divine from its clay body, what had been its story from the time when I had last seen it in my cottage and it turning up here, eight years later, hundreds of miles away? I would never know. All I could guess at was that it had probably changed hands many times. The Gypsies would not have held on to the piece for all those years. It was too long and they were notorious for selling swiftly, often for little profit. They depended on turnover in cash.

I asked the shop owner the price. He said I could have it for four hundred pounds and I bought it.

And now it was mine again I felt as though I had re-entered the full circle of a time warp and returned to that auspicious day in 1967. I drove all the way home as though in a dream, conscious only of the driving rain, the dark, the empty loneliness of a quiet road, wanting to be at home, alone with the knowledge that my jug– Richard's jug – our jug – the start of it all – lay carefully wrapped, in a box, on the passenger seat of my car.

It was terribly late when I arrived home, somewhere near four in the morning – that dead time of the night and I was dog-tired. I unwrapped the jug, placed it on the table, stretched out on my sofa, still in my saleroom clothes and fell asleep.

I have said before that of all the people I have ever known Paul Wernier-King had the most unfortunate sense of timing. I awoke some time late morning, aware that someone else was in the room. He was standing with his back to me, staring up at my portrait of the Tudor woman.

'Paul?'

He turned around.

I tried to rub the sleep out of my eyes. 'What are you

doing here?' I sat up. 'Has something happened? Is something wrong?'

'No.' He held out my bunch of keys. 'You left these in the door. Careless girl.'

'Paul?'

I sensed then that something was wrong. I studied his face. There was something different about it. His mouth looked firm and strong. He looked determined.

Something warned me.

Paul kept his eyes on me and knelt down on the floor. 'Susanna,' he said with the smallest of smiles. His eyes were fixed on me, very bright blue, with an uncertain expression in them.

'Paul,' I said softly. 'What is it? Tell me.'

He paused before he spoke, choosing his words very carefully, picking them out, like fishbones. 'I know you've never really been interested in me. No.' He held up his hand to stop me speaking. 'Don't start saying things, Susanna. Listen. Just listen. Please. Hear me out. What do you know about me? Or about what I want? You've never asked one single personal thing about me because you don't care. I understand that. It's Richard. It was always Richard. I should have realised that back at the sale that day when I saw you kiss him.'

I opened my mouth to speak then shut it again.

'I thought you seemed very beautiful and very loving. I wanted to be on the receiving end of that love.'

Behind him I could see the jug standing on the table, its pale shape a spectre watching over the scene.

Paul's voice was bitter. 'But I think– I like to think,' he corrected, 'that over the time we've been together we've become friends. At least that. So I'm going to tell you what I want for a change – whether you're interested and ask me – or not.'

I watched him quietly. His hair was bright blonde – almost yellow. It had been the one of the things I had noticed on that first encounter. That and the blue of his eyes. Together with the name, had I thought about it I might have guessed at German origins but Paul was right. I never had thought about it.

'Tacoma,' he said, 'is named after the city in Washington State where my great-grandfather first got work when he came over to the States last century. It's called the City of Destiny. Apparently after he built Tacoma he said he would either call it that or Point Defiance – the park.' He gave his lopsided grin. 'I'm kind of glad he chose Tacoma – although sometimes Point Defiance would have seemed more apt.'

He continued. 'I already told you my mother left when I was two and I never really had any contact with her again. She's somewhere in Florida now, I believe.' He licked his lips. 'My father and I were very close. We did everything together but he died a few years back now. When I first saw you I was studying at Oxford.' He smiled. 'Fine Art. I fell in love with you when I first saw you. I don't know what it was – whether it was your looks or your manner or the way you got excited over a little china rabbit. I've wondered lots of times what it was but I don't have a sensible answer. All I know is I couldn't forget you. Every day you were in prison I thought about you. I couldn't bear the idea of you being in that horrible place for something I never believed you did consciously. I hated Richard for what he left you to.'

I looked away.

'I thought you an innocent. I collected the china partly as a way of keeping in touch. I visited your shop many times while you were in prison. And partly because I always planned to use my collection as a lure to bring you to Tacoma. Then you came to my house and you weren't a fantasy figure anymore. You were someone for real. I could see you, touch you. Love you. Make love to you, Susanna,' his face twisted, 'as long as you thought it was Richard. But we've got along together for a coupla years now. We've built up a relationship.'

I nodded. Of sorts.

He gave one of his dry laughs. 'This is where it gets tricky,' he said. 'Susanna, I live in that big place alone. I come from an old family a little like your Richard's but now there's only me left. I don't want to live my life alone. I want a family. Children of my own. I want a son.' The wide grin held a hint of sadness now. 'Maybe even a little daughter who looks like her mother. I want that house filled with life and a future and children, not a shut-up mausoleum. I want a family, Susanna. I want you. I'm asking you to marry me.'

He rested his head on my lap and I could tell he was relieved now he had spoken.

As gently as I could, stroking the yellow hair, I told him that when I had lost Richard's child there had been some damage. I had to tell him that his dream was simply a dream. I could never be the mother of the children he so badly wanted.

He stood up then, his face a blank and he walked out without saying another word.

I glanced up at the Tudor woman and read there a warmth and sympathy as she gazed after Paul Wernier-King. Even some pity for me. I looked across the room at the jug and then I sat and covered my face with my hands, feeling hopeless.

A month later Paul sent me a letter to say that he had married Frances Swanson.

CHAPTER NINETEEN

I did wonder whether Paul would want to wind down the business now he was married. I realise now that I still saw him as someone mercurial, inconstant when he was anything but. I believed he would have other things to fill his mind– his wife, his family. But I was wrong. As 1975 melted into 1976 he rang me up and expressed the desire that we continue importing and exporting antiques in and out of the States. He also told me that Frances was pregnant. He couldn't hide the joy in his voice and though I felt a gut-wrenching twinge of envy I was glad for him. Six months later he rang in the middle of the night and told me he had a son. 'Paul Wernier-King the fifth,' he said proudly. 'I'll be calling him Junior.'

I congratulated him.

We still spoke once or twice a week during the intervening years but I sensed he was not anxious to meet up with me again and I, I told myself, felt the same. I did not know whether his marriage to Frances was happy. I assumed so but there were no more children and Paul never mentioned her. It was obvious that all his attention was focused on his little son whom he always referred to as 'Junior'.

So the Seventies melted away into the greedy Eighties and the antiques trade fired up to its most profitable decade. I spent every spare moment at Hall o'th'Wood with Richard, my stepgrandson. He called me Zanna and accepted me into his life without question, as children do. We did everything together, rode horses, played tennis, swam, sailed. I batted while he bowled and bowled while he batted in cricket. I lurked around the goalpost while he was practising his goal shots. I tested him for school exams and took him to Majorca for the summers. He grew tall and strong, and each day a little more like the Richard I had been married to. I adored the boy. He was my raison d'être, the son I had so cruelly been deprived of, because I always believed that the child Richard and I had lost had been a son.

He was a pupil at the same public school that Richard had attended and Michael after him and held strong to the family traditions.

In 1985 antiques hit the world headlines when the contents of a Dutch East India Company ship called the Geldermalsen, laden with Chinese porcelain, was rescued from the bottom of the South China Seas by a diver named Michael Hatcher. The contents were put up for sale by Christies in Amsterdam. Known as the

Nanking Cargo the sale attracted worldwide interest.

Like many others I was curious and excited by the story of adventure and determined to attend the sale. To my surprise Paul decided he would come too. We had fallen behind with some of the bookwork and it needed a face-to-face meeting. I had not seen him since his visit to my cottage and I was curious to see how he looked.

He was waiting for me on the tarmac as I flew in. I saw him as the plane taxied in and was surprised at how much I had forgotten about him, the bright hair, that awkward grin. I wondered if his son had it too. He was wearing a long, tan, leather coat and looked different – not the Paul I had last seen at my cottage.

He watched me descend the aeroplane steps. 'So,' he said. 'Finally. Susanna.' He kissed my cheek then drew back and studied my face. 'You look well,' he said. He nodded his head in agreement with himself. 'You look very good.'

'I am well.'

He searched my face with those well-remembered, determined eyes. 'Happy too?'

It was an uncomfortable question but I looked away and said yes, that I was happy enough and asked him if he was. His reply was equally unconvincing. We took a cab to the hotel. Our rooms were on the same floor and we arranged to meet for dinner.

Paul was every inch a proud family man. Over dinner he showed me pictures of 'Junior', a confident young lad with Paul's yellow hair and toothy grin. I noticed too that he was wearing braces. I asked him how Frances was and he answered very briefly that she was 'OK'. He was not anxious to enlarge and I did not pry. It was his personal life while I was simply a business partner but I did wonder why they had had only the one child. Perhaps it was enough for Paul – to have an heir.

It was like the old days. We spent hours that evening sorting out the paperwork and took a brandy nightcap together, arranging to meet in the morning and view the sale.

It was fantastic to see the contents of the Nanking ship laid out. Fabulous Chinese porcelain. Acres of it. Eighteenth century. Some pieces were badly damaged but incredibly much of it was perfect, some even encrusted with shells and barnacles. Paul couldn't hide his enthusiasm and bought three or four pieces for his own collection. 'With all this publicity,' he pointed out sensibly, 'it'll fetch too much money. We won't be able to sell it at a profit but there's no reason why I should miss out.'

I admired his reasoning. He was right on both points.

I bought a barnacle-encrusted plate. Like Paul I would add it to my collection. And now the sale was over there was no need to tarry. My flight was early the following evening. He came with me to the airport. He was flying later on that day. I sensed he was reluctant to say goodbye to me. He gave a great sigh, put his arms around me and spoke. 'I wish things had been different,' he said quietly. 'I wish—' This time it was I who shushed him with a finger on his lips.

'It couldn't ever have been different, Paul,' I said. 'It is all written in our destiny.' I tried to make a joke of it. 'Tacoma,' I said. 'City of Destiny.'

'Destiny can be very cruel,' he replied.

I believe then that he wished he had never seen me at the duke's country sale.

I flew back to England in pensive mood.

So we settled back into our ruts. Paul and I continued to speak but we did not meet again.

Then in the autumn of 1986 I received word that my aunt was ill and flew to the Casa Rosada at once, dropping everything.

The minute I saw her I knew she was dying. The fact that she was lying in her bed when she had always had so much energy, the waxen sheen on her face, the way her eyes had lost their brightness. And I knew that she was disappointed in her life. The fame that had promised so much had somehow cruelly eluded her. She had received accolades but never real recognition.

She was having difficulty breathing and the skinny, brown hands clutched at the bedclothes. 'I feel cold,' she said so I lit a fire. Houses in Majorca are not geared up with central heating and the Casa Rosada was no exception. It had one huge log fire to keep the entire place warm. When we had been children Sara and I had loved this. We would sit round it with my aunt and tell stories while listening to the wind howling around the lonely house. We would feel safe and secure and the sun would soon be out to warm us again. It was never really cold like an English winter.

I stayed with my aunt night and day, sleeping in a chair so she could stretch out and touch me at any time. On the second day she rallied a little and talked for most of the daylight hours. 'Susie,' she said, 'I've left you the house. Sara gets most of the rest but I want you to keep the Casa Rosada. It's your home.'

I nodded and she fell asleep.

A little later she started again. 'Susie,' she said. 'You should marry again. You're not old. You have a great capacity to love. I wished you had had your own children.'

'Richard is like my own son.'

'He's not your son,' she said cruelly. 'You're still pursuing the wrong path.' Then she turned her face to the wall. 'But you won't listen to me.'

I remember wondering then how she could make such a distinction when she had brought us up as her own.

'I don't want to marry,' I said. 'My destiny is written up there, Eleanor, in the clouds and the stars. How can I escape? I didn't pursue all that has happened to me. It has simply happened.'

'Maybe,' she said wearily. 'I'm too tired to discuss this now. You'll know all one day.'

I kissed her then and bathed her face. 'Will I?' I asked. 'Will I? Will it all come clear and straight?'

She didn't answer. She had slipped into unconsciousness and died late that afternoon.

It was when the storms hit the sunshine isle. For three days the wind howled and the seas lashed the coast. At times I almost wondered if the house itself would be hurled from the cliffs and thrown into the Mediterranean. On the third day we buried my aunt. Sara and I followed the coffin, hearing the church bell toll and I felt alone. More alone than ever before in my entire life. Now I had no one except my sister and Richard's family.

Sara didn't stay but returned to the UK straight after the funeral while I remained at the Casa Rosada, saying I wanted to pack up my aunt's belongings.

It wasn't true. The real reason was that I wanted to grieve alone and to ponder her final words to me.

She was everywhere in that house. There were paint daubs all over the place. Her pictures hung on every wall, her belongings in every cupboard and drawer. I found I didn't want to pack her things up but leave them out to pretend to myself that she was still with me. And the storms continued to lash around the house.

Late on the third night after the funeral I had lit a fire of pine logs, bathed and wrapped myself up in a towel. As I passed the mirror I caught sight of myself. Instead of moving on I moved closer and studied my face, trying to read the destiny prepared for me but only succeeding in seeing myself in a different way.

I was forty-six years old. I did not look old or fat or wrinkled. My hair was still thick and dark but what held my gaze was a terrible void behind the eyes. A desperation. It had been there ever since Richard had died. I had lost the light, the sparkle and, I believed, the capacity to love. Not to love a child. I loved Richard's grandson but to love a man, to feel a man wrapped around me, holding me, kissing me, inside me. I would not feel that again. I backed away from the mirror. I did not like what I had seen.

So I sat, my arms wrapped around my knees, staring into the flames. In a log fire you can read all sorts of things. Demons and fairies, houses and lives. It hissed and spat at me and I continued to stare.

I did not hear the knocking at first. The storm was too fierce and noisy. He told me later that he had been knocking for many minutes. But I did hear his voice calling me impatiently. 'Susanna, let me in, will you?'

I opened the door to the rainstorm.

Paul was standing there, an inadequate windcheater held over his head. He was getting soaked. Rain poured down his face. I knew then that I wanted him. Physically. I flung myself at him, wanting human contact, wanting something from him.

At first he did nothing but stood still, the rain streaming down his face, his hair, his clothes getting wetter by the minute. He held his arms stiffly away from me. 'Hey,' he protested gently. 'Hey, Susanna.'

I stepped back. 'What are you doing here, Paul?'

'At the moment? Getting wet,' he said, laughing and pulling me to him. Now we were both wet. 'I heard

about your aunt and...well let's just say I didn't want
you to be alone. Not here. I'm sorry I missed her funeral.
Now can I come in out of the rain?'

I laughed and led him inside to the fire.

And now I had broken that taboo I could not let him
go. I remember I asked innumerable irrelevant
questions, how had he known about my aunt, how had
he known where to find me. The answers were all the
same. I had always suspected that he and Sara would
become allies and now he confessed all. They had kept
in touch.

About Frances I said nothing but pushed her out of my
mind. I enjoyed the feel of him too much, stroking my
breasts, touching my mouth with his fingers, his lips,
exploring my body. His hands fumbled under the towel
and then he stopped. 'Are you sure about this?'

'Never so sure about anything,' I said.

We spent an entire week together, hardly leaving the
house – or each other. I have never known such an
intensity of emotion or need. As I had once been greedy
for Richard now I was greedy for Paul and this
rediscovered physical lust. Like a teenager freshly in
love I clung to him as though he was my oxygen, my
life, my colour, my love. My pleasure. And Paul? He was
happy as I had never seen him. He hummed tunes
around the house, cooked simple meals. We rang
Carmina and she dropped provisions off every other
day. We saw no one else in that entire time. We were

sealed off from the world. Alone. The island turned warm and we ate on the balcony, eating sardines, drinking Rioja, watching the stars by night and the sun by day. It was a quiet pool of pure indulgent hedonism. I had forgotten how good it felt to know that your body is being enjoyed.

But happiness does not last.

Eight days after he had arrived I awoke and stretched out my hand, expecting to feel Paul but there was a cold, empty patch. Sleepily I opened my eyes and saw him standing naked, his back to me, staring out of the window. I watched him with a feeling of dread.

He must have sensed that I was awake because he came back towards the bed, bent down and kissed me. 'I have to go back,' he said gently. 'There are things I have to sort out.'

I sat up. 'What things?' I knew once this spell was broken it could never be reworked.

Halcyon days are like that. They can never be recaptured and I had loved these past days too much.

He kissed me again and stared into my eyes. 'I have to divorce Frances,' he said.

I was appalled. 'Divorce Frances? Why? What's she done?'

He lay down beside me, his hands underneath his head, staring up at the ceiling. He still looked cheery. 'It's what I want to do.' He raised himself up on his elbow. 'We can be married, have Junior along with us.'

I did not answer and he must have sensed that I did not approve.

'Susanna,' he said. 'Our marriage was a sham. You can't think I ever loved her? After you?' The wide grin was back. He was more sure of himself now. He sat up, explaining patiently as though to a child. 'You couldn't have children. It was the only way.'

There was a candid innocence behind his eyes and I saw that his feelings for me could not die. Perhaps that makes subsequent events even more cruel. Or perhaps it was part of destiny still laughing at me and him.

I tried to dissuade him.

'We don't have to be—'

He cut in. 'We do, Susanna. Believe me. We do.'

I stared at him. It was the first morning since he had arrived that we had not made love.

We breakfasted very quietly and very slowly and I watched as he packed his suitcases and loaded them into his hire car.

I clung to him and felt that the episode would soon be over.

As he reversed down the drive he opened the window and gave me a small smile. 'Auf Wiedersehen.' He waved.

I put my hands on the window. 'Don't do it,' I urged. 'Don't divorce her.'

Perhaps I believed that to divorce his wife for no reason was tempting the fates again. Perhaps I still didn't understand Paul's psyche or perhaps I thought that he was asking me to share his life in Tacoma and that was against my wish.

Perhaps...

Who knows?

Paul divorced Frances anyway.

I spent Christmas of '87 at Hall o'th'Wood. As I drove up through the snow I reflected that the crooked black-and-white walls looked like the design on an expensive Christmas card.

I stopped the car to gaze up at it and recalled my first visit. The old house still made me catch my breath with its beauty. But now I knew something of its secrets.

Richard, or Dick as I called him, was now a tall, serious boy of fourteen years old and I could see the resemblance to my husband grow stronger every day. He had the same clear, grey eyes and direct way of speaking. He met me in the hallway, Michael and Linda standing behind him. Richard threw his arms around me. 'Happy Christmas, Zanna. Maria says we've time for a ride before Christmas dinner,' he added excitedly.

So we took the horses out for their Christmas morning gallop and dismounted at the lake. I knew Dick had something to ask me. 'Zanna,' he said seriously. 'I want to ask you about my grandfather. People say things but they never tell me the full story.' There was the hint of petulance in his voice. 'He did something very bad, didn't he?'

I nodded. I have never seen the point of hiding things

from children – even unpleasant things. 'Yes, he did. We both did. He died and I went to prison.' I hesitated. 'For three years.'

He had the schoolboys' love of unearthing secrets.

'What was it?'

'We brought some things – letters – into the country illegally.'

His eyes were round, his mouth open.

'My father told me that you did it for money.'

I nodded.

'He said it was to preserve the house.'

We both glanced involuntarily through the trees, at the crooked, white walls with their black timbers criss-crossing, woodsmoke drifting up from the chimneys.

Richard put his hand on my arm. 'I just wanted to tell you,' he said, 'that it's all right. I would never do anything that stupid. Not just for a house. Not even Hall o'th'Wood. It wouldn't be worth it.'

I felt reassured.

We galloped back to our Christmas dinner then.

Christmas fare in every household is full of its own traditions. Mulled wine, the turkey and then the Christmas pudding, brought in in flames. In the pudding in Hall o'th'Wood we had always hidden small silver objects – a shoe, a tiny suitcase, a heart. Portents of our future. We would leave them on the side of our plates and Maria would clean them, wrap them in tissue paper and preserve them ready for the next Christmas – and the next. I was eating my portion when I felt something hard and round. I spat it out and knew the wedding ring had found me this year. Then I looked up. Linda was watching, smiling, Michael too, even Maria from the doorway. They were all part of the conspiracy. The trinkets were not randomly distributed but carefully manoeuvred to the correct person's plate. I spat it out and put it on the side of my plate. Dick, I noticed, was not part of the conspiracy. He carried on doggedly spooning the pudding and brandy sauce into his mouth, oblivious of the drama playing over his head.

Right on cue the telephone rang and Maria returned to the table to say that Paul was asking for me.

He wished me a merry Christmas, said that he was in Tacoma, alone with Junior, that he was having a great time and that he hoped I was too. He sounded happy. He asked me again to marry him and this time I said yes.

I put the phone down, looked round the ring of faces and told them that I would be getting married again. Michael kissed me and opened a bottle of champagne. Linda kissed me and asked me when. Only Dick regarded me mournfully from the end of the table as though I had let him down badly.

CHAPTER TWENTY

Paul was ecstatic. He could talk about nothing but the wedding which he had decided was to be at Tacoma, on the lawn. Every single, tiny detail was of the greatest importance to him – guests, the cake, the dress. He talked endlessly about my living in Tacoma, with Junior, about us being a family.

A week after Christmas he arrived at Horton Cottage very late one night, theatrically bent on one knee and presented me with a huge solitaire. 'You don't need to wear that,' he said, touching the third finger of my left hand. So I removed Richard's engagement ring and put his ring on instead.

Even that small gesture seemed disloyal. He touched my wedding ring and I knew he would soon expect me to remove that too.

I felt I was living a dream. No – not a dream. A lie. I still felt that I had not severed the threads of my previous existence and I could not shake off the feeling that none of this would really happen, that it would somehow melt away, like ice in sunshine.

It made it worse that everyone was so happy for me. Sara and her family, and especially Michael and Linda. Linda came with me one day to Chester to look at wedding dresses. I tried on one after the other and couldn't decide. It all seemed too unreal. I couldn't wear a long, white wedding dress, which was what Paul wanted me to wear. I imagined I would wear a tailored, white, silk suit. Something like that, anyhow.

It wasn't that I didn't love Paul. Admittedly I didn't feel the same as that first passion I had felt for Richard. Love matures as do people and the love I felt for Paul was different; but it was love. He had stuck by me for years. He was a part of my life. In a way I felt I owed it to him to make him happy.

The problem was that I could not see myself as mistress of Tacoma. I would be happier in my own tiny cottage than there.

I couldn't imagine living in the States, away from Richard, away from Hall o'th'Wood, away from Bottle Kiln and everything that was so dear and familiar.

But I let Paul continue planning the wedding. A marquee on the lawn, caterers, a string quartet. Every time he thought of some small extra thing he would ring. Whether it was the cake or the cars or the honeymoon or the service or the hymns. I answered automatically, in a flat voice.

All I can say is that it didn't feel right. Something was very wrong.

Dick had taken me to one side. 'I don't want you to be married,' he said, with all the stilted stubbornness of a fifteen-year-old. 'I don't want you to live in America. I want you to stay here, with me.'

I said nothing but hugged him. It was what I wanted too.

I must make my own life – not bloodsuck theirs.

Two months before the wedding Michael had to go on a business trip to Australia and Linda decided to go with him.

My treat was to stay at Hall o'th'Wood with Dick who was on his school holidays.

I was hugely happy living back in the old house. The furniture seemed to come alive under the attention Maria and I lavished on it. I slept in the same bedroom that I had shared with Richard which Michael and Linda had kept as a guest room and sometimes, when I awoke in the dead of night, I could almost persuade myself that he was still alive, maybe pacing the long gallery over my head, but still here somehow. I could believe that he had never really left the place. I could pretend that young Richard was our son, that none of the nightmare had really happened. I was truly, truly happy and knew that I could never be complete away from Hall o'th'Wood. I spent long hours staring at his portrait, the latest one to grace the collection, looking at the photographs, particularly the one taken of us on the night of our third wedding anniversary, and talking to his grandson about my days in his home. I had brought the jug back with me to its rightful place, where it should have always been, standing on the long, low dresser in the dining room, warning the current owners of the house to take care of their morals. I wished I could tell my husband that I had found it again. I decided that I would search out Mr Cridman, whose ancestor had first retrieved the jug from its enamelling kiln. Perhaps he would be able to shed further light on the circumstances surrounding the jug's beginnings. I would stand beneath the stained-glass window on the landing and commune with the crusader as Richard, my Richard, had done when he was a little boy.

I felt the strongest impulse that this was where I truly belonged.

Once the studded great door of Hall o'th'Wood was closed Paul Wernier-King almost ceased to exist. He was outside the rarefied atmosphere of Hall o'th'Wood. It was a jolt when he rang up. I almost had to remind myself who he was. He seemed a foreigner, an alien. And then I would remember that I was to marry him in a few short weeks.

Good phone calls never come in the middle of the night. No one rings in the small hours for a chat or a gossip. It is always bad news.

I wrapped my dressing gown round my waist and ran down the stairs. Seconds later I was staring into my own future. Because this would change everything. Now I was beginning to understand my destiny.

A car accident on a highway near Adelaide and

Michael and Linda were both dead. I stared at the receiver in my hand and knew that if they could speak they would remind me of my solemn promise, to treat Richard as my own son, to bring him up here, where he belonged, in Hall o'th'Wood. To teach him the family traditions. I must obey my destiny.

I woke him up and told him. He cried and I hugged him and then made the most solemn of promises to Richard's grandson, that I would be here, for him, as long as he needed me.

Now I only had to break the news to Paul.

It was out of the question that I would use the telephone. I wouldn't pay him that insult. I flew to Newark and took a cab out to Long Island without telling him I was coming. I arrived late on a Thursday night, unexpected, to find the house shrouded in a mist that had stolen in from the sea.

I spoke into the intercom and watched the gates swing open sleepily.

I met Paul coming down the stairs in his dressing gown. 'Well,' he said. 'Hi. How's the blushing bride?' He kissed me. 'Did you come over just to take a peek?'

I shook my head.

He must have read something in my face because he took me into the library, closed the door behind us and I told him.

Firstly about Michael and Linda and then what it meant.

He looked shocked at the news and then I watched his

eyes narrow as he absorbed my statement.

'I can't marry you,' I said. 'I'm sorry. I must stay in England, in Hall o'th'Wood, with Richard.'

He went white. 'You can't do this to me,' he said, gripping my shoulders. 'Susanna – you just can't. I won't let you. I have…'

He must have looked at my face and realised it was no good. Mentally I was back there already – not here at all.

He screamed at me then. Shouted at me, threatened, cajoled, begged.

Reasoned. 'We can bring the boys up together here,' he said.

I reminded him of my promise – that Richard would be brought up in England, in Hall o'th'Wood.

'Does it matter where? He's at boarding school.'

He reminded me that my aunt had brought Sara and me up in Majorca.

'That was different,' I said. 'We had no family home.'

At some point he must have realised that I was deadly serious and that nothing would divert me from my purpose.

Something in him froze then.

He left the room and I summoned a taxi to return me to the UK and Hall o'th'Wood.

I turned around to watch the great gates of Tacoma swing closed behind me and knew they would never be opened again to me.

CHAPTER TWENTY-ONE

Paul wasted no time. Within a week of my visit I felt the full fury of the Wernier-Kings. I had letters from his lawyers dissolving the Wernier Oliver partnership.

But I was happy. After fifteen years I was back where I wanted to be, living in Hall o'th'Wood.

Richard grieved for his parents as I had mine but I took comfort in the fact that I was there for him as my aunt had been for me and Sara.

My days were happy. I managed the estate as best I could. Rented out Horton Cottage again and ran my antiques shop. Luckily I had made some wise investments in my earlier, prosperous years and Michael and Linda's finances had been well managed so, for now, we were solvent. Unexpectedly Richard began to take an interest in my work and expressed an intention to join me in the business. He certainly had a talent for it. I loved taking him to the salerooms and watching him pick out the fine pieces or dismiss others which were poor quality, point out restorations or anomalies.

'A levels first,' I warned. 'Then, if you still want to you can come in with me.' He demurred but I insisted. 'Your father and mother gave you into my care,' I said. 'They wouldn't want you to give up on your education.'

He grumbled but did as I asked.

From Paul I heard nothing. I suppose as I had watched the gates of Tacoma lock behind me I had known that it must be the end, not only of our partnership, but our friendship too. I missed him more than I'd thought but never doubted that I had made the right decision.

I did as I had vowed to myself and sought out John Cridman, the farmer whom David had told me about. I took the jug to show him one day. He was in his eighties and lived now in a converted barn. He was bent with arthritis. Even the joints of his fingers were lumpy and distorted. I let him sit in his chair before unwrapping the jug and handing it to him.

'Ah,' he said, running a rheumy eye over it. 'You know, it were such a story in our family. My father kept it hidden from human eye in a box as had his father before him and his before that.'Twere a shameful story.' He looked up, his eyes bright. He was dying to tell me.

'I don't know if I know the full story,' I prompted.

Cridman eyed me with suspicion. 'What's your connection? How did it come into your possession?'

I decided to give him a sanitised version of my life, told him I was a dealer and had bought the jug at a sale and subsequently married into the Oliver family. 'I currently live at Hall o'th'Wood,' I said.

'You are the owner then?'

I shook my head. 'I am the guardian of the current owner,' I said, 'until he is twenty-one. He was orphaned a while ago.'

'Bad business,' he said. 'I'm truly sorry about that.'

I bowed my head.

Cridman eyed the jug. 'I'm not sure this is a story suitable for a youngster's ears.'

'That's why I came alone, Mr Cridman,' I said.

He puffed on his smelly pipe.

'Well now,' he said. 'There are several versions of this tale.'

'If it helps,' I said, 'I believe I know the bald facts.'

Cridman pulled some more on his pipe. His eyes flickered.

'Rebekah Grindall, so the stories say, was a very lovely girl. Strong and beautiful.' He leant forward and touched my hair. 'With a thick mane of very dark hair, like yours, so my grandfather told me his grandfather had told him.'

'And have you told your grandson?'

Slowly Cridman shook his head. 'I have not,' he said. 'When I decided back in '67 to sell the jug I also decided it was time to bury these evil, old tales. Sometimes it's just time to move on.'

I nodded.

'Rebekah was betrothed to a young potter named Luke Chater,' Cridman said, 'who was struggling to manage the factory together with Rebekah's brother...'

'Matthew,' I said.

The old man nodded. '...when Richard Oliver came to visit the factory on his fine horse. They wanted to borrow some money and he was the only one willing to back the potbank. Unfortunately the price he demanded weren't money at all.'

I understood now.

'He took her and kept her at...' The old man's fingers traced the window on the jug. 'Her fiancé were none too happy and tried to take her back. Unfortunately he died in the attempt.' He looked at me through a cloud of tobacco smoke. 'It's no use your asking me exactly what happened. Mr Oliver claimed he had found him poaching on his land and had shot him. Certainly, so the story goes, a bag with some rabbits in were found but I don't know.' His eyes dropped. 'No charges were brought and Mr Oliver were so furious he withdrew his money from the clay pit but kept hold of the girl. Again records and stories are poor – to say the least – but it is certain that Rebekah must have been locked up because she took the only way out she could – through the window. She tumbled into the knot garden which is understandable, all things considered.' He puffed again on his pipe. 'The way I look at it is this – that girl had not saved, as she had thought, the potters' livelihood but had lost her betrothed and gained nothing – only losing her purity – which was the only thing of value that she had. With the result that she threw herself out of the window.' His eyes flickered.

'That is what the story said. But...' His eyes flickered and looked away. 'She did not die right away.'

'*It took her four days to dye,*' I quoted and the old man nodded.

'There was talk,' he said, leaning towards me conspiratorially, 'especially as the master did not even visit her. A maidservant who was caring for her in those last painful days spread a rumour that Rebekah did not throw herself out as rumour had it but had been thrown out.'

I looked at him in horror.

'This rumour reached her brother's ears and before anyone could stop him he took himself up to Hall o'th'Wood and right in front of the tall window...'

'Of a crusader.'

'...he ran him through. Then he returned to the potbank and threw the jug. While it was still in the enamelling kiln they came for him.

Three days later he was swinging on the gallows,' he finished with malicious pleasure.

I started. One of my favourite places to sit was on the great staircase, right in front of the crusader window – Richard's too. Had we then sat on his ancestor's bloodstain?

As I drove home I wondered whether I wished I did not know the full story behind my piece.

But I typed it out and placed it in an envelope inside the jug.

I knew Dick would want to read it one day.

* * *

About a year after Michael and Linda's deaths I was scanning the Antiques Trade Gazette when I saw a picture that caught my eye. It looked very much like the partner of my own Tudor woman. I had removed all my valuables to Hall o'th'Wood when I had left my cottage, amongst them my favourite painting which now hung in my study. I took the paper up there and held the photograph up next to her. There was something about it which made me sure it was the companion to my painting. The brush marks, the way the eyes had been painted in, dead and flat – almost threatening. Certainly disdainful and proud. The date was right too, judging from the style and the costumes of the subjects, also the fact that it too was painted on an oak panel. I dialled the number of the gallery and made some enquiries.

A week later I caught the train to London to see the picture for myself. With me I had a folio of photographs to compare the two paintings.

The dealer had a small gallery in New Bond Street, locked until I pressed the buzzer and was let in. He was Jewish, Obadiah Cricklestone. He was well known in the art world though I had never met him personally before. I had heard about him, however, and knew that he had an awesome reputation for buying and selling period portraits, particularly Tudor portraits of gentility. He showed me into the back room where his portrait hung. 'It was painted by George Gower,' he said, handing me a magnifying glass so I could study the signature.

'My painting isn't signed,' I said.

He looked comfortable with that.

'The paintings were meant to be hung together,' he said. 'It is not uncommon for the artist to sign one and not the other. In some ways...' He was studying my photographs with the same rapt attention that I was giving to his painting. '...it is not surprising.'

I looked up at the face of the portrait with its thick moustache and pointed beard, the dark, cynical eyes. Using the magnifying glass I peered at the ruff around the man's neck. It was this that persuaded me that the artist had to be the same. The detail of the lace had been done with identical brush marks.

Next I took the painting off the wall to see the condition of the panel on which it had been painted. And this convinced me even more. There are a thousand different shades of brown, a hundred different grains of oak. And this one was the same. I would swear it. I knew my painting better than I knew my own face.

'Do you know who they are?'

'Your painting is of Lady Kynnersley,' he said. 'And her husband is Lord Kynnersley. She married him when she was very young and he much older. He died, I believe, when she was still very young and left her with a terrible debt. She was renowned for working on the farm herself to try and maintain the estate. Quite a thing in those days. Very hard work for a woman.'

I felt a curiosity for the woman. I had not known even her name for so many years and now I was learning her life history. 'Did she have children?'

'None of her own. And she never married again but lived a rather lonely life. I believe she adopted a nephew. Brought him up as her own and on her death he inherited the farm. Rather a sad story, I often think. She was about twenty-four when her husband died. Ah well.' He sighed. 'It's a long time to be on your own, Mrs Oliver.'

I agreed that it was, paid the price he asked and took the painting home with me. I hung it adjacent to the Tudor woman so that husband and wife could watch each other for the first time in many years.

But the obvious parallels to my own life made me uncomfortable.

CHAPTER TWENTY-TWO

So the years passed until 1991.

It was early on a Wednesday morning and Dick was reading the Society gossip page in his newspaper over the breakfast table.

'You missed out on something there, Zanna,' he said, giving me a cheeky grin over the top of the page.

I was well used to his teasing. 'What?'

He pushed the paper across the table. It was a picture of Paul, in a dinner suit, his arm draped across the shoulders of a slim youth I assumed must be Junior – the likeness was so strong. In fact, with the blonde hair, he looked very like the Paul I had first set eyes on at the country-house sale. The young buck, as Richard had called him. Underneath the picture the story read... 'Paul Wernier-King and his son share a box at the London Opera House.'

The article continued, 'Paul Wernier-King, whose bank was floated on the stock market yesterday, celebrates with a night out with his son. The Wernier-King Bank has gone from strength to strength since its director, Paul Wernier-King, took over the reins three years ago.'

There was more gossipy stuff about his house and his relationships and it covered his divorce. It finished with the comment that he was considered one of the world's most eligible bachelors.

It was a shock to see him again. I stared at the picture with a mixture of emotions and read something hard in Paul's face which I had never seen before. But I was glad to see that his affection for his son was patently so strong. I passed the paper back to Dick without comment. 'Water under the bridge,' I said. 'Now get on with your swotting.'

At the beginning of July 1991 Dick finally left school and joined Bottle Kiln Antiques. In fact he had excelled in his A levels with two 'As' and a 'B'. He had chosen to specialise in the arts and had studied English and art and oddly enough biology. I was looking forward to him joining me but I didn't want to be selfish. 'Are you sure you don't want to go to university?'

He shook his head very firmly.

It seemed that he had only been in the business for a matter of weeks before we were approached on behalf of a Canadian to furnish his house with 'British antiques'. He gave us a budget of a million pounds sterling and furnished us with descriptions of the type of pieces he would like. He faxed detailed dimensions of the rooms and the number of an interior decorator who was to work with us selecting pieces. It was a huge commission and, even timed with Dick's partnership in the firm, promised to keep us very busy.

The real irony is that unless Dick had joined the firm I would not have accepted such an undertaking. It would have been too much for me alone – too much money, too much searching, too much travelling and too much responsibility. It is hard to choose pieces for another. But I was anxious for Dick to have plenty of work to do. I knew he would welcome the challenge and it was a good start to his new career. So after a brief discussion we took it on.

There was only one drawback that niggled me. The amount of money was so great that for the first time ever I used Hall o'th'Wood as collateral.

I hated doing it but Richard and I talked late into the night and we could see no other way. The Canadian had put the money up front but there were still insurances and shipping costs which we would initially bear until the pieces had arrived in New York and been approved.

The Canadian customer had unusual tastes. He liked chinoiserie, period walnut and Regency pieces, rather than decorative Victoriana, which made each individual piece expensive. We managed to track down two or three pieces of fine Queen Anne walnut and a lovely pair of Regency rosewood bookcases that I was sure would meet with his approval but filling the container kept us both busy.

We bought a few paintings too, mainly hunting scenes which he had stipulated, and two very fine still lifes.

By Christmas we had almost finished our buying. We were nearly up to our million mark and were anxious to gain our commission. So – we nailed down the containers and watched them being loaded on the quayside in Liverpool for their trip. Then we settled down for Christmas.

It was the time of year when we both missed Michael and Linda. We had taken to inviting Sara and her brood but it wasn't the same. Besides, my sister had never really forgiven me for sacrificing Paul and even now found it hard to steer clear of the subject.

Like many families we were relieved when the festive season was over.

The nightmare began halfway through January when we had a phone call from our irate buyer to say that the container had not arrived.

At first I did not panic. There were plenty of possible explanations. His freight trucks had met the wrong boat. The pieces were in the wrong depot. The ship was delayed. My natural optimism found all sorts of rational explanations for the missing containers.

But at the back of my mind a little worm was boring.

If they didn't turn up we were in trouble. I couldn't stand the loss without having to remortgage Hall o'th'Wood. It could even be worse than that.

They would turn up, I told myself. But when, two weeks later, there was still no sign of the four containers, our customer was furious – to say the least. He was starting to call us names and threaten legal action and I began to feel real terror overwhelming me.

A million, we had said so glibly. But it was an awful lot of money.

By early February I was panicking. The containers still hadn't turned up and we were having trouble tracking them down. They had, it seemed, arrived at the dockside in New York and been picked up. The paperwork was faxed over to me. There was a signature purporting to be from our customer's firm of carriers but they denied all knowledge. It was even harder trying to work out what had happened from the UK. In the pit of my stomach I believed they had been stolen and alerted the police who seemed to get nowhere.

Richard and I paced the house endlessly. Our assets had been frozen so business stagnated. Without money we could not buy and without stock we had nothing new to sell therefore no income.

It is a terrible fact that when no money is coming in to a household it seems to spitefully leak out all the faster.

I began to suffer from sleeplessness, to find it hard to concentrate. I would stand in front of the portrait of Richard and try to apologise to him. But did I read forgiveness in his eyes?

I don't think so. He would not forgive this risk to his beloved house. In fact sometimes when I stood in front of his portrait I seemed to read scorn there and I began to feel that I had failed him after all.

And his grandson and I began to argue and point fingers at one another. Whose idea had it been to go ahead with this deal? When we knew we had both been in agreement. It was a terrible time.

And then, right out of the blue, at about three o'clock in the afternoon in the middle of February the telephone rang.

I picked it up, half-hopeful, half-dreading further bad news.

'Susanna.' It was a well-remembered voice.

'You know where I live. You want your stuff back you'll have to come and get it. Otherwise I'll put a match to it.' The phone clicked. The line was dead. I stared at it, wondering whether I had dreamt the whole thing.

Then I was galvanised into action. I ran upstairs to pack a bag and told Richard to book the next flight to New York. I half-explained what was happening but I didn't really understand myself. He drove me to Manchester airport and waved me off. 'Good luck, Zanna,' he shouted. 'Good luck.' Then, 'And don't let him bully you.'

CHAPTER TWENTY-THREE

New York is not cold in February. It is freezing. I landed straight into an icy fog which penetrated even the fur coat I wore over a cream, wool dress and leather boots. I took a cab all the way from Newark to Tacoma and peered in through the gates while the cab driver spoke into the intercom. They swung open and I again saw the façade of Tacoma. It looked still and lifeless and cold. As we drove towards it a flock of Canada geese flew overhead marking the sky with their wings.

I paid the cabbie, knocked on the front door and stood back, watching the car slide back down the drive towards the gates. I watched them close behind him.

The door was opened by a black-frocked maid – no one I recognised. Not Lola or Jemima. I gave my name and she led me into the great hall with its white statues, then along the corridor to the small sitting room where I had been ushered on my first visit to Tacoma.

She opened the door, announced my name and left.

Paul was standing with his back to me, leaning against the fireplace. And even from behind I could see he had changed. He was not the Paul I had once known but a stranger. His once yellow hair was paler. He had put on a bit of weight, only a few pounds, but it made his frame look more powerful. He was not the slim youth he had been but a middle-aged man. And he was wearing a lounge suit which made me smile. The Paul I had known had practically never worn a suit – except occasionally a dinner suit.

I stood awkwardly.

He turned around and I saw the hardness I had read correctly from the newspaper photograph. He regarded me steadily and with some hostility for a while before speaking.

'You look older.'

'I am older,' I said angrily. 'And it might not have escaped your attention that I have had a worrying time lately.'

The shadow of a smile fleeted across his face and I saw that he was the same Paul. Memories flashed through my brain: the day I had first met him – the gangly youth in white trousers who had tried to speak and provoked such fury in my husband; his face – vulnerable when I had told him I could not have the child he so wanted; the day he had turned up at Casa Rosada and we had become lovers; his joy when I had agreed to marry him which had turned to white-hot anger when I had told him I was staying at Hall o'th'Wood. The lopsided, awkward, uncertain grin. He had threaded through almost my entire life but I had been too blind to see it. Blinded by Hall o'th'Wood and Richard, blinded by what I had thought was my destiny and blinded by my duty to young Richard. I stared at him, speechless with the realisation of all that I had got wrong and he stared back.

I spoke first. 'The furniture,' I said. 'What have you done with it?'

'It's safe,' he said.

'Surely,' I asked curiously, 'you wouldn't really burn it? Knowing about antiques as you do.'

'Why not?'

'Because you value it. You would be destroying so much of beauty.'

He moved a step closer, his eyes burning with emotion. 'And what were you prepared to destroy?'

I had no answer.

'You walked in here, took everything away from me. You didn't care about all the plans I had for us – and Junior. How do you think I felt cancelling the wedding, telling everyone that you'd walked out on me?'

'I don't know,' I said. 'I didn't think. Only of my promise to take care of Richard.'

He nodded. 'It was still Richard,' he said.

I stared back at him steadily. 'It was still Hall o'th'Wood and my stepgrandson,' I corrected.

'Well now you have the choice.' His eyes were very bright. They reminded me of the day he had fished me

out of the sea. 'If you lose all that furniture you'll have
to sell Hall o'th'Wood now that Richard is a partner in
the firm.'

I listened.

'But you can have it back after you've married me.'

'What?' Even for Paul it was stunning.

'You heard,' he said softly.

I felt my face smile. 'OK,' I said.

'Tomorrow.'

I raised my eyebrows.

He moved closer still. 'I'm taking no chances this time
around,' he said.

We ate dinner early. Paul excused himself saying he
had things to do and so I wandered, alone, through the
house, to revisit the octagonal room and look again at
the pieces of Staffordshire pottery which had, after all,
brought us together.

Perhaps it was in this pretty room that I really
understood the depth of emotion Paul felt for me. I knew
then the constancy of his love. The room was neglected,
dark and cold, the figures thick with dust. I opened a
cabinet door and ran my finger over the face of Queen
Victoria. No one had touched them for years. And in this
house which bristled with servants this told me, more
than anything, how deeply I had hurt him. I set Her
Majesty back down, next to her consort and resolved
that I would finally make him happy.

I had thought I would not sleep that night. I had plenty
on my mind but I must have been exhausted because I

fell into a deep, black, dreamless sleep and was awakened the next morning by a soft tapping on the door.

I sat up. Paul manoeuvred his way into my room carrying a dry-cleaning bag and a welcome mug of steaming coffee.

He grinned. 'I got your frock cleaned,' he said and handed me the coffee.

He sat on the side of the bed. He was relaxed and smiling. 'It's OK, Susanna,' he said. 'I wouldn't really want you to go through with all this unless it's what you want.'

I eyed him over the rim of the mug. 'You didn't need to go to all that trouble, you know. You only had to pick up the phone.'

'And what? Ask you again? Did you never hear of something called pride? Besides.' His grin broadened. 'It kind of suited my sense of drama. I enjoyed planning it all, watching and waiting, getting the timing just right.'

I nodded. It figured.

'The JP's coming at eleven,' he said. 'Do you want any help with your hair or…?'

I shook my head.

I reflected as I dressed on that morning that it was a far cry from our original, planned wedding but as I descended the wide staircase of the great house I was happy. The library was filled with flowers. Junior was there and two of Paul's closest friends. It was a very quiet wedding.

So finally, Paul Wernier-King and I were married at Tacoma on 14th February, St Valentine's Day, in 1992 and the first person I told was young Richard Oliver.

CHAPTER TWENTY-FOUR

The Lodge House, August 2005

I am sitting at my desk, in my small study, penning my memories and waiting for my husband to come home.

Paul and I spend some of our time here, at Elijah Hobson's lodge house, in the grounds of Hall o'th'Wood. Through the open window I can see Richard's children playing, Richard and his wife, Janner. And on the ridge at the end of the field, I see the great house.

Richard and Junior are walking up from the tennis courts. They are sweating and laughing. A pair of chums.

My eyes leave the window and swing round the room. Over the fireplace hangs my aunt's swirling painting of Hall o'th'Wood which I see now fairly represents the turmoil the place has caused. The couple, standing at its side, wooden, like Rousseau's figures, are almost oblivious to the objects swirling around them – furniture, pieces of pottery, hearts and flowers. The man, in a grey suit, is tempestuous with fiery eyes and the woman serene in a long, white nightdress.

My eyes drift away from the painting. On the mantelpiece stands the photograph of Richard and me on our third wedding anniversary. Next to that is a wedding photograph of Paul and myself. Happy at last.

In the corner, in a glazed cabinet, stands the jug, the beginning of it all. Knowing its story Richard insisted it stay with me where, he felt, it belonged. Next to that, a small, grey, pottery rabbit nibbles a piece of lettuce and beyond that sits a barnacle-encrusted Chinese porcelain dish with the Nanking label on its undersurface. My Tudor portraits hang in our sitting room.

All these inanimate objects are the silent witnesses to the drama which has been my life.

When Paul and I are not in England or the Casa Rosada we live in a wing of Tacoma. I have learnt to love this place too, learnt to accept what I cannot change and adapt to a different life. I have laid all my ghosts to rest and remain in love with Hall o'th'Wood and its occupants while loving too my husband.

And Paul? Well Paul is Paul. Irascible, unpredictable but above all loyal and constant. Clever and easily bored. He will not change but will always be as he is.

And this I can accept.

Richard now manages Bottle Kiln Antiques and when I am in England I help him.

I find plenty to do in Long Island also. There are

museums and art galleries who are often glad of my help and advice and Paul and I share a good life there when we are not travelling.

I never knew the true story behind the jug but I found clues. The bedroom I shared with Richard, the same room which had imprisoned Rebekah Grindall, has low windows. It is possible that she leant out – too far. There is an old repair in the stone mullions. I cannot say how long ago the stonework crumbled except that it was not recent. Paul and I were invited to name a rose by an American rose-growing society. Blood-red and robust, with a strong scent. We decided to call it after Rebekah Grindall, whose fate became bound up with my own. I have replanted parts of the knot garden beneath the fateful window with this lovely flower and breathe in the fragrance whenever I walk through this part of the garden. It brings me pleasure now – not pain.

The final piece of the complicated jigsaw which is my life finally slotted into place last week so I knew I had arrived at my final destiny.

I was in the Guggenheim museum in Bilbao, standing in front of a painting which had been bought for a huge amount a few months before.

An Australian couple were behind me, discussing it. 'Do you see that?' the man enquired of his wife. 'It's an Eleanor Paris. Now she was a genius.'

It was the moment that I had waited for.

I hear the front door open, footsteps along the hall. Another door opens and I feel a light hand on my shoulder. 'Susanna?' There is always that faint question in his voice, some slight anxiety in his eyes and I know he is wondering what I am writing.

When I am finished I will let him read it but not until then.

Destiny has stopped using me for her sport. She has stopped mocking me and instead allows me to lead my autumn years in peace. Sometimes I wonder. What would have happened if I had not bought the jug on that day but it had been knocked down to someone else – perhaps Eric Goodwood or John Carpenter – and I reflect that if that had happened my entire life would have turned out quite different. And so I close – again on a question. What if...?

Written this day by Susanna Wernier-King, who used to be Susanna Oliver who once, long ago, was Susanna Paris who attended Sotheby's sale and bought a jug.